BOOK ONE
THE MORRIGAN CANTICLES

Whisper Music

J.B. TONER

An imprint of Sunbury Press, Inc
MECHANICSBURG, PA USA

Whisper Music

an imprint of Sunbury Press, Inc.
Mechanicsburg, PA USA

NOTE: This is a work of fiction. Names, characters, places and incidents are the product of the author's imagination or are used fictitiously, and any resemblance to actual persons, living or dead, business establishments, events or locales is entirely coincidental.

Copyright © 2019 by J.B. Toner.
Cover Copyright © 2019 by Sunbury Press, Inc.

Sunbury Press supports copyright. Copyright fuels creativity, encourages diverse voices, promotes free speech, and creates a vibrant culture. Thank you for buying an authorized edition of this book and for complying with copyright laws. Except for the quotation of short passages for the purpose of criticism and review, no part of this publication may be reproduced, scanned, or distributed in any form without permission. You are supporting writers and allowing Sunbury Press to continue to publish books for every reader. For information contact Sunbury Press, Inc., Subsidiary Rights Dept., PO Box 548, Boiling Springs, PA 17007 USA or legal@sunburypress.com.

For information about special discounts for bulk purchases, please contact Sunbury Press Orders Dept. at (855) 338-8359 or orders@sunburypress.com.

To request one of our authors for speaking engagements or book signings, please contact Sunbury Press Publicity Dept. at publicity@sunburypress.com.

ISBN: 978-1-62006-080-3 (Trade paperback)

Library of Congress Control Number: 2019938762

FIRST HELLBENDER BOOKS EDITION: April 2019

Product of the United States of America
0 1 1 2 3 5 8 13 21 34 55

Set in Bookman Old Style
Designed by Chris Fenwick
Cover by Chris Fenwick
Edited by Chris Fenwick

Continue the Enlightenment

For Ellen

TABLE OF CONTENTS

I: QUEENS

1: Moonlight in Medjugorje
2: Old Memories
3: Going Home
4: A Bleak Century
5: The Devil's Kiss
6: Six Words
7: Unexpected Guests
8: Space-Lungs
9: Into the Dark
10: A-Slaying We Will Go
11: Trust
12: Blood and Fire
13: Out of the Depths

II: KINGS

1: Blasphemies
2: When We Were Very Young
3: Back to Work
4: A Quiet Drink
5: Fang-Chasers
6: Pride Goeth
7: The Shepherd
8: A Mustering of Ravenings
9: Rex Mundi
10: Time
11: Miss Morrigan
12: Things Fall Apart
13: The Valley of Shadow

Whisper Music

III: ACES

1: After This Our Exile
2: War
3: Season of Lent
4: How Long, O Lord?
5: Dancing in Golgotha
6: Dying of the Light
7: The Thirst
8: Behold His Rising
9: Good Friday
10: Time to Fuck Shit Up
11: Apotheosis
12: It All Comes Down to This
13: Settling Dust

A woman drew her long black hair out tight
And fiddled whisper music on those strings
And bats with baby faces in the violet light
Whistled, and beat their wings
And crawled head downward down a blackened wall
And upside down in air were towers
Tolling reminiscent bells, that kept the hours
And voices singing out of cisterns and exhausted wells.
- "The Waste Land," T. S. Eliot

I QUEENS

Chapter 1

MOONLIGHT IN MEDJUGORJE

I never wanted to be a goddess. I only wanted to corrupt what was purest. I wanted to make *her* like me, and that was enough to bring me across the sunlit sea and all the long bright empty miles.

The part of me that was still American couldn't even pronounce "Medjugorje" when I came gliding down through the darkening purple clouds. It was just a forgotten town on the Croatian border, with a 16-ton crucifix brooding over its little brooks and valleys from the peak of Mt. Krizevac. But now the town rustled with a thousand murmuring pilgrims every day, ever since 1981. Ever since she first appeared there.

Shades of dusk were lengthening as I perched on the giant cross, and a few high stars already glimmered on my face, cold and pale. That gaudy yellow toy was failing in a wreck of shadows beyond the western mountains, and a winter wind was prowling in the chimney smoke below. It was Christmas Eve tonight. A time for wonders.

I stepped easily from the top of the cross to the rocky slope thirty feet below me. There were two pilgrims huddled at the foot of the crucifix, praying and shivering: a very old man and a very young girl who might have been his great-granddaughter. The old man's eyes were closed as he muttered over his beads, but the girl had seen me falling from darkest heaven like a black-robed, golden-haired raven. She stared in silence, trying to decide between delight and terror. I smiled at her and let her see my fangs. All the blood left her face, but she didn't run or scream—just stared and stared, with her mouth drawn tight and her eyes like lidless corpse-eyes in their sockets. How do you think *she* felt when that winged thing told her what was growing in her virgin body?

"I'll see you again, little one," I whispered. Then I turned and walked away, but I've since kept that promise.

My name was Danyaela Morrigan, once. Twelve years before that Christmas Eve, I'd been a Catholic myself. When She came, I too prayed to that lady in blue. When She bit me, I begged her for deliverance. When She turned me, I cried to her for death or even Hell, if it could keep me from becoming what I am. But not all prayers get answered.

St. James Church awaited me at the bottom of the hill. From within the chapel, I could smell the incense drifting on the cold December breeze and hear the soft hymns rising from a crowd packed inside like prisoners on a death-train. Above its twin spires, a gibbous moon was rising. I strode to the massive double doors, hauled them open, and stepped over the sacred threshold.

I loathe hallowed ground. We all do. The air is like slime, a clinging, clogging filth that creeps into every pore and stinks in the deepest corners of the mind and heart. Like the sewer-reek of the sun, it doesn't burn us, but it twists us and fouls us with shame. I shuddered and cursed as I passed the holy water fount, and a towering Scotsman who could have been a lumberjack turned toward me with a kind look.

"All right there, sister?" he asked. I placed a hand, very gently, on his chest and shoved him backward into the shoulder-to-shoulder horde, opening a broad space to walk through as the people behind him were swept aside. It made me feel a little better.

All eyes were on the altar, and only a few of the faithful had noticed my entrance. I walked lightly down the aisle, parting all those warm, breathing obstacles like a warship passing through water-lilies. When I reached the front, I looked up at the altar and saw the man I'd read about. The priest.

He was old and stooped, a random Bosnian cleric chosen long ago to keep watch over the Medjugorjean flock. Each night he picked a few pilgrims, as the spirit moved him, to enter the room upstairs where she appeared to the visionary children. His face was wise with decades of piety and pain, but his eyes were merry and serene. I pushed my way to the foot of the communion rail and called out, "Father!" He turned and looked into my bright green cat's eyes. Just for a moment, a strange look of wariness came over him, but then I breathed out, *"Father."*

Slowly—very slowly—his hand rose and pointed to me. The masses roared their ignorant approval, and I stepped up to the altar where the old priest stood dazed and empty, a flopping little puppet to my whims. Beyond the altar was the sacristy, and beyond that were the long wooden spiral stairs that only the blessed few had ever trodden.

Upstairs I found a broad, plain chamber of bare plank floorboards and rafters, filled with roses. A few chairs and a crucifix on the wall were the only other furnishings. Three unremarkable peasants knelt on the floor, mouthing unimaginative prayers. They didn't stir as I entered the room, and I amused myself by counting all the ways I could slaughter them. But a moment later, the air in the room began to change.

The sickly, cloying odor of roses grew stronger, and the candlelight seemed to focus itself in the center of the open space. When her outline appeared, it didn't seem to be materializing—rather, it seemed as if we were just now noticing what had been there all along. And then the shadows drew back in a gentle azure glow, and she was standing there among us.

"My children," she said softly. She wasn't speaking English, but somehow, I understood her, and so did those ignorant barbarian peasants. They bowed before her, and I could feel the palpitations in the air as they shivered with happiness. I stood behind them with my fists clenched, glowering, and she spared me a glance. "Children, you must leave us now. I must speak with my lost daughter."

Without a word, the visionaries rose and left the room, and she and I stood gazing at each other. She was beautiful—so beautiful. She was tall and straight and robed in blue, and a fair blue wimple wrapped her hair, but a few dark strands strayed out across her face. Her eyes and skin were Hebrew-dark, her nose and mouth were strong and tender and perfect, and a soundless hum of grace pulsed steadily from her quiet form. I feared her. I wanted her.

"Danyaela," she said. "I have missed you."

"No need. I've been feeding on souls that were close to you."

"I know, dear one. But your feeding leaves you ever emptier."

"That's why I'm here. Since you're so full of grace, I thought you could spare me some. Maybe if I taste you, I'll never have to feed on your people again."

She didn't bat an eye. "You ask for your own unmaking."

"Then what are you afraid of? There's no ecstasy in earth or heaven like the Devil's Kiss, you know."

"So you say, but you have turned from what you once knew of paradise. All these passions are only the faintest of echoes."

Anger stirred in me. "I didn't turn, I was turned. You couldn't be bothered to save me."

"Salvation comes in its own season. You trusted in that, once."

"Spare me the official rhetoric. I have a new mistress now, and She doesn't lie to me. She never offered freedom."

"Why have you come here?"

"To trade perspectives. I think it will be instructional for both of us."

"I know your perspective, child. I too lost our lord once, and I remember that suffering. But now he is risen."

"So am I."

She shook her head. "You are in the tomb."

"Because you left me here!" I shouted. "I want you to wake up craving human blood like I do. Why should you be happy?"

"I take no happiness in seeing my beloved daughter embrace

a destiny so petty and vile."

"Bitch!" My wrath took over and I lunged at her. I grew up as the only girl in a family of boys, and I knew how to throw a punch. I launched my fist at her skull, a fist that could demolish skyscrapers—but she raised her hand as if in benediction and caught that fist neatly in her palm.

There was a loud, flat smack like a suicide hitting the asphalt, and the jolt of impact nearly ripped my shoulder out of its socket. I hadn't felt pain in over a decade, and it drove me berserk. With a deafening chorus of howls, I exploded into wolves.

Not a flock of bats or a murder of crows, but a whole pack of huge black snarling, slavering wolves, swarming through that little chamber in a maelstrom of talons and frothing, snapping jaws. My mind burst into a swirl of splintered images from every direction, sharp scents of blood from multiple nostrils and the sight and sound of prey roaring in through dozens of eyes and ears. Rational thought was gone, but sheer raving ferocity guided the scattered pieces of me as I thronged the room, circling and leaping at her from every direction at once.

But now the craven cheater was intangible. My wolf-selves could still see and smell her, but I kept plunging straight through her body as if through a mirage, colliding with myself and tangling myself in myself. Insane with rage, I sent up such a baying from all my throats that dust came sifting down from the rafters. Then, from the chapel beneath, I caught the scent of fear. Hundreds of her faithful were stuffed into that teeming space, and only one door led out. None of *them* could turn intangible. Instinct and raw, seething hatred guided all my yowling shapes out of the upstairs chamber and back down the steps in a black stampede of bloodlust.

I crashed through the stout oaken door of the sacristy and rampaged out onto the altar. All those huddled bodies—terrified, helpless—all that quivering, unprotected flesh. I stood multiform, with my fur bristling and my teeth bared, growling deep in my many thirsty throats. As I stalked across the altar, the first few screams began: the overture to my crimson Yuletide symphony.

Then the vast window over the altar shattered in a glittering stained-glass cloud and a scorching gold ray of pure sunfire blazed through. The stone floor at the edge of the altar boiled and burst into a wall of fire, cutting me off from the sweet-smelling victims beyond. Pandemonium erupted.

And the pandemonium died. I looked up—all of me looked up—and there she was, hovering above the masses like a Christmas star. Peace and trust flowed out from her hands and her face, flowed over her flock and calmed them; not an irresistible peace, but an offering, an unfolding, that anyone could accept. It was cool and free, unlike the hot salty compulsion of my gaze. Even I could feel it, and it quieted my wolven selves for a moment or two. All those people fell silent, trusting in her, and they filed out of the church unharmed while I slunk about the altar with my muzzles dripping foam.

Enough of this. All the wolves of me reformed, pulled together and became a woman once again. In one high bound, I hurdled the inferno and landed in the aisle, flanked by tumbled pews. "Fight me," I hissed. "Fight me now or they die."

She dropped gracefully to the floor. "Danyaela," she said, with the slightest hint of a smile, "you have no strength for such a fight."

"We'll see." True, she had stopped my best punch. But I had other weapons. My canines grew to their fullest jugular-tearing length and my nails grew into claws as sharp as needles and stronger than steel. Then I unleashed my full speed.

One by one, the remaining windows exploded in a series of sonic booms as I circled around and around her in a long comet-like streak. To my eyes, the falling shards of glass and the leaping tongues of flame were frozen in time as my thoughts and senses accelerated. Around and around and around, in a hypersonic prowl, probing for some flaw in her defense. She was powerful but human, and nails had pierced her family before.

But always her eyes were on me, following my movements

effortlessly. I couldn't even see her turning, but no matter where I went, she was facing me, her hands folded, with that loathsome glow of quiet joy in her beautiful monstrous face. At last, I charged her head-on, swinging my demon-claws in a blur of bullet-fast strikes—but now a soft blue aura rose from her unmoving form and my talons glanced off its surface like raindrops on a mountainside. Her eyes closed as I flailed against her halo like a child.

"Coward!" I raved. "Hiding in your heaven while we suffer here below. Just like that bearded weakling, you told Joseph was his son."

At that, she opened her eyes again—and for an instant, I caught a glint of anger. But I didn't see it for long, because in that instant her aura flared into a dazzling white radiance that slammed into me like a thousand freight trains all at once. I went sailing through the air at a sharp upward angle, smashed through the ceiling, and hurtled out over the town, spinning end over end. Finally, I gathered my energy, caught myself, and hung there, dazed, half a mile above the snow-clad earth. Before I could clear my head after that blow, I caught her scent again and whirled around; and there she was behind me, already waiting, standing on thin air with her previous tranquility restored. Her garments shone in the moonlight.

"Kill me!" I shrieked. "Just kill me!"

"You did not come here seeking death."

"Then give me my desire."

"Your will is bent, child. You do not want what you want."

It was time to play my final card, my trump card. I focused all my fear and fury. I called the Darkness into me, opened myself to it, magnified it through my spirit and my gaze. Then I breathed out: *"You will bare your neck to me."* No mortal, no saint, could have resisted that command. There could be only submission, prostration, everlasting servitude to everlasting Night.

She paused, and for the first time, she appeared to exert herself. But a moment later, she shook her head and smiled.

"My will is given to the lord. No force can take me from him, and no might can change the lord."

I lunged at her, desperate and hopeless, and flung one last blind claw-strike. She raised her forearm to deflect it, and I felt my nails bite into the skin of her wrist. A few tiny blue tatters of her sleeve went wafting away, and that was all I could accomplish against her.

"Now," she said, and she raised her arms to the sky. The million stars above awoke and blazed like plummeting suns. A great soundless thunder filled the air, a billion otherworldly trumpets. And a trillion bitter seraphim descended with a trillion gleaming swords, filling the black unfeeling firmament. I cowered at the blasting, crushing weight of her awful frowning god, and my powers left me, and I fell.

Plunging from that starry vault, I bashed into the icy stony turf like a meteor. A gigantic mushroom cloud arose from the crater of my impact, and debris rained down on my head as I lay there trembling in despair. I had gambled everything, and such was my loss.

I heard and smelt and felt her as she came floating down through the air. She landed softly just a few yards away from me, and I could feel the weight of her gaze. I knew there was pity in her eyes, and I hated it. I hated *her*. If only I could—

And then I smelled something else. I smelled a few droplets of her blood, fallen from the tiny scratches on her forearm along with the shreds of her robe. That blood had dribbled on the earth mere inches from where I lay. I raised my head and glared at her and saw her smiling sadly back at me. And before I could think or feel anything else, I scrambled across the open ground and snatched at the damp red patch of earth with my damp red fingernails.

She could have stopped me—I see that now. She could have destroyed me a hundred times over. But in her own strange way, she gave me both the things I'd asked her for. Angry, fearful, lost, and hopeless, I pressed my bloody vampire mouth to the soul of the Blessed Virgin Mary.

CHAPTER 2

OLD MEMORIES

The coffee was like acid and mud. Sergeant Belson used to make the stuff so well we looked forward to coming in each morning. Could've been a French gourmet. But it was over a year now since he stumbled into a dope-for-arms deal and took a fistful of buckshot in the lungs.

"It's not that it's *bad* coffee," my partner was saying as he wrestled with the waffle-iron. "I mean, not that it's *not* bad. It's obviously hideous. I'm sure there's a clause in the Geneva Convention about this exact specific cup of coffee I'm drinking right now. But that's not the point. The point is its *weak* coffee. I could endure bad coffee if it fulfilled the fundamental function of coffee—hmm, lotta F's in that sentence—but what's the point, if it doesn't wake you up?"

The waffle-iron was his own small contribution to the precinct when he was promoted to detective. Just a moment ago, we had passed fat old dour Detective Robarts coming out of the little kitchen with a giant waffle on his plate—Robarts, who had teased Danny mercilessly about the thing when he first brought it in a few months back. "Oooh, can we have Lucky Charms too? Let's all bring sleeping bags and have a sleepover!" and so forth. Robarts gave him a hostile glance as he passed, but Danny just gave him the same big smile he gave everyone. He was a good kid. In the old cop movies, he would've gotten blown away in the first scene.

"—which might make it espresso instead of coffee, but then at least it would have some character to it, you know? It's not like it could taste any worse. Maybe we could even—"

Whisper Music

"Danny," I said quietly. "Let's wrap this up. We've got work to do."

"Okay, yes, sorry. Twenty seconds."

He was ready in ten. We headed out the door, he with his waffle folded like an ice cream cone, half-filled with blueberries, and I with my Styrofoam cup steaming in the frigid Boston air. As we climbed into my battered old Honda Civic, Danny took a huge bite of waffle and then remarked with his mouth full, "Heck of a day for a murder, huh?"

"I doubt our perps keep Christmas in their hearts."

Harry Blake's my name. I've been a cop since I was twenty-two—half my life, that year. I was a Marine before I joined the force, and I still carried more muscle than fat on my 200-pound frame; but between the grey hair and the dingy brown trench coat, I looked older and wearier than I felt. On the other hand, my new partner Danny McArdle was a skinny twenty-six-year-old prodigy whose happy face and tousled sandy hair made him look like a teenager. People had even taken us for a father-and-son act, which amused him to no end.

Our crime scene was at the corner of Charles and Chestnut, on the fifth floor of a trendy apartment building. I knew the patrolmen on the scene, and we nodded to each other as Danny and I stepped past the yellow tape. Just inside was a tidy, unremarkable living room with green couches, a potted fern on a table, and a human body sprawled face-down in the largest pool of blood I'd seen in years. A trained investigator like myself could hazard a guess at cause of death: his entire spinal cord had been ripped out of his back and discarded several yards away.

"Yeesh," Danny said cheerfully.

Whoever had helped himself to the victim's backbone had gone on to use it as a paintbrush, decorating the far wall with a bizarre symbol that sprawled from the ceiling to the floor. I stood gazing at it, tapping my finger on my coffee cup, frowning. I'd seen that symbol before.

"Any idea what the hell could've done this, Detective?" one of the uniforms asked me.

I shook my head.

"How 'bout that thing on the wall?" Danny asked.

"Can't place it," I said. "Let's come back to that."

A trail of red footprints led away from the corpse. We followed them through the tidy, unremarkable kitchen into a tidy, unremarkable bedroom. There was a sharp chill in the air, and we found the window standing open. The blood-trail ended at the sill. I leaned out and glanced downwards. "No prints on the wall."

"Maybe he slid down a rope? No, that doesn't—wait, what if he climbed *up* a rope? There are two more floors above us. You can climb up a rope without using your feet if you've got good upper body strength, which, you know, judging by the state of the vic's vertebrae. . ."

"Well, it's not as if they did it with their bare hands, is it. Can't say what the weapon was yet. But apart from being disturbed, this guy is well-prepared and determined." I chewed my lower lip for a moment. "Yeah, climbed up a rope is a good bet. No prints in the alley either. Let's find out who lives in the rooms above this one."

Danny threw a sharp salute for a non-Marine. "Yes sir, Officer!"

He stepped out to make a call, and I stood there alone in the cold draft, peering at nothing. I'd promised Beth I wouldn't sneak a smoke today, so I stuck an unlit cigar in my teeth. A circle, with four smaller circles at the four points of the compass and four inverted crosses at the mid-points, and a staring eye in the center. Devil worshipers, I supposed, too dumb to know that inverting the cross gives honor to St. Peter, who was crucified upside-down. But it wasn't the gaps in their logic that bothered me. It was the gap in my memory. Where had I seen that damned thing before?

I pulled on my gloves and started poking around the bedroom. It was possible that the killer had simply taken off his shoes and walked back out, leaving the footprints to confuse us. But somehow, I doubted it. There was an elegant savagery about

Whisper Music

the whole scene that didn't feel consistent with someone who was worried about what the cops might think. The good news was, this meant a better chance of finding fingerprints. The bad news was, that level of confidence doesn't just come out of nowhere.

Under the bed was a small black wooden box, sealed with a lead clasp. I pulled it out and hefted it in my hands. Weighed maybe ten, fifteen pounds. No markings. I opened the clasp and raised the lid. Inside was a flask engraved with a cross, a long, curved knife, and a crucifix with no arms. I'm not a metallurgist, but the knife didn't look like steel—too shiny—silver, at a guess. I lifted the crucifix and examined it. Why would anyone want a crucifix without—then I squeezed the base and the folded arms popped out like twin switchblades, snapping into place with a gratifying clack. I tapped the box and shook it, in case the bottom was false, but it looked like this was it. I sat back and chewed on my cigar.

"Huh."

Danny came back in. "Hey, Blake. Looks like the apartment right above this one is vacant. Up above it's just an old married couple—prob'ly not the spine-ripping type, although you never know. Whatcha got there?"

"Looks like the makings of an amateur inquisitor's kit. I feel safe in hypothesizing that Mr.—what's our cadaver's name again?"

"Petrucci."

"—that Mr. Petrucci stumbled into something a little more real than he was prepared for. Which. . . wait a minute. . ." I sat there on the floor, my hands full of damp cigar and spring-loaded cross, with my mouth and eyes open wide as a sudden recollection flooded my brain. "Oh, man."

"What's up? Coffee kickin' in?"

"Must be." I got up and handed him the cross. "Start cataloging this stuff. I gotta make a call."

"What's with the arms on this—oh, *sweet!*"

"Don't play with it, Danny, just make an inventory."

"Awww."

I walked to the bathroom, closed the door, and sat down on the edge of the bathtub. I didn't need to call anyone, I just needed a moment to process. I'd seen pictures of the symbol on the wall in connection with a case from eight years ago—a case I wasn't allowed anywhere near because I had known the victims. What I hadn't known, until after he and his wife were found butchered, was that my old friend had been mixed up in some kind of damn fool religious crusade decades earlier. I never learned much about it, but the abrupt re-appearance of that symbol, dripping scarlet over another dead self-appointed crusader, didn't strike me as a likely coincidence.

My first thought was that I had to keep quiet about any connection, at least for right now. Didn't want to get yanked off this case too. Might be my chance to get justice for—

"Oh, man," I said again. I'd forgotten something else. David and Alicia Gunnar had left someone behind: a boy, Patrick. He was nine when they died, which made him, what, seventeen now? I'd kept in touch with him for a few years afterward, but I lost track of him somewhere along the line. 'Far as I knew, he was still in Boston. Lived with an aunt, or something. Maybe it was time to catch up.

But that would have to wait. Right now, I needed to call in an old favor. I got to my feet and strode back into the bedroom. "Danny."

"Speaking."

"Get your stuff. We're off to see the Bishop."

He hopped up, beaming like a kindergartener. "The wonderful Bishop of Oz!"

.

CHAPTER 3

COMING HOME

*oving over dark waters. Rising up ahead, a galaxy. Silver sparks filling the void, innumerable. A dim, quiet hum, building. Building slowly, rising, rising. Stars ascending, swirling, ever faster, rising, rising, rising, rising.*

It was like a dream, in that I couldn't remember where I was or how I'd gotten there—yet it also felt like waking up. It felt like I was seeing reality for the first time, Reality itself shimmering above me in the darkness. Half of me stretched and yearned toward it; half of me shrank away with bared teeth. The conflict sent me into a tailspin, sea, and sky wheeling over me like a titanic kaleidoscope, the waters reflecting the cosmos until I lost all sense of up and down in the ever-growing storm of luminescence.

Stop! I screamed without sound. *Stop it!*

Somehow in the turmoil, my memory was awakening. I had tasted her blood, the blood of the lady in blue. She had said it would be my unmaking. The deep bass humming in the air grew stronger, and I could feel my bones vibrating as I tumbled toward the light, toward the unyielding bedrock of the universe.

But when the lights engulfed me, I wasn't burned or shattered. The points became rays, stretching out over a vast field of crystal that scattered and reflected and refracted them in a terrible, beautiful bewilderment. The hum became a babble of voices, and the babble became a chorus of souls from every corner of the earth, all chanting:

	hail		hail		
HAIL		hail	*hail!*		hail
	Hail				
Hail	(hail)		Hail!	Hail	**HAIL**

When I tried to cover my ears, I found that my hands were gone. So were my arms, and the rest of my body. I was one of those insufferable rays, shooting across that crystal landscape. When I intersected another beam of light, I saw a face: the little girl from Mt. Krizevac. And in that instant, I knew her like a sister. I knew her name and the names of her parents and her brothers and her dogs and her weather-beaten old stuffed lamb. I saw her dreams and I shared her fears (of me), and just for a moment, I felt her deep love for that horrible woman in blue.

Then I went flowing on past her, flowing past thousands of others, crossing them and knowing them, feeling their faith and hating it, scalded by the piety of a whole planet. Up ahead was a great shelf of crystal, multi-faceted, looming like a cliff above the plains, and I saw that I would strike it any second. I tried to steer myself away, but I couldn't yet control my path or my speed in this place: I struck the cliff and felt myself shredded like a light in a prism, and I saw through many eyes.

I saw a huge menacing shape, wreathed in smoke, striding through green fields and plucking out the hearts of all those mewling sheep without a shepherd, laughing at their weakness—demonic, mighty, invincible. A warped and splintered mirror, my image of myself. I saw the Dark inside of me as *she* would see it—an ugly squalid thing, a creeping bug on a banquet table, furtive masturbation in dim-lit alleyways round behind cathedrals, a playground bully hiding from the grown-ups, peering and muttering with aimless empty spite. And I saw myself as she did: a daughter, loved and lovable, playing on the edge of a cliff, ignoring the cries of her mother as she danced ever closer to the brink.

Enough, I snarled. *Enough of this.* ***Enough!***

And I felt the earth and snow beneath my body once again. I

shook my head and rubbed my hands across my face, clearing away the wisps of that wretched vision, and found myself still kneeling in a crater in Medjugorje. I looked up, expecting to see her watching me with those piercing, pitying eyes, but she was gone.

I looked around. I was just outside the village. The townsfolk were rushing toward the burning church with buckets of water. In all the clamor and confusion, no one glanced in my direction. I climbed to my feet and turned away from them. I would return to wreak vengeance on this rabble, these fools she loved so much, for their bovine devotion to her. But not tonight. I needed time and solitude to assess whatever damage she'd done.

My powers were intact. I rose into the night sky, veiled by darkness and mist, and flew eastward as fast as the strength of Hell could carry me. We didn't lean forward, my mistress and I, when we took flight; we stood in the rushing winds, watching the earth drift by below, as if we were at ease in a parlor room.

"Hold your head high, Danyaela," She told me once. "We are the last empresses of this world. All that crawls upon it must look up and behold us standing above them in our glory."

"Are we the only vampires left, Mistress?"

"No. There are hundreds, perhaps, still walking the mortal lands. But thin gruel runs in their veins. I was the last one turned by the Darkness itself, before that puny Nazarene came and changed things. Since then, the true Lord has been barred from this sphere, and we have been lessened. Each of us can create only one offspring, no matter how long we exist. My peers have all been destroyed, and their children's children have grown ever weaker. I have watched our decline for centuries, waiting for a mortal who was worthy to be turned by me." She reached up and placed a hand on my cheek, and all my nerves tingled at Her touch. "That is why, despite your youth, you are stronger than any of our kin."

"But, Mistress—why me? There's nothing special about me."

A soft red smile curved Her lips. "Not yet. But no more questions tonight. Let us feed."

That was a dozen years ago, just after I was turned. I'd rarely been apart from Her since then—until last year when She vanished. I'd been drifting along without Her for months, lost and void of purpose, when I heard rumors of the Apparitions in Medjugorje by sheer chance. I hadn't expected to succeed; but whether I found success or death or nothing at all, it was good to have a mission again. Since both my queens had now abandoned me, maybe I could take revenge on one of them. I hadn't counted on what I would find in those sinless veins.

When we taste your blood, we touch your soul and know you. We take in a part of what makes you who you are. But when I tasted hers, I took in more than my spirit had room for. Her mind surveyed the whole of Creation and hearkened to the prayers of all her flock at once. A glimpse of that enormity nearly broke me.

But I'd been caught off-guard—that was all. I needed to regroup. Back over Europe and across the Atlantic, I went, four thousand miles of freezing waves rolling forever in the starlight. As I flew, I debated which of my two strongholds I would return to: the penthouse in Boston, or the desecrated church in the old Maine ghost town of Tarn. My first instinct was to head for Maine, to cleanse myself from that cesspool of sanctity I'd just been plunged into; but the church was Her lair, and I found that I wanted to be on my own ground tonight. I veered south over the hills of Massachusetts.

Up ahead on the skyline, the high-rises glinted. I swooped low over the tenements, rattling their windows in my wake, and then glided up to my balcony, sixty stories high. Their little satellites and radars couldn't see me, any more than their cameras or their mirrors. I landed on my feet in the same relaxed pose in which I'd just soared across the globe.

The sliding glass door was unlocked. I paced through the living room, feeling the lush carpet under my toes, glancing at the old Impressionist paintings on the walls. There were no lights—I didn't need them—but I hit a button by the gas grate and started a fire in the hearth. Then I poured a glass of wine

Whisper Music

and sank onto the grey divan.

There were nights when I missed being American. I was undead, a citizen of perdition; one did not order pizza and turn on the TV. I didn't even have a TV in this place. Before Her, I'd lived in a little third-floor walk-up on the east side. I had a movie collection and a chubby Siamese called Mr. Darcy, and a crush on a guy at school. It all seemed so small and commonplace now. My province was the wind and the moon, the smell of fear and the spray of blood, and the worship of weak spirits overthrown.

And yet. . .

CHAPTER 4

A BLEAK CENTURY

"I mean, I'm sure it's a lot of responsibility being a bishop. But you do get to wear one of those bitchin' hats. So, I feel like it would balance out, you know? I wouldn't mind bishoping for a while. I could call myself the Bitchin' Bishop of Boston. I wonder if 'bishoping' is an actual verb. I bishop, you bishop, he/she/it bishops. Prob'ly not, but you never know. English is funny."

A quarter of my brain was listening to Danny as we cruised down Washington Street. The rest was brooding on the unhappy fate of Petrucci and the Gunnars. What kind of man used his victim's spine as a paintbrush? It was brutal—but that wasn't the thing about it. Thing was, it was whimsical. It was the kind of thing you would do if murder was your idea of a swell time.

Up ahead, the Cathedral of the Holy Cross came into view above the rooftops. I pulled off into the parking lot of a little grocery store where I knew the owner and he wouldn't have me towed; finding a space at the church on Christmas morning was not a feasible plan. We walked the last couple of blocks, trotted up the steps, and elbowed our way into the crowd inside.

We were in luck: Mass was just wrapping up. I led the way down a side aisle toward the offices in the back. It wouldn't be easy getting an audience with on such short notice, and on this day of all days, but I had an in.

The old Irish lady at the desk looked up with the same bespectacled mixture of squint and scowl I remembered from my last visit, some years earlier. She was tiny, wrinkled, and older than dirt, but her long white hair was still bright orange at the roots, and I suspected she'd been quite the looker in her day.

"Merry Christmas, I'm sure," she said in a raspy lilt. "But what's bringin' you two all the way back here when the Mass is all the way out there?"

"Good morning, Mrs. Darrell. I'm Harry Blake with the Boston Police Department. This is my partner, Detective McArdle."

"Oh, I know who you are. Never forget a silly coat like that one, would I."

I cracked a smile. "S'pose not, ma'am. I need to speak with Bishop Damascus right away."

"Did I mention it's Christmas, Detective? And there's a Mass on? D'you think His Excellency might be just a wee bit busy at the moment?"

"Is *that* what they call the bishop?" Danny whispered. "Now I need be one!"

"Shut up, Danny. Mrs. Darrell, there's been a murder—" she made the sign of the cross "—and I believe it's connected with the case that brought me here a few years ago. It's very important that I speak with him."

Mrs. Darrell heaved a sigh. "Well, I'll see what I can do. You two wait here, and don't be makin' yourselves too comfortable."

"Thank you, ma'am."

She got to her feet and shuffled out of the room.

"Okay, so how do you know Bishop Damascus?" Danny asked.

I lowered myself into a chair. "Coupla years back, we had a serial killer with a thing for offing priests."

"Oh yeah, I remember. The Collar Killer."

"That's the one. I had a hand in catching the bastard. Damascus told me to look him up if I ever needed anything."

"But how's that connected?"

"Norman Grey—the Collar Killer—was part of some cult here in town before he went off on his own. Devil worshipers. I don't know if they're the same folks that painted that symbol back at Petrucci's, but it's a good place to start. And Damascus will know what they've been up to."

"Makes sense."

It did. And the part about Grey was true. But it wasn't why we were here.

A few minutes later, the door opened and His Excellency, Bishop Damascus, walked in. "Detective Blake," he said, taking my hand in a grip like a vise. "It's good to see you again. Let's talk upstairs."

He was a short, sturdily-built fellow in his sixties, broad-shouldered and silver-haired, with smile lines at least as deep as the furrows in his brow. He'd been a Marine before he joined the priesthood, so he and I had always gotten along well. This morning he was clad in his best white robes, smelling of incense. We followed him up a long spiral staircase to a big red-carpeted office, where he offered us chairs and took a seat behind a mahogany desk adorned with a picture of the Sacred Heart. Handel's *Messiah* played in the background.

"My apologies," Damascus said as he sat down. "I should have wished you both a merry Christmas earlier."

"That's all right, Father," I said. "It hasn't been merry so far. This is my partner Danny McArdle."

"It's a pleasure to meet you, Detective."

"You too, Father," said Danny. "Thanks for talking with us." The kid knew how to behave himself when he had to.

"Allow me to get straight to the point, sir," I said, pulling out my phone. It was one of those fancy new phones that take pictures and go on the Internet and navigate for you when you're driving. Damn thing was handy, I had to admit, but I wasn't thrilled about a one-pound piece of plastic being smarter than me. "What can you tell us about this symbol?"

He gazed at the screen for a long moment, expressionless. He'd be a tiger in a poker match. With a grimness, he raised his eyes to mine. "Who was the victim?"

"Guy called Willem Petrucci."

His shoulders lifted. "I don't know the name."

"But you know the symbol."

His shoulders sank. "Yes."

"Tell me."

"Are you a Catholic, Detective?"

"By upbringing. I don't practice."

"Do you believe?"

". . . Eh."

"We believe there are things older, and stronger, than men like Norman Grey. Things that drive such men to do the things they do—to be their proxies here on earth. But once in a great while, they show themselves openly."

I said nothing. Even Danny, for once, was silent.

"It's said—whispered—that these things sometimes fight amongst themselves. That on a handful of occasions, some have even allied themselves with the Church. And the ones they allied against—the darkest ones of all—formed their own group. The symbol of that group is said to be the one you've just shown me."

"What's the name of this group?"

"They call themselves the Golgotha Dancers."

I sat chewing on my lip. I felt a deep urge to smoke something or hit someone.

"So," I said. "We have a group of people who think they're some manner of hobgoblins and another group who think they've been hand-picked by the Almighty to defend the innocent against the onslaught of said hobgoblins. And the two groups are now butchering each other in my town. This is faith at work, I take it?"

"There's no call for disdain, Detective. Whatever you may believe of the first group, they have killed countless innocents over the years. And if this second group exists outside of your own inferences, then they have doubtless saved countless innocents in their turn."

"Glorious stuff, padre. But you and I know what glory comes to when you're face down in your own guts."

He shrugged. "Follow what may, great deeds are not lessened in worth."

Danny raised an eyebrow. "Shakespeare?"

"Tolkien."

"Kay. I just assume people are quoting Shakespeare when it sounds like they're quoting something."

The old bishop smiled, "It's usually a safe assumption." Then his face grew serious again. "Gentlemen, our race endured a bleak century to arrive at where we now stand. At the end of the 1800s, Pope Leo XIII suffered a vision of what lay ahead: world wars, gulags, the Holocaust. He knew it would be the work of Satan unleashed on earth. He warned us back then, although few listened. But by the time we reached the year 2000, we had all seen so much that we no longer have any excuse for not believing in Evil."

"I believe in evil, sir. I just don't see the need to give it horns and a pitchfork. Now, where do I find these Dancers?"

"I'm afraid I've told you as much as I can, Detective Blake. It is the will of Our Lord that quite ordinary men and women are meant to do most of the fighting in the great war with Hell, which is why I've told you as much as I have. I would like you to have at least some forewarning if you should cross paths with the Wailing Ones in person. But there are details I'm not at liberty to reveal."

I held his gaze. It was time to ask the question that brought me here. "How does all this tie in with David and Alicia Gunnar?"

He looked surprised for a moment, and then his smile resurfaced. "If you're aware of that connection, then you already know more than I would have told you myself."

There was a brief silence. I could've waved around the authority of the state, and he could've waved around the authority of the Church, and nothing would've come of it, and we both knew it. He'd told me as much as he was going to—and if it wasn't much, it was still a good deal more than I'd known fifteen minutes ago.

Whisper Magic

"Thank you for your time, Father." I got to my feet, and the others followed suit.

"Yeah, Merry Christmas," said Danny.

"Merry Christmas, Detectives. And God be with you both."

Chapter 5

THE DEVIL'S KISS

We all have our tastes. My mistress says we seek prey that resembles the one who turned us. She often feeds on tall, gaunt men with pale features—such was the form taken by the Darkness long ago. I favor women like Her.

When the sun showed its hateful face again, I pulled voluminous indigo curtains over the windows and retired to my silken sheets. I once asked Her how the ancient vampires had ever been destroyed when they were so powerful, and She said, "No matter how great our strength, we have one thing in common with those little mortal playthings of ours: we all need to sleep." Lasers and tripwires guarded my bed.

Christmas holds a special place in our calendar, but not because of *him*. We remember King Herod, who slaughtered the children of Bethlehem in his efforts to destroy that upstart godling. (If only his soldiers had been less incompetent!) I spent the time of daylight in slumber and arose at the violet hour, ready for a Yule-feast of my own.

First, I poured dark wine and bathed in my luxurious tub. Last night's battle had shaken me, but I was recovering now. I had achieved what I sought: I had tasted her blood and survived. I dried my body and clad myself in red: a long scarf and boots, and a short sleek blouse and skirt. No one who felt the cold could have worn such garb tonight, but I felt a longing to be longed for. I bound my golden hair with silver braids and draped it over my shoulder. She had resisted me, but no one else would do so. My private elevator brought me to the street, and I

Whisper Music

stepped smiling into the sharp December chill. A city of victims awaited me.

I had no goal; the night would bring what it would. I walked the street with long sure strides, swinging my hips, in a straight line as the crowds parted before me with stares of admiration, envy, and desire. This town was mine.

A thousand faces, faceless, passed me by. The moon climbed and the stars were kindled, and the evening breezes blew with winter's breath. In time I found myself walking past that old stone joke, the cathedral of the "holy cross." And there on the sidewalk, I saw the one I sought.

She was slender, graceful, with dark hair and keen grey eyes, dressed in a simple coat and jeans. Her face was perfect, like my lady's—and, I realized, like *hers*

"Hello," I said, and she stopped. She was walking alone, huddled against the cold, with a rosary dangling from her fist. Just heading home from Mass, no doubt.

"Hi," she said uncertainly. "Merry Christmas."

She was young—twenty, at a guess, about the same age I was when I stopped aging forever. I could see the conflict blossoming in her eyes, after just three sentences between us: her instincts warned her against me, but something else, something deeper, drew her near.

"Oh, I hope it will be."

She stepped closer, already melting. "Well—there's twelve days of Christmas, you know. So even if today wasn't merry, you've got a lot more chances still."

"Today isn't over." I offered both my hands. "I'm Danyaela."

She hesitated, snared in my gaze, then took my hands in both of hers. "I'm Rose."

I smiled. "Walk with me, Rose."

And the last of her hesitation evaporated. "All right."

We walked arm in arm down Washington Street. A few flakes of grey snow drifted in the bitter air, but she no longer noticed the cold. "You have a beautiful name," I said.

Her smile was angelic, her eyes adoring. "Thank you,

Danyaela."

"You trust me, don't you?"

"Yes," she breathed.

"Good. Close your eyes, love. I want to show you something."

We stopped in the shadow of a tall brick building. As her eyelids fluttered shut, I stepped closer and put my hands on her waist, and a tiny sigh like a whisper escaped her lips. Then we were rising into the air. All the way up we floated and touched down weightlessly on the gravel of the rooftop. Rose opened her eyes, looking puzzled, and then gasped.

"What—how did we—what did you—*what?*"

"Don't be afraid. I wanted us to be alone."

She took a step back. "Who are you?"

"I've told you my name."

Another step back. "Our father. . . who art in heaven. . ."

"Hush," I said. I raised a languid finger and beckoned, and she took three steps forward into my arms. The little string of beads fell from her hand. "Don't be afraid," I said again. It's what She said when She lured me into Her embrace. I remember. Every night I remember.

I could feel the sweet warmth of Rose's breath on my lips. Our noses brushed together. I bent forward and kissed her softly on the jugular. Her body trembled against mine, and a low quiet moan crept up her throat. I kissed her again at the base of her neck, just above the collarbone, and felt the pulsing skin-deep blood against my mouth. My teeth grew sharp

When She took me, it was in my home, in my bed. I'd never seen her before that night, but She showed up at my door and smiled at me, and I was helpless. I let Her in. I gave Her wine. I let Her unclasp the cross around my neck. Oh, I remember the fear and confusion, and the aching, smoldering desire. I remember the moment.

My fangs entered her, and she gasped, and her hands clutched at me, pulling me closer against herself. There is no pain. A jolt like electricity, like love's first kiss, as the skin breaks—and then, as we start to drink, the touch of Darkness on your soul. Everything forbidden, every midnight passion, all the sweet allure of evil: these are but hints, promises, of that ultimate soul-transforming rapture. When She bit me, She made love to my innermost heart, my innermost self, and made me Hers. In the same way, Rose was now mine. Her fingers ran gently through my hair as I drank, and every part of her accepted me, surrendered to me, wordlessly whispered *yes, oh yes, oh yes.*

For me, the ecstasy was even greater. As I drank, the Dark moved through me, made me its conduit as it entered Rose, and filled me with unspeakable things. When my mistress drank of me, She drained me to the point of death and then gave me Her own blood to drink. *That* was what changed me. It was like what I felt now—the spreading shadow within—but that first time, it was infinite, absolute horror. It was rape by Hell itself. But now I welcomed it, craved it, reveled in it.

Only once in my endless lifetime could I create another like me, and tonight was not the night. I drank enough of Rose to slake my thirst, and then I lowered her to the gravel. Her eyes were closed, and she still moaned and shivered with the bliss of it. I leaned over her ear and said, "Go home, Rose. You'll forget all of this."

"Yes, my lady."

The wounds would heal impossibly fast, and her mind would not recall. But deep inside, she would always know that part of her belonged to someone else.

I was ready now. It was time to pay a visit to my lady's lair in Tarn. Once again, I rose into the cold black skies and headed north.

CHAPTER 6

SIX WORDS

We spent the rest of the day cataloging evidence, coordinating with CSI, interviewing neighbors, filling out reports—cop stuff. Danny didn't ask me who the Gunnars were, but I knew that kid: as soon as our shift ended, he'd be digging through the old files. He was both curious and smart, which meant I wouldn't be keeping any secrets from him. Nor did I want to. He was my partner. I don't know why I didn't take five minutes and fill him in; I guess I wasn't ready to talk about it yet.

I turned off my monitor, pushed back from my desk, and said, "All right. I'm going home."

Danny waved. "G'night, Blake. Tell Beth I said hi."

"Will do."

The streets were deserts. I drove home on auto-pilot, my thoughts full of emptiness. We lived on the second floor of a halfway decent apartment building; I trudged up the steps, put my key in the lock, and headed inside.

She was in the armchair by the tree, already in her flannel PJs, reading some goofy novel by the red and green glow of the string lights. She glanced up as I entered, and hoisted her Guinness at me, and I almost found a smile.

"Evenin', darlin'," she said.

"So it is."

Last night was Christmas Eve. We made a honeyed ham together and ate it with Riesling by candlelight. Sometime that same evening, a man had his spine ripped out. Tonight, we'd have leftovers.

Whisper Music

"How's work?" she asked.

"Same's ever." I took off my tie and headed for the cabinet over the fridge. I keep two bottles of Scotch on hand: the everyday stuff and the good stuff. This was a night for the good stuff. I poured myself a glass of Laphroaig and fished a single ice cube out of the freezer. "How's Christmas?"

"Lonely. Pull up a chair, handsome."

I wandered over to the stereo and turned on some Warren Zevon. She pushed my dad's old wooden chair toward me with her slipper, and I slumped into it with the ice clinking in my glass.

Beth was a couple of years younger than me—I'm not at liberty to state her age, but you can do the math—and we'd been married seventeen years. They told us early on that we couldn't have kids of our own, but she taught English at Our Lady of Lourdes, and dozens of high schoolers knew her as their surrogate mom. She was pretty and plump, with long brunette hair in a braid. We sat together for a few moments, sipping our drinks and listening to the wind. Then she said:

"What's wrong, Harry?"

I sighed. "I gotta get back in touch with Patrick Gunnar."

She nodded and said nothing.

"Someone got killed. Same way David and Alicia got killed. Talked to Bishop Damascus. He said—" I shook my head "—well, he said a lotta crazy shit, but he said there's a group of people who do this. It's not random."

"Is Patrick in danger?"

"Nah. Prob'ly not. I dunno." I sipped my Scotch. "Maybe."

"It's been a long time since we saw him, hasn't it?"

I thought about it. Jesus, five years? How had it been five years?

"Yeah, I guess it has."

I remembered him at nine years old, with flaming red hair and piercing blue eyes, lost and angry and scared. Over the next few years, the fear had burned out of him and turned colder, and the anger had gotten quieter, more focused. I remembered thinking the last time I saw him that this kid would make one hell of a cop. But things happen. People drift apart. It's just life. It wasn't my—

Oh, hell. I was a son of a bitch.

"Is he still with his Aunt Clare?" she asked.

"Expect so. I'll look him up in the morning."

"What did you tell Danny?"

Beth thought Danny was the nicest cop in the continental states. She may have been right.

"Haven't told him anything yet. Needed to mull it over."

She nodded again. "Danny will be able to talk to him."

"Mmm."

"Are you okay?"

I shrugged. "Still got a spine in my back."

". . . Hungry?"

Shook my head.

She finished her beer. "You know, you should go back to Mass sometime. Father LaValley said something this morning you might have liked. He said there's two phrases in the Gospel, two three-word phrases, that sum up the human and divine sides of Jesus. One of them is, 'And Jesus wept.' It shows Him feeling sorrow for His friend's death, the same way any of us would. But the other is, 'Lazarus, come out!' And that shows Him triumphing over death. That's the whole reason He was born."

I didn't answer. She knew where I stood on religion. I didn't *not* believe.

"Want to lie down?" she said.

I didn't answer. The song ended. I finished my drink.

"Yeah."

Whisper Music

We went into our room and lay down on the bed. She put her head on the pillows and I put my head on her chest. My shoes were still on. I could feel the calm steady beating under my cheek. She hummed something soft, some old Irish tune. I fell asleep to the music of her humming and her heart.

CHAPTER 7

UNEXPECTED GUESTS

Innocent blood throbbed within me as I went tearing through the stratosphere over eastern Maine. I knew Rose's secrets, and I felt her sweetness and purity curdling in the cauldron of my heart. Part of me mourned; part of me was mad with glee. To know there are forces in the world that can take away your eternity, your everlasting soul, is a darkening knowledge. To be such a force yourself, is beyond all darkness.

There was no epiphany, no vision, as when I tasted Mary's blood. That had never happened before and would never happen again unless she and I crossed paths once more on some distant battlefield. No mortal blood contained the whole world the way hers did. But there was always a great force coiling and flexing inside my body, and a thriving keenness in my intellect, in the hours after I fed. I was focused now. I had found one queen in Medjugorje. It was time to find the other.

Tarn was abandoned in the '60s. A subterranean vein of sulfuric gas was ignited by construction workers, and never stopped burning. Spurts of flame still lick out from cracks in the street, and a shroud of smog veils the town to this day. My mistress had many strongholds throughout the earth, but this was Her favorite place in America. She had taken over the old church of St. Gabriel the Archangel and changed it to Her liking.

I glided down through the pale moonlit smoke and landed in the street outside. There was a smell in the air I knew, but one I'd rarely smelt apart from my mistress. The smell of our kind.

I felt a scowl contort my face. Who were these lesser ones that dared to walk here? This was no halfway house for any undead passerby.

The oaken doors were cracked and rotten, and I strode through them without concern. This ground was no longer hallowed—it had been the scene of many a ghoulish murder through the years. The giant windows were boarded up, and human skeletons hung over each one, crucified with iron nails. The altar was defiled with old dry gore and viscera, the crucifix cast down in pieces in the aisles. At the highest point of the ceiling, five stories up, another body had been nailed into place, staring down at the chapel below.

I sensed twelve vampires in this place. Two of them I knew by scent, and neither were friends of mine.

The deep gloom hid nothing from my eyes. I paced down the center aisle, glaring at the four figures lounging on the altar. Two intruders were lurking above me in the rafters; the rest were scattered in the pews. One of those at the front of the church was called Demarius, a massive bearded fellow nearly seven feet tall and with over three hundred pounds of thick, knotted muscle. He wore a 19th Century coat and a stovepipe hat. By his side was a vampiress called Rain Vissarian, with waifish features and a slim build, looking even smaller next to Demarius. Her auburn hair was in pig-tails, and she wore a pink sundress that stopped midway down her thighs. She also had brown calf-skin boots, which I rather liked. Perhaps I would take them when I finished dismembering her.

"This place is consecrated to Lady Claudia," I said as I mounted the steps to the altar. "Are you here at Her bidding?"

Demarius grinned at me. He was leaning against the broken stone table of sacrifice with his arms folded over his broad chest. "Nice to see you again, Danyaela."

"Not at all. I will allow you, this one time, to depart with your head still attached, but the penalty for trespassing is your eyes. Give them to me now and go. A real vampire could grow them back overnight; for you, it will take a few weeks."

His smile faded. "I've been of the blood for a thousand years, little girl. That's a hundred times longer than you."

"And yet you're only the great-grandson of a great-grandson."

Rain stepped in between us. "Now, now." Her voice was low and sweet. "We're all here for the same thing."

"I doubt that."

"So, you didn't come here tonight looking for Claudia?"

I bared my fangs. "Looking for *whom?*"

"*Lady* Claudia." She held up her hands in a gesture of peace and apology, but there was a mocking blue twinkle in her eyes. "Forgive me."

"Forgiveness? You're in the wrong church for that, Rain. If you know something about Lady Claudia, then speak."

"We know She's disappeared. And we know She's done it before."

My eyes narrowed. "Before? When?"

"Before your time," said another voice. I glanced over at the sallow-looking old man sitting at his ease in what used to be the priest's chair. "Long before."

I was weary of bantering with these idiots. I moved to the chair, faster than their dull eyes could track, and caught the sallow one by the arm. He jumped up, startled, and tried to summon power from the long-diluted droplets of the Darkness in his blood, but his strength was that of an infant next to mine. I stomped a foot into his chest, shoving him backward as I yanked with both hands, and there was a ghastly rending sound as his arm tore away from his body.

The air was full of screams, screams of agony from the sallow one, screams of anger and fear from the others, and a scream of laughter from myself. This was what I'd been needing.

The fourth vampire on the altar, a dark-eyed woman with a permanent sneer, dove at me with her claws extended. I turned in her direction, swung the spurting arm like a baseball bat, and knocked her forty yards through the air. She crash-landed in the pews, and dust billowed up from the impact. The others came running and leaping up the aisle to join in the assault; I watched them coming in slow motion, smiling at their inability to fly.

A tremor in the air alerted me that the two in the rafters were descending. I launched myself upwards, passing between them as they dropped, and they caught themselves in midair. These ones could at least levitate, if not take actual flight. They rolled over and snarled up at me, hovering fifty feet above the ground. I shot up to the ceiling, flipping over as I went, and pushed off with my feet, shrieking back down at those poor fools with my hands outstretched. I caught them both by the throat and drove them to the marble floor, shattering it and them.

The weaklings from the pews were almost upon me. I unsheathed my talons and blurred past them as they advanced, then spun to attack the stragglers in the rear. The first one lost her head before she could even turn to face me. The second had just time enough to screech before I stabbed my hand through his ribs and took him by his unbeating heart. As I was wrenching it from his body, a third one whirled and slashed my face with his claws, but they barely broke the skin. I smiled at him and stood still for a moment, letting him see those meager scratches heal before his eyes. Then I took his head. The others fled, but I could track their scent across an ocean. None of them would see the sunrise.

"Danyaela!"

Demarius and Rain were still standing on the altar. She was cowering, but his claws and fangs were bared for combat. He leaped high into the air and then, at the height of his jump, banked and went soaring out over the pews, circling above me like a vulture. So, this one could fly in earnest, eh?

I ascended, grinning, with the blood of his underlings dripping from my skin. "You should have given me your eyes, Demarius."

"I will bathe in your marrow, whore."

"Enough talk." I flew straight at him, and he at me, and we collided so hard that my teeth rattled. He went sailing backward into a stone pillar, cracking it in half, and his hat went drifting away. Bits of masonry peppered the floor, and rats scattered from beneath the benches. But he didn't fall.

I was half-stunned for a half-second, but I shook it off and floated closer to my enemy. I could see he was struggling to stay in the air, and my smile returned. I gave him a playful swat, opening four long gashes down his chest. He cried out in pain and then attacked me, swinging his razored paws like a mad bear. I gave ground, weaving through the columns and arches, keeping just out of his range, and we danced a nightmare dance through the upper vaults of St. Gabriel.

Tiring of the game, I reached out and caught him by the forearms. He was stronger than I expected, and we hovered there grappling for a long moment. I could hear his teeth grinding together, and a groan of supreme effort came from his throat. I almost admired it. But then I remembered his trespass, and with a sharp twist, I snapped both his wrists. He howled and kicked me in the stomach with all his might, flinging me back into a wooden rafter, and the bats surrounded me in a storm of flapping wings. I laced my fingers into a single fist, reared up above him, and brought it down on his head like a club of stone. He plummeted to the floor and lay still.

I landed next to him and knelt to place my hand on his chest. My mistress had taught me we were not invincible. Fire and silver could harm us, and to lose our heads or hearts meant final death.

"W—wait," Demarius croaked. "I came here to help you."

"You've never shown my mistress the proper respect. I think She let you live all these years because you amused Her, but my sense of humor isn't as developed as Hers. A symptom of my youth, no doubt."

"But I know where She is. I'll tell you everything. Anything."

"Oh, I think Rain will tell me what I want to know." I raised my voice. "Won't you, Rain?"

I could hear her cringing from halfway across the chamber. "Yes, Lady Danyaela."

"You see?" I let my claws extend further, digging into his sternum. "I don't need you, Demarius."

"But I can help you! *Please!*"

"There it is. I wanted to hear you beg."

Whisper Magic

Then I ripped his heart out.

Now let's see, I thought as I approached the altar once again. Four had fled, including the woman I hit with the arm. Four were dead. The two from the rafters were incapacitated, but I thought I might spare their lives for now; they seemed plucky. That left Rain and the sallow one.

Gone were their bluster and condescension. As I mounted the steps a second time, Rain fell to her pretty knees before me. The sallow one was huddled next to the table, cradling his severed arm and whimpering. I ignored him for the moment and gazed down at Rain.

"So," I said.

"Please, my lady," she whispered. "Please don't kill me. I meant no offense."

I put one bloody finger under her chin and raised her eyes to mine. "You have information for me, don't you?"

"Yes! Demarius told me all he knew. Coming here was his idea."

"Good. Then all that remains is for you to demonstrate your loyalty. Some small act of devotion." I made a show of glancing around the room. "Ah, yes. Why don't you dispose of this vermin for me?"

The sallow one gaped. "But—but I—"

"Silence," I hissed. "Keep still, and your death at her hands will be far less horrible than it would be at mine."

Rain was already rising to her feet, cruel joy replacing the terror on her face. "I told you twenty years ago I'd end you someday, Maximilian."

I wandered around the altar as the wails and thrashing began. I'd been here several times of late, hoping to find a trace of Her, but I couldn't seem to pick up Her trail. Almost everything looked as I had left it, apart from the carnage of the last few minutes—but I noticed an odd symbol on the stone table that hadn't been there before. It was a circle marked with crosses and smaller circles, with an eye in the middle.

[39]

When Maximilian's pathetic death cries ceased, I walked over to Rain. Her face and torso were splashed with blood, and she was smiling like an angel. "Well done, dear heart," I said.

"I live to serve you, my lady."

"Tell me everything you know."

SPACE-LUNGS

Danny was already at his desk when I got in. I hoped he'd gone home last night. Not because I was concerned about his getting enough sleep—damn kid could go for days on sheer nervous energy—but because they'd been getting strict about overtime.

"Mornin', Blake."

"Hey." I swished around the abominable coffee in my cup. "So."

"So, I looked up the Gunnars."

"Yeah."

"I'm sorry about your friends."

"Thanks."

"Looks like they had a son."

I nodded. "Lives with his aunt Clare down on Dorchester."

"We goin' there today?"

It was a groggy day in the precinct. People were shuffling around half awake, mumbling mornin's and merry Christmases and get the fuck outta my ways. A light fall of sleet was rattling at the windows, and the old clock over my desk ticked slowly. I watched the steam curling up from my coffee and drifting away into nothing.

". . . Yeah."

Traffic was still thin this morning. Danny babbled about his sister in Oregon as we cruised along, providing an upbeat counterpoint to the blues on the radio.

I'd printed out Patrick's high school records. It looked like he was a smart but troubled kid, good at math and English, introverted, with a tendency to beat the crap out of older and larger boys who made the mistake of trying to push him around. There was a photo, only a few months old, of a good-looking young man with kerfuffled red hair and a wounded glare he couldn't quite hide behind a smile. Someone should've been there for him.

Clare Gunnar was a nurse. They had a duplex near Carney Hospital. There was a tidy welcome mat on the doorstep and a big pine wreath on the door.

"Nice place," Danny remarked.

I grunted. I was not looking forward to this. Taking a breath, I raised a finger and pressed the doorbell.

There was a long pause. Maybe they're not home, I thought. Maybe—

Then the door opened, and there he was. He was sharply dressed, with tan slacks and a blue polo, but there was a faint wildness in him that made the clothes look like a costume. His frame was lean and tense; even standing still, he looked fast.

"Hello, Patrick," I said.

His eyes widened. "Detective Blake. It's been—boy, it's been a long time, huh?"

I opened my mouth. Nothing came out. What the hell do you say?

"Hi there," Danny said, offering his hand. "I'm Detective McArdle. You can call me Danny."

Patrick spared him a glance, let a beat go by, and then shook his hand. "Well—come on in, I guess."

Just inside the door was a cozy living room. A wood fire was crackling on the hearth, and a nearby table was laden with plates and bowls of food left over from yesterday. The walls were lined with photos of Patrick and Clare. I remembered her. Good woman.

A bearded man in his thirties rose from the couch as we entered. He was a big guy—not huge, but taller and broader than I was, and with hands that were large even for a large fellow. He looked Middle Eastern, and his accent was British.

"Gentlemen!" he said. "God rest you merry, both."

Danny beamed. "Thanks! You too."

As a matter of course, I pulled back my jacket to show the badge on my belt. "Good morning, sir, we're Detectives Blake and McArdle, Boston PD."

"Welcome, welcome. Paulson Cormorant, at your service. Friend of the family. Ms. Gunnar isn't home at present, but please make yourselves at ease."

"So," Patrick said in a tone of studied neutrality. "I bet you're here to tell me about Willem Petrucci. He died the same way as my parents, right?"

I nodded. "We don't know yet if there's any connection."

"It would be hard to tell since you discovered nothing about the first case. Kinda like solving for y when you don't know the value of x."

"That case didn't have me on it. This time'll be different."

"Well, I'll look forward to an update in another decade."

"Detectives," Cormorant interjected. "Won't you join us for some eggnog? There's a batch without bourbon in it, as you're no doubt on duty. Mind you, I'm not sure which one it is."

"That sounds great," Danny said. "And don't worry, bourbon won't make me any dumber."

"I can believe it, sir! Detective Blake?"

I shook my head. I knew he was trying to smooth over the social awkwardness, but I could've done without the interruptions. "Patrick—if you already know about Petrucci, then you're keeping an ear to the ground. Is there anything you know about this case that could help us?"

Patrick grimaced. "I know what the cops tell the news. I sure hope you've got more to go on than that."

"You haven't talked to anyone unusual? Seen anyone hanging around your house or your school? Anything out of the ordinary."

"Define ordinary."

Cormorant glanced over from where he was pouring Danny a glass of nog. "Now there's a point. We live and breathe every day in the realm of the ordinary, but it's almost impossible to articulate."

"Hard for a fish to explain the ocean, I guess," Danny said and took a sip of his drink. "Hmm—no bourbon." He sounded disappointed.

"But fish aren't just in the ocean, Detective McArdle! They're also in outer space, like everything else on Earth. Whizzing along at—oh, I don't recall, some impressive-sounding speed, surrounded by things we can't understand or even survive unless we're protected."

"Or unless we grow space-lungs," Danny said. "Whatever that means in this metaphor. We *are* doing a metaphor, right?"

"Guys," I said. "Let's focus. Have you ever heard of a group called the Golgotha Dancers?"

Patrick glanced at Cormorant.

"I know the name," the big man said, still cheery. "Are you planning to pursue this connection?"

"I'm planning to pursue the people who murdered this boy's parents, Mr. Cormorant. I'm planning to end them. You find that amusing?"

"I try to take things only as seriously as I have to, sir. But I set great value on the lives of good men. May I suggest that if you plan on stepping into this world, you develop a tolerance for its atmosphere. For instance, are you familiar with Medjugorje?"

"No."

"It's a small town in Bosnia-Herzegovina where, for the last thirty years, the Blessed Virgin Mary has been making regular appearances. Two nights ago, the chapel where she appears was attacked and burned halfway to the ground."

"All right. And that's relevant?"

"I don't know, Detective, but I suspect so."

"Paulson," Patrick said. "He doesn't need to know this stuff."

"Oh, I'm not so sure. When men of honor appear in a time of need, it is rarely mere chance."

"Yeah," the kid muttered. "Honor."

I sighed. "Patrick. . ."

"Believe me," Cormorant said, and his voice lost some of its jolliness. "The longer one lives, the faster the years go by. As one grows older and busier, it's easy to lose touch, even with people for whom one cares. Such is the price of living with a mission."

There was silence.

"So!" Danny said and smiled. "How's being demon hunters workin' out for you guys?"

CHAPTER 9

INTO THE DARK

"Demarius' master knew Her a long time ago. He was afraid of Her. He said She was the last of the Dark-bloods, the last one turned by. . ."

She trailed off. I was sitting in the priest's chair, vacated by the discourteous Maximilian, and she was sitting at my feet. The two survivors of our little debate, slammed into the floor with enough force to embed them in the marble, were beginning to stir. The others were shriveling into brittle grey husks like tumbleweeds.

"Go on, Rain," I said quietly. "I know who turned Her."

"Yes, my lady. Guureg—Demarius' master—he said every few centuries, She would disappear from the earth. He said Her Lord, the True Lord, would take Her away to the place of shadows."

I recognized the name of Guureg; She had mentioned him in passing a few times. Unless I was mistaken, he had displeased Her and come to the end of his immortality. "For what? And for how long?"

"For—for the pleasure of the Darkness. Sometimes for years in our time."

"Our time?"

"They say time flows faster there—that a night in Hell can be months on earth."

"How do I find Her there?"

"I don't know, Lady Danyaela. No one knows."

"Then you're of no use to me. Why did you come here?"

"Because She has enemies! While She's been gone, they've been gathering."

"What enemies?"

"Our own kind. We call them the Apostate. They work together with slayers from the Vatican, to hunt down the elders of our race and destroy them."

"Why?"

"Power," she whispered. "The Apostate covet the power of the ancient ones."

"So, they take their blood when the slayers are finished with them. But that can only give them a fraction of the original strength."

"It's still more than they have now."

"I suppose." I glanced toward the altar table. "What is that symbol you've drawn over there?"

"It's the mark of the Golgotha Dancers. We banded together decades ago to hunt down the Apostate. To punish their treachery against the Darkness."

I made a wry face. I might be young in the blood, but it didn't take much experience to know that vampires did not work well in groups. "So, you wanted to enlist me while my mistress was away and hope I could convince Her to adopt you when She returned."

"Y—yes, my lady. As a patroness."

"Well. Perhaps things would have gone otherwise if you'd shown more respect from the outset. But no matter. Who are those two?" I gestured at the ones from the rafters.

"Nikosk and Petrov. They're brothers."

"They work for me now. Once they're back on their feet, tell them to prepare the sleeping chamber in the catacombs and find me some hikers or some such. I expect I'll be hungry and tired when I return."

"As you wish, Mistress." She bowed low. "But where are you going?"

I got to my feet. "I'm going to Hell."

Then I was out the doors and hurtling up toward the waning

moon. After feeding and fighting, I was energized and confident. I could sense the four cowards fleeing through the rubble below me, but I decided not to bother with them tonight. They might be useful later, as servants or as sport. For now, I had business with the Darkness. I might be only the second strongest vampire on the planet, but I had one thing even my mistress didn't: the blood of Mary herself inside my flesh.

Last night, I was hurled against my will into the crystal sphere that her spirit inhabited, far above Creation. But now I was prepared. Now I would enter by choice, and by an ability which had become my own.

I called up her face in my memory. Her eyes, her lips. Her scent. I called up the taste of her blood. Her memories and power. I hung there in the starlight, high above the earth, and felt the desert wind of Israel in my hair. I heard the oxen chewing in Bethlehem and the waves on the seashore of Galilee. And I felt her life-force dawning in my core, suffusing my limbs, radiating from my body—luminous, limitless. I envisioned that crystal sphere again and willed myself there.

My head went light.

My eyes went dark.

Up ahead of me was the galaxy of lights, rising once more above the dark waters. I willed myself faster. This time I would not be dragged into that place but would take it head-on. *Faster!* I shot across the endless sea and went speeding across the crystal fields. As before, uncountable millions of rays surrounded me, the souls of all mankind. And as before, whenever I touched a shaft of light, I *knew* that person. For the first time, I realized what incredible vistas were now open, what heights and depths of knowledge. All the earth.

The crystal cliff appeared on the horizon, growing ever closer. If I struck it, I would be lost in that terrible sevenfold vision of my inner self. I gathered my will and tried to steer myself in some other direction, but I had no rudder here. I couldn't slow down either. But then I crossed the path of another soul—Tomás, from Guatemala—and I clung to him as if to a low-

Whisper Magic

hanging branch in a flood. My headlong flight stopped, and I was suspended within his beam. My general knowledge of him became specific: he was reading a book, and if I focused enough, I could see the page through his eyes.

Perhaps I could navigate this place. I thought of Rose, the rooftop maiden. I summoned up her image, reached out to it with my mind—and there she was. No longer flying aimlessly across the plains, I blinked to her location. I could feel her stumbling through her apartment, drained and puzzled, probing at the disappearing marks of my unhallowed fangs on her neck.

Now: could I find a vampire in the same way as a mortal? I thought of Nikosk, my newest acquisition—and there he was, back in Tarn, shaking stone dust out of his hair as he helped his brother Petrov to his feet.

Good enough. I focused all my will upon my mistress. *Lady Claudia. My lady.* I called out to her with my whole being, stretching forth invisible hands, yearning for her. *My queen!*

There was nothing. She was nowhere in the cosmos.

So be it, then. I would plunge into the chaos. I shook loose from Nikosk's mind and headed for the crystal cliff. Last time, I was subjected to a perception of myself and the Dark through the eyes of Mary; this time I would seek a perception of Mary and myself through the eyes of the Dark. And perhaps from there, I could somehow enter the Heart of the Darkness itself.

I struck the cliff and was shattered. As before, my first glimpse was a self-image—that of a warrior princess, wielding the stolen sword of heaven in the service of Hell. It was followed by the image of a stubborn child in her father's workshop, demanding to play with his tools, until he let her mash her own thumb with a hammer. I ignored all that and turned my thoughts toward my goal.

There was the Darkness as she saw it, wailing and gnashing its teeth in the void, dreadful but impotent. I moved closer, opened myself, invited it into me—and then I saw her. I saw her like the sun, blazing, blinding, and I had no lids, no veil, to shut her out. She was the scourge of clean water to a pig hiding in its own refuse, the smell of savory foods to a man starving himself in the grip of heroin. She was a cyclone of shining silver doves; she was holiness and flame. My resentment of her was swallowed up in terror.

And then I saw a marionette dancing on strings that were chains of iron. I saw a nail that believed it was a person, a talon on a vast gnarled hand, gouging strips from the back of a man crowned with thorns. Here was its image of me; unflattering, but at least it was a direct connection. I bent all my energy upon following that connection back to its source.

The images faded. Light and dark both faded. Grey were the heavens and grey the earth, and I stood in a broad dull wasteland of salt.

Hello, Danyaela.

I turned and beheld a young woman, green-eyed and golden-haired, clad in red. I hadn't seen a mirror in twelve years, but I recognized my face gazing back at me.

Who are you? I demanded. *What is this place?*

It waved its hand. *Redundancies. Don't squander what time we have. I know why you've come.*

Where is She?

She is dreaming. The thing that bore my face pointed its finger, and a shimmering window opened in the air. Through it, I could see a great stone chamber, black as pitch, empty but for a single bier on which my mistress lay on her back like a corpse. Her hands were at her sides, and a viper was coiled between her breasts with its fangs buried in her heart. *She will dream a long time yet.*

No. My fists clenched. *No, you will not have Her. Give Her back to me.*

It leered at me. *Do you love her, Danyaela? Is this love?*

I glared and said nothing. We did not use that word.

You cannot enter this place with love in your heart. Why do you care what happens to this vampiress?

She gives me purpose. She's all I have.

There is no purpose.

I want Her!

Ah—that's better. But you still can't enter as you are now. We too have our Purgatory.

What do I have to do?

It stepped closer. *Do you accept me?*

I hesitated.

Well, as you wish, it said, and the window to my mistress closed.

Wait! Yes, I accept you!

Good.

Its eyes began to glow an eerie purple. Its power all around me, and I thought of what Rain had said about the young ones who craved the power of the ancients. That same craving awakened in the pit of my stomach, and I stood there staring at that thing with my face, wanting what it had, grinding my teeth in envy. I wondered if I could defeat it in battle—if I could take its blood and seize its antediluvian strength for my own—and I was wracked with greed at the thought. I was a force to be reckoned with, a creature of might and beauty, a haughty and alluring demoness of the night. I looked upon that countenance, my countenance, with a towering sense of pride. And then I felt something different.

I felt a warmth spreading through me, rising to my throat and sinking to my thighs. My hips moved forward of their own accord, and my hands pressed against my stomach. I gazed at the smooth skin and perfect form of that being, and a deep ravenous lust took me in its jaws. Helpless, shuddering with need, I stumbled forward and took it in my arms. But at that moment, I realized how it was toying with me, and my heart burst into wrath. I seized it by the hair, wrenched its head back, and chomped into its neck.

Hot blood came boiling into my mouth, and I gulped it down, slurping, gobbling, letting it spray over my face and chest, gorging myself like a rapacious hyena. It kept on coming, more blood than could ever fit inside a human body, but a hideous gluttony had taken me, and I couldn't tear my mouth away. And the blood grew cold, thick, congealed—became foul, cadaverous, leprous—became maggots—became endless mouthfuls of buzzing, churning flies, crunching in my teeth and wriggling down my throat.

At long last, it ran dry. Stuffed beyond all capacity, I sank to the ground and lay with my face in the dust. I could not have moved if I had wanted to; and in that moment, I cared for nothing so much as that one small bare patch of earth. If a portal to my lady had opened right in front of me, I would not have cared enough to drag myself to my feet. Absolute sloth possessed my will.

I don't know how long I laid there. When the weight of that torpor lifted, I got my feet under me and rose shakily, groping for something to steady me. I had forgotten the sensation of fatigue.

The thing with my face was gone. But as I swiveled to survey the bleak terrain, I found that my view of the salt-scape was broken by a free-standing door behind me. It was a plain pine door with a tarnished brass knob. There was nothing else for as far as my vampiric eyes could see.

Well—I'd come this far. If I'd been human, I would have taken a deep breath. As it was, I simply turned the knob, opened the door, and stepped through.

CHAPTER 10

A-SLAYING WE WILL GO

Some jobs are more a part of you than others. You can be a lousy line cook and still be a great guy. But if you're a bad cop, then you're not a good man. I was dedicated to this job, and I'd been doing it over two decades now. You pour yourself into something for that long, you develop a sense of when things are going right.

When Danny asked that bizarre question—*seemingly* bizarre question—I opened my mouth to tell him to stop clowning and be serious for once. But before I could form the words, I saw the looks on Patrick and Cormorant's faces, and I fell silent.

Cormorant's expression was complex; he was a canny one, to be sure, and I saw multiple shades in his smile. There was a dash of "Well played, sir," and a hint of "Good luck proving it," and a very distinct smattering of "Now, if I had fifty men like this one!" But Patrick's expression was simplicity itself: it was the exact look I'd seen a thousand times when I presented a smug perpetrator with undeniable evidence of his own guilt. The verbal equivalent of that look was, "H—how did you know?"

Not two seconds went by, but a lot can happen in two seconds. "I'm not sure what you mean, Detective McArdle," Cormorant said with unruffled calm, but it was a bit late for that.

I took a step closer to him and jabbed my finger at Patrick. "Are you dragging this boy back into the same business that killed his parents? Is that what's happening here?"

"No one's dragging anyone into anything. Calm yourself."

"You think he's in a position to make a rational choice about this?"

"Hey, I'm standing right here, *ass*," Patrick interjected. "I haven't even seen you in like, what, five years? So, spare me the Uncle Harry routine."

"Kid, this ain't a comic book. You get mixed up in vigilante shit like this, it's gonna come straight back to the people you care about. A guy like Norman Grey will FedEx your aunt's severed legs to your doorstep just to say hello."

Patrick scoffed. "They'd be in for one hell of a—"

"Patrick," Cormorant said, and the kid stopped short.

"Ohhh, boy," Danny said under his breath.

I stared at them until it felt like my eyeballs would drop out of their sockets and dangle by the retinal nerves. "Are you. . . Clare is in this too? *Clare?*"

"Detective," Cormorant said in a low voice. "Recall what I said about atmospheres. You're edging into another world here. Take shallow breaths."

"What does that even mean?"

"It means you should be wary of assuming you comprehend the situation in which you find yourself. There are many threads interwoven in this tapestry, and none of us perceives them all."

I exhaled. "Fine. Then unravel me this. I'm not a Protestant, but I know my Bible, and St. Paul tells us to respect the authority of the government. So why do you insist on hindering appointed representatives of the law?"

"I have no desire at all to hinder you in your proper duties. But note, sir—the law has many levels and many offices. A wronged man will seek different agencies of the law, depending on the nature of the wrong. But you and I, in our different ways, are fighting the same battle."

"I'm sure you believe that, but you lose me at 'demons.' Do you realize what millennium this is?"

"Oh, I'm aware of the millennium. I'm also conscious of its irrelevance. There have been atheists and believers in every age, and always will be. The mere spinning of the clock will never alter the burden of final choice that is laid upon every soul."

"You're good, Cormorant. That's genuine guru talk right here. I bet wounded people come to you from all over."

"You don't know what you're talking about, Blake," Patrick said. "I think it's time for you to leave."

"Now hold on a second—"

Just then, the front door opened behind us. I turned, and there was the lady of the house. She looked a lot like her nephew—tall and thin, with a tautness about her that belied that grey in her hair. Yet she had a pleasant face, creased with old smiles, and you got the impression that she would dominate a room not by talking the loudest but by mothering the most.

She stood in the doorway for a long moment, backlit by the sun, like she'd just swaggered into a saloon. Then she snapped her fingers and said, "Why, Harry Blake or I've lost what little wits I had."

Despite everything, I found myself smiling. "Hello, Clare. Been awhile."

"That it has. Merry Christmas! And who's your handsome friend? You bringin' me suitors, now?"

Danny gave her the grin. "Danny McArdle ma'am. Nice to meet you."

"Nicer if you drop the ma'am. Now, are you lummoxes gonna help an old lady with her groceries, or what?"

We stepped forward and took her bags. Behind her on the step were three people I didn't recognize, two men and a girl in her teens. At a glance, they had no obvious family resemblance either to her or to Cormorant. All three looked athletic and confident, and all were dressed in dark leather. They followed her into the living room without a word, and the reptile part of my brain started leaking adrenaline into my system.

But then Clare made a general wave of introduction. "Folks, this here's Detective Harry Blake, old friend of the family. Harry, this is Leah, Rigby, and Brother Joseph."

Leah was blond and pretty, with a cheerful face and a caffeinated demeanor. Now that I got a better look at her, I decided she was closer to her mid-twenties than her late teens, but she was the small, vivacious type of girl that gets carded at bars well into her thirties. Rigby was a broad-shouldered fellow with a ponytail. He looked to be in his early thirties, still just young enough to be cocky, but not to be underestimated. He had a solid air about him. Brother Joseph was rail-thin and specter-tall, with dark African features, a shaven head, and sunglasses. He seemed tranquil, but I suspected he could tear shit up if provoked. When he took off the shades, his eyes were surprisingly merry in that stony face.

"So, you're the rag-tag monster slayers," I said. Rigby bristled like I'd said something unflattering about his yoga instructor. Clare and Joseph had no reaction at all; I might as well have been clearing my throat. But Leah's eyes twinkled.

"Dibs on that for a band name," she said. "Harry, you play bass?"

I almost smiled.

Then Danny once again reminded me of why he was the youngest detective in the department. "Ms. Gunnar," he said, in the same quirky, pleasant tone, "did you know Willem Petrucci, the man who had his spinal cord ripped out of his back the other day?"

Leah subsided. Rigby bristled even more. "Hey, buddy," he said. "We're trynna have a quiet get-together. We don't need you barging in here talking about spines and backs in front of the ladies, all right?"

"Keep your shirt on, Rigby," Clare said. "It's their job to ask questions. And no, Detective Danny McArdle, I did not know Mr. Petrucci, although I heard about him on the news."

"Be a shame to get Patrick involved in something like that, don't you think?" I said.

She held my gaze. "Be a shame if he grew up without a spine, that's for sure. Now it's been nice catchin' up, but if you don't mind, I got a lotta cookin' to do."

I tipped my hat. "Good to see you again, Clare."

"Likewise."

Whisper Music

They parted to let us pass, and we headed out the door. "Merry Christmas, gentlemen," Brother Joseph said in a soft voice.

"You too," Danny said. The door closed behind us.

As we headed back to my car, Danny paused beside Clare's old red pick-up. "Hold on a sec, my shoe's untied." He knelt for a moment, then hopped back up and trotted over with a smile. "Okey-doke, let's hit the road."

I put the Civic in gear and pulled out of the driveway, shaking my head. "Buncha maniacs. What in hell is that woman thinking."

"Dunno. Maybe we can tail her for a while."

"Yeah, maybe. But we'll need actual evidence to justify a stakeout."

"Mm. Or, you know, we could just keep track of where she goes on our own."

"How would we do that?"

He raised his shoulders. "I *might* have planted a GPS behind her license plate."

". . . Is that legal?"

"I was hoping you'd know. I bet not, though."

"I bet you're right."

TRUST

The door slammed shut behind me. I paid it no heed but went forward into the vast dim chamber. It was like a dungeon, filled with tall stone pillars that rose into an endless gloom overhead, and the far-off walls held neither door nor window. Ahead was the bier where Lady Claudia lay bound in slumber.

After my ordeal, I felt ugly and dirty inside. Part of me was ashamed to look upon my mistress; another part of me resented Her for putting me through this. But I forced myself to keep moving forward. She was my mission, my purpose.

There she lay, in a grey funeral shroud. Her body was strong and slender, her face beautiful and cold. Long raven hair framed her antique Roman features. Even in repose, she exuded the age-old temptation of the forbidden: a siren, a succubus.

The hateful serpent was still coiled in Her bosom. I plucked it out, ripped it in half, and threw the pieces away. She did not stir.

"Mistress," I said. "Mistress!" I shook Her and patted Her face, but She made no sign.

I knew what She needed. I pried open Her mouth, sliced open my wrist, and let the blood dribble onto Her tongue. Still, She lay motionless. Furious, I smashed my fist on the bier and cracked the cold stone. "Wake up!" I screamed.

The holes in Her sternum from the viper's fangs had already closed, but two tiny spots of blood remained. Moved by some impulse, I wiped her blood with my fingertip and touched it to my tongue.

Danyaela?

"My lady!" I cried. "I hear you!"

Her eyes did not open, nor Her body move. But Her voice came into my mind, first faint and then stronger.

My sweet slave. My precious plaything.

"Yes, my lady. I'm here. I found you."

How did this come to pass? Is not my body still in the underworld?

"It is, Mistress. But I've gained a new power. I can take you home."

I fear not. The ascent back to my body from Deep Hell will take long months yet.

"I don't understand."

The place where you stand now is only the anteroom to the Abyss. But my spirit is still in the depths, and it is a long climb back to wakefulness and union with my flesh. It will take hours for me—many weeks for you.

I clenched my fists again. "But Lady, there must be a way to bring you back!"

There is no way that I know of. She paused. *Save one, perhaps.*

"What is it?"

There is a man who calls himself Cormorant. Paulson Cormorant. His blood has properties unlike those of other men. Perhaps it could revive my body, and so bring back my spirit from the Deep.

"I will find him, Mistress." I knelt and took her cold hand. "I will bring you his dripping heart."

Do not slay him, Danyaela. Take only enough of his essence to anoint my lips.

"But why? Who is this Cormorant?"

That is a tale for another day, little one. You have done well to find me. Your loyalty pleases me.

"Thank you, my queen." I rose. "I will be back soon."

I gathered my powers and willed myself back to the crystal sphere. Once again, I flashed across the glittering fields among the millionfold beams of every spirit, and this time I focused on the name of Paulson Cormorant.

I found him quickly enough. He was in Boston, of all the places in the world—an odd coincidence, if such it was. And what was this secret of which my mistress had spoken? What made him so special?

But now I found something even odder: I couldn't seem to read his thoughts. He carried within him some hidden force that blinded me.

Well, that was as it might be. There would be time later for the unraveling of mysteries. First, I would hunt him down, and then we would have words. I directed my energies back to the mortal world.

And there I was once again, hovering high above the Maine countryside. The moon was setting, and that wretched yellow thing was breaking over the eastern hills. I found that I was weary—weary to the bone. Finding Cormorant, I decided, could wait until nightfall.

I floated back down to the desecrated church and slipped inside as the last of the shadows surrendered to the daylight. There was no one upstairs, so I headed down to the catacombs.

Rain was waiting for me. She had built a fire and prepared the bath. My mistress had chosen the largest room and reclaimed it from ruin, laying out lush carpets and installing a huge silken bed. Tapestries hung on the walls, and dozens of black candles smoked on ebony tables. There was no running water, but those of our race could carry an enormous basin to the river and bring back water to heat at the fireplace. There was a grate in the floor where the bath could be drained.

"Lady Danyaela," Rain said and curtseyed low.

"Hello, Rain."

"You're tired, my lady. Will you bathe?"

I nodded. "I think so."

"Nikosk and Petrov haven't returned with your meal yet, but I'm sure they'll be back soon."

"Ugh. I want no blood today. Only sleep."

Whisper Music

"As you wish." Then she lowered her face a little and smiled from beneath her eyelashes. "Shall I attend your bath?"

I smiled back, despite myself. So many of these vampires were from an older time when such things were commonplace. No one had ever attended my bath before. "Why not?"

She came closer. "Your clothes become you, but I think they're past saving at this point." Extending a single claw, she cut away my tattered blouse and skirt. Then she knelt and removed my blood-stained boots. "Come, Lady." She took my hand and led me to the ivory tub.

I sank into the steaming water and closed my eyes. Rarely had my body been so grateful for a bath. Rain slowly poured soapy
water over my hair and began to scrub away the filth. She made me lean forward and sponged my back and my arms. She made me lean back, and she cleaned my face, my neck, my skin. She hummed softly as she tended me, and then she sang an eerie melody:

To moonlit holy ground with footsteps sure
The beautiful and ghastly demons come,
To touch the souls of those most fair and pure
And turn them from the light of God and sun.

With languid lips they smile at mortal faith—
The wills of saints bend softly at their gaze,
And blood and flesh yield to the whims of wraiths
Who haunted dusky Nod in elder days.

A dark Communion and a dark Baptism
To their unblessed chosen ones they bring,
Anointing them with sanguinary chrism
While somber choirs of devil-voices sing.

When the water in the tub was red, she drained it and then refilled it with the heavy buckets heating by the fire. Then she peeled away her own garments, slipped into the tub, and began washing my feet.

"How long have you been of the blood?" I asked idly, my eyes still shut.

"Just under four hundred years, my lady. An old pirate called Dandervoort turned me and took me away to sea. We had a lovely time until the slayers caught up with him."

"Mmmm." She was cleaning my legs now, in long caressing strokes. "And what became of the slayers?"

"Oh, the usual. I tracked down some of them, and time tracked down the rest. They keep dying but more keep coming along. They're always recruiting, it seems."

"We slaughter and corrupt their flock, I suppose."

"Of course, we do. That's what they're for."

"I used to be a nice girl, Rain. I cared about people. I tried to be a blessing to everyone I met."

She kissed me on my closed eyelids. "That life was a dream. We're awake now. We're *real* now."

"Are we." I thought of what I saw when I passed through the crystal cliff. The image of myself as a tool and a toy of the Darkness. I thought of the old baptismal words, half-remembered from Easter Masses long ago: "I reject the glamour of Evil, and all its empty promises."

She made a lithe movement and knelt on either side of my legs, straddling me. Her arms encircled my neck, and her forehead rested on mine. "Oh, Mistress," she whispered. "Will you not drink of me? Will you not bind me to you? You're troubled by echoes from your mortal self. Let me help you forget them."

I pressed my palms to her shoulder blades and ran them down the curve of her back, and she made a small sound like the purr of a cat. I cupped her hips and pulled her closer. Yes—the glamour of Evil. My fangs began to lengthen.

Then I stopped. I could make her my servant (*my sweet slave, my precious plaything*), but I had no real power over her. I belonged to Claudia and She to the Dark. We were all puppets. Rain would betray me in a heartbeat at the command of a higher authority, and so would my mistress. And perhaps I would betray them. Why bother with this illusion, this lie?

"Drink me, my queen," she breathed in my ear. "Make me yours."

"I'm not your queen," I said in a flat voice. "Leave me."

"But—"

With one hand, I seized her by the hair and tossed her thirty feet across the room. "Leave me!" She picked herself up and fled the chamber, closing the heavy reinforced door behind her.

My hand plopped back into the water like a bored toad. All these creatures—either my masters or my subordinates. I'd almost forgotten what it felt like to have an equal. I had friends, once. People I trusted. But there was no trust in this undeath of ours. Only power and lust. Perhaps I should forget my quest, leave Claudia to molder in the shadows.

But no. This was all I had, all I was. At nightfall, I would track Cormorant down. There was one thing in which I could still put utter trust: if I took my claws to a mortal man, he would never fail to bleed.

CHAPTER 12

BLOOD AND FIRE

Sunset came early that day. By 5 o'clock it was full dark. Danny and I were back at our desks, wrapping up paperwork on an older case and getting ready to head home for the evening, when he shifted in his seat and clutched at his hip pocket.

"Psst—Blake."

"Yeah."

"She's on the move."

For half a second, I frowned at him, wondering what the hell he was talking about. Then I was out of my chair and pulling on my coat. "Let's roll."

She was heading north along Dorchester. Making for I-90, maybe? I resisted the urge to put on the siren—she could be going out to buy flour, for all we knew—but I drove fast. Roads weren't great; the sleet had continued off and on all day, and it was still drifting down in an icy mist. Traffic was heavier than I would've liked. I pressed my lips together and put my foot down a little harder.

"She's not going for the interstate," Danny said. "She turned east."

"Got it."

"Now she's heading north again."

"Public Garden," I guessed.

Turned out I was right. We pulled onto Beacon Street just two minutes after she did and cruised along the Common till we spotted her truck. Then we drove on by, parked about fifty yards down, and waited for the next move.

Whisper Music

Two people got out of her truck, and three more people got out of a car next to it. Visibility was poor, but I felt safe in betting this was everyone we'd met today except for Patrick. And that could well mean that whatever Clare was up to, she was leaving the boy home because it was illegal, dangerous, or both. We waited till they'd moved off into the Garden, then quietly got out and followed them.

The lampposts threw dim circles of light in the frigid gloom. As we passed the first one, hunching against the wind, the Christmas wreath tied to it came loose in a gust and went skittering out across the frozen lake. We could barely make out our quarry up ahead, passing beneath the branches of a great elm. They didn't emerge.

We hung back. "Must be meeting someone," Danny said in a low voice.

I nodded. "We get close enough to hear, they're bound to make us."

"Maybe if we split up?"

Then, from right behind us: "I wouldn't bother." We both jumped a foot in the air and spun around—then we both forgot everything.

She was like gold in the snow light. Her hair was long and bright and fair. Her face was pale and flawless. And her eyes were cold green suns.

"Now who are you two?" she asked in a voice like a razor in silk.

"Boston PD," I heard myself say. Something azure was fluttering in the damp wind, and I tore my gaze away from those eyes of hers to see what it was. I realized she was clad only in a diaphanous blue gown that rose to her chin and fell to her ankles but hid almost nothing of her perfect body. For a moment I stared—then I thought of Beth, and I shook my head and looked away. "You must be freezing, miss," I said, and shrugged out of my trench coat. "Here, take this."

She laughed a soft, strange laugh. "You're very kind, officer. But I'm not cold. Are you following Paulson Cormorant?"

"What, uh—what makes you think that?" I asked, trying to raise my guard.

"I'm curious about the man. But it doesn't matter. My business is not with his soul tonight."

What the hell is that supposed to mean?

Danny spoke in the most subdued tone I'd ever heard him use. "Who are you?"

"Pray you don't find out," she said. And then she passed right between us.

I'd never seen anyone move that fast in my life. I felt a spatter of sleet as it was pulled along in her wake. I snapped out of the weird half-dream I'd slipped into, grabbed Danny by the collar, and took off sprinting after her. She was already at the elm where Clare and her confederates had taken shelter.

As we came barreling up behind her, I saw that my earlier assumption had been right: Clare and Cormorant were there, along with Leah, Rigby, and Brother Joseph. And there with her back to us was the woman in blue. But there was another figure, one I didn't recognize, a gaunt man dressed in white. The woman was speaking to him as we came into earshot.

"Well, well, well. Conspiring with the slayers, are we? You must be one of the Apostate I've heard so much about."

Clare and the others were brandishing some serious hardware. I saw Glocks, Sig Sauers, Mac-11s, and holy crap, an AK-47 (Rigby, of course). They looked startled and angry, but ready to fight; the gaunt one looked terrified. All this for an unarmed woman?

"I know who you are," the gaunt one was saying. "Please, give me a chance to explain what—"

"Spare me your sniveling," she said. "I'm not even here for you, but your skull will fill an empty spot on my mantel."

"*Police!*" I bellowed, pulling out my Beretta. "Nobody fucking move!" At my side, Danny was hauling out his Ruger.

Clare ignored me. "What do you want, bloodsucker?" she demanded.

"I want to burn down Heaven." She moved again, impossibly

fast, blurring in the shadows, and caught the gaunt one by the throat. The others sprang back, leveling their weapons, but the gaunt one was between them and the woman. Only Danny and I had a shot.

"Okay, lady," I said, taking aim. "Let the man go." I realized that her hostage's feet weren't even touching the ground: she was holding him in the air, negligently, like he weighed nothing at all. Was she on some new super-advanced PCP? A military experiment gone berserk?

"You desire the power of the ancient ones?" she said to her writhing captive. "Here is a taste of it." And she stabbed her free hand right through his torso.

Sometimes the biggest decisions happen in the part of you that exists outside of time, and they translate straight to your will without ever consulting your conscious mind. As I saw her blade-like hand emerge from the gaunt man's lungs, I squeezed my trigger and fired at her head.

After that, something happened that my eyes registered, but my brain couldn't accept. I was looking at her, and she was looking back at me, and her other arm was stretched out toward me, and her fist was clenched on something in the air. But I had shot her. I had shot her. Where was the—where was the bullet?

The gaunt man, still impaled on her other arm, was screaming and struggling, and Clare's desperadoes were fanning out around him to get a clear shot. I stood there staring, trying to wrap my head around what I'd just seen.

"Harry!" Danny shouted, and tackled me to the ground as gunfire erupted all around us.

The woman in blue shrieked. Their bullets were having more effect than mine. She hurled the gaunt one like a rag doll, and his body knocked over three of them. "I'll kill you all!" she raged.

"Suck on this, bitch!" Leah yelled and unleashed a billowing column of fire. Crazy little minx was packing a flamethrower under her windbreaker.

The shrieks grew louder. The woman in blue lunged at Cormorant and slashed him with her nails—then she did something else that made my eyes and brain disagree. She leaped into the air, higher than anyone could jump, and higher, and higher still. And she kept on going. She sailed upwards and upwards, faster and faster, and she flew away into the night.

CHAPTER 13

OUT OF THE DEPTHS

Vermin, scum, upstart monkey filth! Defying me with their childish pyrotechnics and their accursed silver. I'd never been shot before, nor burned, since I became a child of the Dark. As I rose through the weeping clouds, I could feel my body already healing itself, closing the holes where the bullets had passed through and pushing out the lumps of silver that had lodged in the wounds—but that didn't assuage my fury. I could find those crawling insects anywhere on earth now. Nothing would hide them from me.

But for now, I had other concerns. My right arm was covered in meaningless undead gore, but the nails of my left hand carried the blood for which my mistress had sent me forth from Hell. All I had to do now was venture back to that otherworldly dungeon and anoint her lips. My azure gown was riddled with bullet-holes and half-incinerated, so I tore it free and let it drift away on the night breeze. Naked I came into this world and naked I would leave it yet again.

I returned to the crystal sphere and the endless whispering music of all those billion voices. I dashed myself once more against the crystal cliff and went searching for the condescension of the Darkness. This time, however, the visions were different. Somehow, I could peer more deeply than before into the spirits that peered into me.

Through Mary's eyes, I saw the crystal field spread out across the universe, lit with glimmering souls—but I saw it as if from some higher dimension above time itself, and all of history, past and to come, was stretched upon that field. I saw one dark thread running through time and space, casting out webs as it went, tying the other threads to its own course and bending them from their paths. I saw that one lost thread plunging itself into the chaos beyond the ramparts of Creation, not in service to some greater plan but in sheer flailing loneliness and spite. And I saw it dragging everything else down with it.

Through the eyes of the Darkness, I saw mirrors—a raging, lashing tempest of mirrors, each reflecting every other drop and all the reflections in all the other drops, over and over in a senseless infinity. I was seeing myself through its eyes, and it saw itself through me, and each of us saw ourselves jumbled up in each other. I realized now why my vision had deepened: I had tasted the blood of Satan Himself. Now His will was at work in me.

But I had tasted Mary's as well. She had allowed it, for whatever reasons of her own. And I knew firsthand how afraid He was of *her*. I might not have a plan or design like they had, but I didn't have to be a slave to theirs. I was still free to choose.

I knew my task. I followed the Darkness back to that chamber of stone, the anteroom to the Abyss. And there lay my lady, and the viper was back at her breast.

"Foul thing, begone!" I snatched the serpent and hurled it away. Delicately, I traced my mistress' lips with my reddened claws. For good measure, I opened her mouth as well and touched Cormorant's blood to her tongue.

There was a long pause. Then, almost imperceptibly, her fingers moved. I watched her face for some sign, and after a few more moments, her eyelids fluttered.

"My lady!" I cried. "My queen!"

And then from the shadows, I heard a long, dire hiss. I looked up and saw the serpent rising before me, and now its size was that of an elephant. Its forked tongue flickered through its venom-dripping tusks, and its swirling crimson eyes bored into mine. Perhaps it hadn't bothered with me before, thinking I could never awaken its prey and would soon leave empty-handed; but now that she was stirring, it was roused to poisonous wrath.

I sprang back and unsheathed my talons. I carried a wrath of my own, and here was a worthy object for it. The snake kept growing; it was five stories tall now, and its fangs were ivory spears. Exhilaration prickled my scalp as I bounded high into the air. "Come on!" I screamed. *"Come on!"*

Despite its bulk, it struck as fast as any adder. I barely dodged its giant head, but I managed to get underneath it and dig my claws into its chin. Then I dove downwards along its underbelly, unzipping its flesh as I went. A torrent of vile milky pus spewed forth, flooding the stone floor.

With a hiss that shook the air, the serpent crashed to the ground to roll and grind itself against the vast stone pillars. A moment later, it had shed its ruptured skin and emerged unscathed, even larger than before.

"Fine," I snarled. "Let's try something new." I flew straight up until I was high above the thrashing form of my foe—and then I burst into wolves.

Howling like the host of Hell, I plummeted through the darkness in a pack of bristling black forms. Mary, Claudia, Satan, all were forgotten in the storm of rage that was now my whole cosmos. All I knew, all I needed to know, was nails and teeth and pounding red hate. I tore into the spurting flesh of the great viper from every angle, ripping it to pieces again and again.

But it kept regenerating, and now it was growing new heads. I was bitten, shaken, hurled across the room in a dozen different forms, and even my vampiric body was affected by whatever awful stuff was in those fangs. My wolven selves regrouped, and I found myself huddled behind a pillar, back in human form. I gazed up at my enemy, shaking my dazed head and clutching at my injuries. It had seven heads now, and it was over ten stories tall.

I got to my feet, feeling heavy and drugged. Fourteen gigantic eyes glared at me with insane malice from a hundred feet in the air. I wondered how high the ceiling was in this place.

And that gave me an idea. I couldn't destroy this thing by

cutting it. But perhaps. . .

The heads were sinking down toward me, hissing, flicking their tongues. I gathered my energy, crouched, and then blasted off into the air. But this time I wasn't trying to avoid its bite: instead, I flew at top speed right into its mouth and down its gullet.

I tunneled through its innards, digging and scooping with my talons, blinded by viscera, till I reached the tip of its tail. Then I rose into the air. I rose straight up, dragging its tail with me, and felt the weight of it growing greater and greater until I knew I had lifted the entire serpent off the ground. Straining under the tremendous burden, I forced myself upwards ever further into the vaults of that chamber, up and up and up. I could feel the shuddering all around me as the serpent coiled and flexed and struggled, but I ignored it and kept on rising. Rising, rising.

If that dungeon has a ceiling, I never found it. I toiled up through the air for over fifteen minutes, bearing my adversary at least a mile high. At last, my strength ran out and I knew that I would soon sink under the weight. So, I wielded my claws once again and slashed my way out through the viper's tail.

And it fell.

I hung there in the dark, naked, covered in slime, and listened for the distant crash. It seemed to take forever. But at last, I heard it booming up through the topless pillars, reverberating into silence.

Wounded and weary, I came floating back down to the earth. The seven-headed snake lay sprawled and motionless, its many eyes gazing nothingness, its many tongues hanging out in the settling dust. The stone floor was riddled with cracks from the titanic impact, and the stone bier had tumbled. I limped over to it, searching for my lady.

She was lying on the ground just behind it. I knelt beside her, and she raised her head and smiled at me.

"Danyaela," she said. "We have work to do."

II KINGS

CHAPTER 1

BLASPHEMIES

I was eighteen when I joined the Corps. I was a tough kid, just like everyone else—maybe even a little bit tougher than most. And I lived on dreams of being the unstoppable badass every eighteen-year-old boy wants to be. But when I joined the Boston PD, one of my instructors told us something that always stuck with me. He said, "You get in a fire-fight, you remember this: the other guy grew up watching all the same movies you did. And in his head, he ain't the faceless goon that's only there to get blown away by the hero. You are." That one simple observation has saved my life more than once, and I keep it chiseled on the forefront of my mind that, however, he might appear, my enemy is always my equal, or even my superior.

But that night on the Common, I was no one's equal. I was disposable, a ski-mask-wearing henchman to be flicked aside by the true badass on her way to vengeance or whatever the hell she was looking for. *She caught my bullet in her bare hands.* What higher standard of toughness can there be?

Danny and I got to our feet and brushed the snow off our coats. Clare and her slayers gazed at us matter-of-factly. The wind around us groaned and muttered.

Clare nodded a greeting. "Heya, Harry."

"Heya, Clare."

"So, what do you think now? We still crazy?"

"What was that thing?"

"You know what it was."

I shook my head.

"You know what it was, Harry. You saw the claws. You saw the fangs. You saw it fly away like a bat outta Hell."

"It's not possible."

"Nope. But there it is."

Danny scratched his head. "So, like. . . vampire?"

She spared him a glance. "Vampire, kiddo."

"*It's not possible,*" I snarled.

Brother Joseph was helping Cormorant to his feet. The big guy was clutching at his chest where the girl in blue had slashed him, but he seemed to be still in one piece. "You failed to—develop your lungs, Detective," he said through clenched teeth. "I did—try to warn you."

"You okay, Cormorant?" Danny asked.

"I will be, Detective McArdle. Thank you."

I took a breath. "What about the other guy?"

"Oh, him?" Clare said. "He's fine."

"Very. . . generous." The guy in white climbed to his feet, unsteady but alive. Even in the snow-blown glimmer of a waning moon, I could see the branches tossing on the other side of the hole in his torso.

"Oh hell, don't tell me."

"'Fraid so," she said. "We work with what we've got."

"He's one of them?"

"Yup."

"And that girl."

"Don't know who she was. But a much stronger one. A closer descendant of the Enemy."

"The Enemy?" Danny asked.

"Think about it," Rigby said, shouldering his Russian assault rifle.

"Oh. Gotcha."

"This is nuts," I said. "I don't even care if it's possible or not. That's not what bothers me. But if God's there at all, then why in damnation's fires would He allow such an abomination to exist?"

"We get used to things, Detective," said Cormorant. "Have you ever reflected upon the staggering, monumental *blasphemy* of the central tenet of our creed—that Almighty God was murdered?"

". . . I guess not. Not in those terms."

"We've gotten used to it, you see. We hear it every day. 'Jesus died for your sins.' And it's true. The holiest of all truths. But that doesn't change the fact that it's monstrous. Monstrous that God Himself could be tortured to death."

"I'm straining to see the relevance, Mr. Cormorant."

"He's saying it's a fucked-up world," Leah put in. "Who knows what God would or wouldn't allow, and why?"

"Well," said the man in white. "It's been scintillating, but I should be on my way."

Suddenly five guns were pointing at his head. "Not yet, I think," said Brother Joseph.

"What more do you people want from me? I've already told you what little I know about Bosnia."

"You know somethin' else," Clare said. "You know who that girl was."

He hesitated. "I might."

She thumbed back the hammer on her Glock.

"All right, all right. Her name is Danyaela Morrigan. She's the offspring of Claudia Procula, the last true Dark-blood."

Cormorant drew in a sharp breath.

"Her mistress vanished over a year ago, and things have been quiet. But if Morrigan's out for blood, then you're in for a war the likes of which you've never seen."

"Was she the one who torched the church at Medjugorje?" Rigby demanded.

The—the thing, the vampire—shrugged. "I don't know. But it wouldn't surprise me."

"Paulson?" Clare said in a low voice. "Could she have—is there any way she could have—"

He shook his head. But whatever "no" Clare was hoping for, she wasn't getting it. It wasn't a head-shake of negation, but of ignorance.

"Quite the abomination, isn't it?" the vampire said, almost smugly. "Almost makes you wonder: does your God allow these things, or is He too weak to stop them?"

Clare jabbed her pistol at him. "Get the hell outta here, Nalfar."

He sketched a bow. "Merry Christmas." Then he went tearing away through the snow—not as fast as the girl, but faster than any man could run.

"Well." Clare holstered her piece, and the others followed suit. "You know where to find me, in case—you know."

"In case we wanna join the Inquisish?" Danny asked, with hideous cheerfulness.

I winced. "Danny—do me a favor and see if you can make it to the grave without ever using the word 'Inquisish' again."

"Second that," said Clare. "But yes. We're always hiring."

"Short life expectancy equals high turnover," Leah remarked in the same merry tone. Good Lord, I could already see her popping out Danny's jabbering little offspring.

Slowly, feeling old, I turned to go. Then I turned back. "Clare—is this the life you want for Patrick?"

"'Course not. But those things are out there hunting us, whether we hunt them back. At least this way he's got a chance to go down swingin'."

"Yeah." Once again, I turned away.

Danny and I walked back to the car, not speaking, and climbed inside. I started the engine, and the wipers began their slow hypnotic swish. We drove quietly through the slushy streets. A few blocks from Danny's apartment, he glanced over at me.

"How you holdin' up?" he asked.

"I'm fine, kid."

"So—turns out vampires are real, huh?"

"Looks like."

"Gotta say, I'm not all that surprised."

In a moment of time, a whole career of war and murder

flickered through my memory. "Me neither."

"You sure you're okay?"

"Yeah." I pulled up to the curb in front of his door. "See you tomorrow."

"You sure you don't. . . Okay, Blake. See you tomorrow." He put a hand on my shoulder and got out.

I drove on home. Parked outside in the sleet and sat listening to the tick of the engine and the rattle of the frozen rain. Lit a cigar and let the smoke enfold me like the night. And I heard my voice in the stillness and the dark, whispering old words I hadn't uttered in a long, long time.

"Hail Mary, full of grace, the Lord is with thee. Blessed art thou amongst women. . ."

I said the words and smoked my cigar and made the sign of the cross. Then I clenched my fist around my keys and got out and headed inside.

Beth was in the kitchen. She had on a pink blouse and a purple skirt, and she looked as lovely as anything I'd ever seen. She was making whipped cream with electric beaters and a childhood loathing of the store-bought stuff.

"Hey, babe," she said absent-mindedly, still focused on her creamy endeavor. "Perfect timing—I gave up on you coming home and started making sundae fixin's. You missed all the work. Laura says hi. We were out at the museum earlier, catching up. She might be pregnant again, or she might just have the flu."

I paced closer, not responding. She sniffed the air and frowned.

"Have you been smoking?" she said and raised her head. Then she froze. "Harry?" And then she was there, taking my hands and pressing her forehead to mine. "Honey, what's wrong? What happened?"

"Had a weird night, baby."

CHAPTER 2

WHEN WE WERE VERY YOUNG

Saturday was beautiful. A sleet storm had swept the city in the small hours before dawn, and the bare-boughed trees outside my window were encased in ice, glistening like dryads. The clouds had rolled away by the time I threw back my curtains, and the sky was a pale, endless blue, full of sparrows and mourning doves. The cold air coming in through my drafty old window felt bright and pure, washed clean by the storm, and it smelled faintly of the joyful, patient secrets of the sea. It was one of those days when you long to stare straight into the sun.

I said my prayers and brushed my teeth and made my tea. I found my dad's old copy of *Paradise Lost* and settled into my grandma's old rocking chair in my mom's old bathrobe. And I spent the last untroubled morning of my existence reading the grand, sweet poetry that chronicles the filthiest thing that ever happened to us.

It was my senior year, and Christmas was twelve days away. Finals were coming up fast, but I wasn't too worried; I'd finished slogging through my core courses last semester and would never have to look at a hypotenuse again. I was finally alone with Shakespeare and Chaucer and Dante.

When noon rolled around, I got up to shower and dress myself. I wore blue jeans that day, and a hand-knit grey sweater I still miss sometimes. Then I threw on a jacket and headed out the door of my little campus apartment.

Gretchen was waiting for me on the sidewalk. "Late!" she said. "By like fourteen seconds."

Whisper Music

"Late is late, chica. Those mimosas aren't gonna drink themselves, you know."

"They wouldn't be much use to us if they did."

Gretchen Barrett was my best friend. We were roommates in freshman year, and both turned out to be Lit majors. We'd whiled away many an over-caffeinated night debating the hidden symbolism of this or that play or novel, reaching many an earth-shaking epiphany that neither of us could remember when we crawled out of bed the next afternoon. She was a tiny red-headed girl with a sweet smile and a million freckles, never ever to be seen without her trademark ponytail. She could also drink most linebackers under the table, and she loved being a bad influence on me.

We traipsed down the street to our favorite cafe for Norwegian eggs Benedict, our inevitable brunch. Frank, the world's best waiter, brought us the first round of mimosas before we even placed our order.

"I love Frank," Gretchen said. "I shall marry him, I think."

"I'm pretty sure he has grandkids."

"Sweetie, that just means he's good in bed."

"Reeeal classy, Gretch. How'd your paper on Raskolnikov turn out?"

"Awesome! If he weren't a fictional 19th-century axe murderer, I would marry him too."

I raised my glass. "Here's to high standards."

"Amen." She clinked my glass, swallowed about half of her own, and then got an impish look on her face. "Speaking of which. . ."

"Oh, don't start."

"Robbie's coming out with us tonight. You'll be there, right?"

"Maybe."

"Danyaela, dearest, he'll never fall in love with you if he never gets a chance to hang out with you."

"We've had five classes together. If he wanted to hang out with me, he could've just asked."

"He's intimidated by how ridiculously pretty you are. *I* would be if I were into girls."

"Does this mean I'm not on your list of people to marry?"

"Don't try to come between me and Frank, you shameless hussy. You can't destroy our love."

After brunch, we headed back to her room to do some nominal studying in between chain-watching Jane Austen movies. We made tacos at around six, and then Gretchen got ready to go out. "You *are* coming, aren't you?" She batted her eyelashes at me. "Pleeeeease?"

I made the face she so often made me make, that grimacey trying-not-to-smile-and-failing look that English has no word for. "Okay, okay. How do I look?"

"Is that supposed to be funny? You never don't look good. Come on, let's rock and roll."

The Angry Donkey was a hole-in-the-wall pub about ten minutes' walk from Gretch's place. It was never too loud to talk in there, and the jukebox had a good selection, and they sold Pabst in two-pint mini-pitchers for the price of a regular beer. A few of our friends were waiting for us when we got there, so we each ordered a Pabst and pulled up a chair around our usual table. (In the Angry Donkey, it was uncouth *not* to drink straight out of the pitcher.)

It was a very typical late semester evening. We talked about class. We comforted the worried and quelled the overconfident. Robbie arrived, and we traded shy glances over mugs of beer. Nothing momentous came to pass. Eleven o'clock rolled around, and I said my goodnights and headed for home. There was no urgency—I'd be seeing everyone tomorrow. I cleaned up and threw on a bathrobe and got myself ready for bed.

Then the knock at my door.

My soul knew what She was as soon as I saw Her. I'd never seen such beauty. Her eyes entranced me—but my soul knew. Not that it mattered; my mind wouldn't listen, and my will was already Hers. I heard Her voice in my ears, in my heart: "Hello, Danyaela."

My lips moved: "Hello."

She entered and smiled. "I've been looking for you, sweet one. For a long time."

"Who are you?"

"My name is Claudia." She reached up and took my face in Her hands, this perfect stranger in flowing black silk, and I realized when She touched me that I had longed for Her touch all my life. She stared into me, and there was nothing else. There was never a time when I could have resisted Her, or even wanted to. "Let us drink together."

". . . Yes."

The 200-year-old bottle of Merlot was the last present from my grandfather. I opened it without a thought and poured a small measure into my two best glasses.

"To rebirth," She said, and we drank. Then she let the glass drop from her hand and shatter on the floor. "Come to me, Danyaela."

I obeyed Her. I was beginning to feel a cold fear in the pit of my stomach, but there was something else as well—something stronger, something lower—a throbbing feverish desire, drowning out thought and volition. *Hail Mary*, I said silently. *Hail. . .*

"Don't be afraid," She whispered. Her fingertips traced my lips, so delicately, and slipped down the curve of my neck. With a negligent tug, She snapped the chain that held the crucifix around my neck and let it fall. She kissed me.

Oh, I yearned for Her, for the beautiful Hell of Her. My whole body yielded to Her kiss. She took my hands and led me to my bed. My robe was gone—Her hands on my skin—Her lips on my mouth, my throat, my breasts. It was sudden and senseless as a nightmare, but I felt more awake than I'd ever been before. This was real, this was reality itself. *She* was reality.

And then the fangs. Ecstasy I had never, never dreamt of. And dread, for I knew then with my whole being what She was and what She wanted. *Lady*, I prayed, *oh Lady*, but only a part of me was praying to the Virgin now. And with each passing moment, more of me was praying to Her. The shadow was filling me as the light drained out. She drank—she drank—the pleasure grew and grew, and I heard myself moaning and moaning with it, but my flesh grew weaker and my heartbeat slowed. I was dying in Her arms.

When She stopped, I was on the brink of the final fall. I saw Her smiling down at me with crimson lips. I saw Her nails slitting into Her own wrist, and I felt Her blood dribbling into my mouth. I woke then from the nightmare to a far, far greater nightmare, and a blackness from which I've never emerged. God was gone. I knew once and for all he had been real, had been there all my life, and was now snatched away from me forever, and all my hope of heaven was destroyed. Evil filled me, Evil and Darkness. I felt my heart stop beating. And my soul and body died.

There was void

Void and

whispering

I hung in the nothingness. I hung before a throne that filled the void, a throne of red nails. Upon the throne was

was

For one timeless, flickering moment, I saw the face, its face, *His Face*. Eyes with teeth, eyes that stare forever. Staring into us, into you, peering at you from the mirrors, from the corners, peering into your dreams, hovering behind you even now. Eyes full of acid, eyes that see you seeing them and cannot be unseen, that watch and know, that glare and glow like suffering stars, eyes that knew you and hated you before you were formed in the womb. All this I saw in a single instant, and then everything faded away.

Please, Mama, I prayed for the last time. *Please let this be the end.*

"Now rise," said Claudia. "Rise and let your everlasting life begin."

I rose. I knew Her now. Ten minutes ago, I had belonged to

the light by choice and by grace; now I belonged to the Dark, and to Her. She was my will, my heart, my fate. After death and damnation, I had nothing left to fear. And as I rose, I felt how light my body had become, energy and strength filling my limbs, and gravity was nothing now. I found myself smiling as I stood naked before Her.

"Lady Danyaela," She said with relish. "I have so much to show you."

"Yes, Mistress."

She led me out into the hall and up to the roof. I was awakening more and more. I could feel the cold night wind on my flesh—could see every particle of wind-blown dust with a clarity I'd never experienced—but I felt only a pleasant coolness. Below us in the city, the streets were full of sounds and smells that grew sharper when I focused on them. I realized I wasn't breathing. My body was relaxed, yet taut with power. I felt as though I could leap across the block to the next rooftop with ease.

"How do you feel?" She asked.

"I feel strong."

"Good. You are a lioness now. You will prowl with me, seeking whom we shall devour."

No one had said the word, but I knew what I had become. I saw now what that would entail, and what I would be called upon to do. My former self, my whole life up till tonight, glinted through the sharp, lucid certainty that was enveloping me. "No," I whispered. "I won't kill."

She laughed a cruel, sweet laugh. "Oh, you'll kill. You'll love to kill. But one step at a time. For tonight you will need only a small taste." She pointed to the ledge. "Step up."

It was like succumbing to a hopeless addiction: when She commanded me, my will became irrelevant. I stepped up to the ledge. She stepped up next to me, and we gazed down—twenty floors down to the concrete abyss of the alley below.

"Feel the Dark inside of you, Danyaela. Feel its strength. Open yourself to it. Let it grow."

I could feel it. I could feel its power filling me, possessing me.

"Gather it into your center. Feel it like a ball in your stomach. Let it rise."

Gradually, as I concentrated, my body seemed to grow lighter. I let it rise and rise, and my heels came up off the ground. I was standing on the balls of my feet, then the points of my toes, as if the earth was slipping away beneath me. There was a moment of exhilaration, and then a moment of terror—and then She put Her index finger between my shoulder blades and pushed.

A long fall in a cold wind. I would have gasped, or screamed, but my lungs had stopped forever. My hair floated in the fall; the ground came soaring up to meet me. But the power in my core was still rising, and my descent grew slower as the windows whipped by. I focused everything I had on willing myself upwards. The rush of air around me died down. My hair settled back to my shoulders. I came wafting down like a feather on a breeze and set my feet to the alley floor.

Claudia dropped to the earth beside me, smiling like a seraph. "Well done, my darling child. Now come, let's find you some clothes."

She led me out of the alleyway to a limousine waiting on the corner. I could smell the driver inside—he smelled warm, alive, different from Her. She had no smell of pulsing blood, only the faint lavender perfume of Her hair. "Wait in the car," She told me. "Only those whom I choose may set eyes upon your body. I climbed into the back seat. The partition between me and the driver was up. I sat in silence.

Then the door opened, and a young woman climbed in. She was my age and my size. She had nut-brown hair and pretty eyes, but they looked glazed. My new mistress climbed in after her.

"Let's teach you the trade," She purred. "This one is already half-dominated, so it should be easy for you. Look into her eyes."

I turned my gaze on my first victim. When our eyes met, I felt a slight pressure in my mind. Somehow, I knew that pressure was her will and that I could push back against it with my own if

I wished. I pushed my new power against her freedom, and said, "Tell me your name."

The force of her will receded. "Isabel."

"Isabel," I breathed. The Dark inside of me was grinning now. "You want to give me your clothes, don't you?"

"Yes, I do." Slowly, as if of their own accord, her hands rose and unbuttoned her blouse.

"Look at her neck," Claudia said.

I saw. I heard. I smelled. As Isabel peeled away her garments for me, more and more of her warm innocent aroma filled my senses. I could feel my canines growing longer—sharper. I could feel my body responding to a craving I'd never felt—or was it a craving I'd always felt but never acknowledged before? Now she was naked, we both were naked, and I leaned forward to enfold her in my arms, and I *was* the Darkness, and I embraced it. I bit her, and she spurted against my tongue, and I shuddered with the black abysmal joy of it. Some part of me meant to stop before she died—that much I still recall. But I was lost in the bliss of the Kiss, and I never heard the moment when her heart stopped beating.

That was my Last Rites and Baptism. Every story has a turning point. Some are subtle and quiet, some fiery and grand; some are tragic, some exultant, some perilous or magical, the stuff of all those poems I once loved to read. On the surface, my turning point was a beautiful mysterious darkness—but underneath, it was so much less. It was brutal and shameful and mean. In the years that followed, Claudia taught me arrogance and cruelty and vengeance, and there was no one to help me or show me any other path. And yes, I learned to revel in the power and passion of my hellish destiny. What else did I have to revel in?

CHAPTER 3

BACK TO WORK

Dawn came cold and grey, and Danny came knocking at my door. Beth and I were on the couch. She was slumped against my chest, dozing, and I had one arm around her shoulders and the other busy with a half-empty glass of Scotch. I was staring up at the ceiling fan as it turned in the gloom. Hadn't slept.

She stirred at the knock, and I kissed her forehead and got up. I found my other hand gripping the Beretta that was still strapped at my hip, and I didn't argue with it. Sometimes your hands are smarter than you. I wondered if the old stories were true—that those things couldn't walk in the daylight.

I peered through the spyhole and relaxed my gun hand. Scotch hand stayed vigilant, though.

"Hey, kid," I said as I opened the door. He came in with a big Styrofoam cup in either hand.

"Hey, Blake. Hi, Beth."

She got up and found a smile. "Hi, Danny. Good to see you."

"You too. Sorry, I didn't think to bring a third coffee."

She waved it aside. "I think I'm in a tea mood, anyway."

I knocked back the rest of my Scotch and accepted the coffee in its place. Dunkin Donuts—excellent choice. "Thanks."

"No problem. Get any sleep?"

I shook my head. "You?"

"Nope."

He and I sat at the counter. Beth started boiling water for tea. The light through the blinds kept growing. We'd have to be heading in to work soon.

"So," Danny said.

"Yeah."

"You saw them too?" Beth asked him.

"Sure did."

"You don't seem upset," she remarked.

She was right, I realized. He was trying not to show it, but he was excited about this. He sat for a moment, and then he blurted out, "Beth, it means everything's true. Everything impossible, everything insane, it's all true. And there's real evil out there to fight, not just strung-out gang-bangers knifing each other over hubcaps, but real actual *evil* we can look in the eyes and shoot in the face. It means there's such a thing as a quest."

She heaved a sigh. "Oh, Daniel."

"Okay," I said. "Let's not sign up for the Children's Crusade just yet. There's a lot we don't know."

"But you heard what Clare said. Those things are hunting us, even if we don't hunt them back. And that Morrigan lady was mad. She might come after any of us."

"I'm not arguing. But you and I aren't knights of the Round Table. If we're gonna do this, we're gonna do it as cops. We've got a lead—we'll follow it. Let's start by seeing if there's a missing person who answers to her description."

He nodded, no longer bothering to conceal his excitement. He looked like a puppy set free at a dinosaur exhibit. "I'll drive."

"Be down in a minute."

"Kay. Bye, Beth!" He waved and scuttled out the door.

With great care and precision, Beth meted out honey for her tea. "Harry, my love."

"Beth, my lady."

"You are to stay alive and come back to me. Is that clear?"

"Always has been. Nothing's changed."

"Except now the bad guys can catch your bullets."

"But not all bullets. I'll just have to start dipping them in holy water, or whatever one does." I came around the counter and took her face in my hands. "I'll see you tonight."

"You'd better. And keep an eye on that sweet buffoon of ours."

"'Course. He's my partner."

"Here." She took one of my hands and pressed something into it. "Will you keep this with you?"

Her rosary. I clenched it tight. "Yeah. I will."

She leaned close and kissed me on the mouth. "Now go do your job."

Danny's Mustang was parked at the curb, idling. I took the shotgun, gestured sloshingly with my coffee, and said, "Hit it." And off we went.

Didn't take us long to track down the name Nalfar had given us, despite the unusual spelling of "Danyaela." Sure enough, a girl by that name had disappeared twelve years ago—and there was her face on my computer screen. She hadn't aged a day, but the face on the screen didn't have the ethereal majesty I'd seen last night. On the other hand, there was a crinkle of kindness in the eyes, and a relaxed innocence about the smile, that she had lost somewhere in the interim. I supposed that being turned into a monster would tend to do that.

"Wow," Danny murmured.

"Stay focused."

"She's really pretty."

"She eats people."

"Maybe it's not her fault, though."

"Maybe you're right, but I doubt that'll cheer up your mom and dad when we're burying you in a mop bucket. Can you make this printer machine work, please?"

"Oh, sure." He reached over and made a few deft clicks with my mouse. "So, she's from Beantown, huh?"

"Looks like. Twenty-one years old—as of twelve years ago, that is—born and raised in Beacon Hill, went to Boston College for English Lit. Disappeared in the middle of her senior year."

"Hey hey hey!" The dulcet voice of Detective Robarts, over by the printer. "Who's the hottie? You guys downloadin' porn at work again, or what?"

Danny got up and walked over to him, so close they could've chewed each other's gum. "She's a kidnapped girl, Robarts. Now gimme that file before I pull your asshole over my feet and wear you around like I'm at a *fucking sack race.*"

"Fine, take it!. . . Psycho."

Danny sat back down and put the photos on my desk. "You okay?" I asked. He nodded. "All right, well, we found Miss Morrigan. Now let's see if we can find the other lady Nalfar mentioned."

"Oh yeah—Claudia something, right?"

"Procula. Easy to remember, sounds like Dracula."

"Yeah, her."

We looked her up in the database. No hits. On a whim, I looked up the name on a civilian web browser, and it came up right away. And I heard myself say, "Oh, bloody hell." Claudia Procula: wife of Pontius Pilate.

"It might. . . it might be someone else," Danny said. "You know—with the same name."

"Sure. Might be." I rubbed my hands across my face. "I'm too old for this shit."

"Not compared to her."

Somehow that snapped the tension, and I burst out laughing. "Good point."

"Well. Whether or not it's the same person, it doesn't help us find Danyaela."

"We're on a first-name basis now? Danny, have you thought about the likelihood that your buddy Danyaela's the killer we're looking for? The symbol on Petrucci's wall belonged to one group, and she tried to kill Nalfar for being part of the other one."

"But Cormorant said Claudia wouldn't belong to either group. So, if Danyaela's her protege or whatever, then she wouldn't belong to them either."

I exhaled through my nose. "True enough. There's a whole political structure here that we don't know anything about."

"You think we oughtta go talk to Ms. Gunnar?"

"No," I said. "We're not getting sucked into this world. At least, not any deeper than we can help. Let's just work the case."

He lifted his shoulders. "Okey-doke. Looks like the investigating officer was a Sergeant Bill Lochran from the 9th Precinct."

We took an hour to familiarize ourselves with Miss Morrigan's history. She sounded like a very nice girl. Her family was unremarkable. And Lochran's case report was unhelpful; no one had seen or heard anything out of the ordinary in the weeks preceding her disappearance. She had gone out for drinks with a few friends on the evening of December 13th, headed home, and vanished forever. The only thing resembling a lead was that, before her disappearance, her name had been accessed in a national database by a Mr. Evan Slade of Manchester, New Hampshire. Sergeant Lochran, however, had concluded that this was unconnected.

Danny sat brooding with his chin on his fist. "This is pretty vague. Lochran just says he interviewed Mr. Slade and 'determined his non-involvement.'"

"That *is* odd. It seems like Lochran was a good cop; three commendations, no reprimands. And it's not like we have protocols in place for dealing with the undead. He ran the whole case by the book, except for this one lead."

"Which is also the only lead that looks promising."

"Huh." I ran a quick search. "He's still over at the 9th. Why don't we go pay him a visit?"

"Done and done."

Sergeant Bill Lochran was a lean, tidy fellow with a stern face and thinning grey hair. His coffee mug said USMC. "Help you gents?" he asked as we converged on his desk.

We introduced ourselves and shook hands, and he offered us chairs. "Thanks," I said. "How long were you in the Corps?"

He didn't quite smile, but his eyes lightened. "Eight years. Things were a lot simpler then."

"Ain't that the truth."

"So, what brings you, boys, around?"

"Sergeant, we crossed paths with an old case of yours and we're hoping you can give us some insight. Do you remember

Danyaela Morrigan?"

He didn't miss a beat. "Sure do. Missing persons. Woulda been, what—ten, twelve years ago now. Never found a trace of her."

"What can you tell us about Evan Slade?"

"Evan Slade. . . Oh, right. He worked at some weirdo rave club in Manchester. Ran an online search on her name a couple days before she vanished."

"And you didn't think he was involved?"

"Well, no." A sudden look of perplexity came into his face. "I mean, he—he was—" He blinked a few times and shook his head as if recollecting something. "No, he wasn't involved."

"You interviewed him?"

"Of course. Funny coincidence, him looking up her name just prior. But things like that happen all the time."

Danny spoke for the first time. "Sergeant, did you happen to meet a lady who called herself Claudia after you talked to Mr. Slade?"

"Say what? I don't—" He stopped again. "That name sounds. . . I can't remember." He frowned. "Got a damn good memory too. I don't—what was the question?"

Danny and I glanced at each other. "It's all right, Sergeant," I said. "I think we've got what we need. Thanks for your time."

The confusion left his face, forgotten. "No problem. Merry Christmas."

"Same to you."

We got back into Danny's car and sat for a while. "Are we thinking what I think we're thinking?" I asked.

"I think so."

"It's not enough they can fly and catch bullets, they can hypnotize people too?"

"Looks like."

"Shit."

"Yep."

We sat again.

"So!" Danny said. "Wanna head up to Manchester?"

I sighed.

Morning traffic was clearing by now, and the weather was good. Once we reached Manchester, we cruised the grubby avenues, following the voice on my GPS, until we found the rave club Lochran had mentioned. Our records indicated that Slade still worked there, and he wasn't answering his home phone. A club like this wouldn't be open so early in the day, but maybe we could bang on the door till a janitor let us in or something.

The club was a big building poised between the better and not-so-good parts of town. The front was windowless red brick, nondescript, with only one door. A sign hung over it, cursive silver lettering on indigo: THE ABYSS.

Luck was with us. As we drove on by, we saw a Budweiser truck parked in the side alley and a couple of guys carrying boxes inside. We parked on the street and moseyed down the alley in their direction.

The deliverymen paused when we got close. One of them nodded and said, "Hiya, fellas."

We showed them our badges. "We're looking for the manager," I said.

He jerked a thumb toward the open door on the side of the building. "Right in there."

"'Preciate it."

Inside the door was a broad, shallow anteroom lit by fluorescents. The far wall was lined with kegs, hooked up to taps on the other side. A very tall thin man in his fifties, with a pointed white beard and impeccable black bow tie, was holding a clipboard and inspecting the crates of beer. He raised an eyebrow as we came in.

"Man, once believed that his enemies could not cross a threshold unless the master of the house invited them. But in these latter days we know better, do we not?"

I held up my badge. "We're sorry to intrude. Are you the manager?"

"I am. Bartholomew Vortok, at your service."

"Detectives Blake and McArdle, Boston PD. We're looking for

Evan Slade, is he here?"

Vortok gazed at the ceiling. "How readily we surrender our true names in this age, despite the power they confer. So much wisdom lost to us."

"We'd like to speak with Mr. Slade. Is he here or not?"

Vortok glanced back at us as if surprised to find us still standing there. "I don't imagine you have a warrant."

"Yeah, as a matter of fact, we do. It was signed by Danyaela Morrigan and Claudia Procula. You know those names?"

His face betrayed no flicker of emotion. A beat went by. Then he smiled a bright arctic smile. "Perhaps I do. Such names should not be spoken aloud; but as I say, we have forgotten much. Please follow me, gentlemen."

The anteroom must have been sound-proofed. As soon as he opened the door leading into the main club, we were assailed by sinister organ music overlaid with a shuddering techno beat. The lights were dim and shot through with flickering strobes. Mind you, this was at about eleven in the morning and the place was deserted. They must have kept the arteries of decadence pulsing away at all hours of the day and night in here.

Behind us along the back wall was the bar, fed by the kegs in the anteroom. It was huge and black and marked with crimson pentagrams, and two men in hooded black robes were moving around behind it, polishing glasses and organizing the bottles on the shelves. One of the side walls was covered in a massive mural of Gustave Dore's illustrations of Dante's Inferno; the other was lined with glass cases full of writhing snakes. A lurid swirl in the light made me glance up: the ceiling was dominated by a titanic glass fixture full of thick red fluid, agitated by what looked like industrial-size blender blades. The floor, I realized, was a giant mosaic of a bearded profile with thorns on its brow. They were dancing on His face.

Vortok led us up a spiraling flight of stairs to a tiny office sealed away from the venomous atmosphere outside. Like the anteroom, it was sound-proofed and lit with normal-people lights. The only furnishings were a desk and a chair. A cadaverous man in his forties was sitting at a computer, and I recognized him from the files despite his pallor and wasted cheeks—Evan Slade, looking not at all well.

"Mr. Slade," Vortok said. "These men are detectives, with queries regarding old friends of ours. They are very interested in speaking with you."

Slade raised his ashen face and glowered at us. "Whattaya want?" he rasped.

"Let's cut the crap," I said. "You tracked down Danyaela Morrigan, and Claudia Procula took her. When our man came around to investigate, Procula brainwashed him into thinking you weren't involved. That about the size of it?"

"What if it is?" He didn't sound defiant; he sounded bitter.

"I understand Claudia's MIA these days. Who do you think's gonna brainwash us? Or the ones who come after us? You don't look so good, Slade. You look like a man who's outlived his usefulness."

"Excuse me," Vortok said in a pleasant, urbane voice. "I brought you up here because you implied that you'd been in contact with Lady Claudia. Am I to understand that you've come under false pretenses?"

"Shut up, Vortok," Danny said. "No one's talking to you." His face was grim; he didn't like this place any better than I did.

"There's no point in keeping secrets for her anymore," I said, still talking to Slade. "Why don't you get it off your chest while you've still got a chance?"

He turned his fading glare on Vortok. "Her blood was the only thing that kept the cancer from eating me alive. Just a drop every six months, and I was healthy as a horse. But she doesn't care what happens to me, just stays locked away in Tarn with her—"

Danny and I were both intent on the man in the chair. When Vortok's gun came out, neither of us was ready. There was a blast and a smack as Slade's brainstem hit the wall behind him, and then Vortok was out the door and heading down the stairs.

I lunged through the opening, drawing my weapon, and went

Whisper Music

thundering down the steps on his tail. Danny vaulted over the railing, dropped a whole story to the floor, and rolled to his feet with a grunt. Vortok turned and shot at us, and we both hit the floor and returned fire. The hooded men came running across the dance floor, hauling ordnance from under their robes. One of them opened fire with a sawed-off shotgun, shattering the glass case behind me, and a brood of vipers came slithering out.

The other hood was firing a sub-machine gun at Danny. These guys may have been talented amateurs, but they weren't trained—otherwise, they'd have known better than to run across an open floor with no cover. Danny put three rounds through his center mass like he was drilling a paper target on a practice range, and the hood flew backward, firing wildly into the air. We heard the crack of bullets hitting glass overhead, and I had just enough time to say, "Ohhhhh, shit." Then the fixture burst and five hundred gallons of hot, churning pig's blood came dumping down on our heads.

Half-scrambling, half-swimming, I floundered out from the wall to get away from the snakes. We were all too gagged and blinded to shoot at each other for the moment, but I still had a sense of where the guy with the shotgun was. I could hear him splashing around over there—too far away for me to use the snakes against him. I wiped frantically at my eyes, looking for a target. "Danny?" I shouted. "Danny!"

"Over here," he yelled. "Where's Vortok?"

"I see him. Freeze, asshole!"

There was a sudden click from the direction of the other barman. His clumsily modified shotgun was misfiring, clogged with blood. Let's see if my Marine-maintained side-arm has the same problem, I thought and shot him through the solar plexus.

Vortok had reached the cover of the bar. He stuck his head out and resumed fire. I was pinned down, and the serpents were fanning out in all directions from their broken prison, weaving their way through the red slime much more easily than the bipeds in the room.

"Throw down the weapon, Vortok!" I called. "Don't make us

kill you."

"Let me see if I can recall the colloquialism," he yelled back. "Ah, yes: You shall never take me alive, coppers!"

"Needs work, bro," Danny called.

Vortok fired again, and then I heard the clack of an empty magazine. I jumped up, blew the head off a serpent that was just opening its jaws to bite my heel, and went sprinting toward the bar.

Our quarry burst into the anteroom, where the deliverymen were wrapping up their stacking of beer crates. They hadn't heard the shooting from inside, but they reacted predictably when confronted with a man covered head-to-toe in blood and waving a smoking pistol: they got the hell out of his way. By the time we got to the bar and followed him outside, he had already leaped into the cab of their idling truck. As it went tearing down the alleyway, Danny made a magnificent bound and caught hold of the rear bumper.

I pounded after him as fast as I could, but the truck was picking up speed. "Keys!" I bellowed. As he was dragging himself up through the open door into the rear of the truck where boxes of Bud were spilling and tumbling every which way, he dug in his pocket and throw his car keys to the pavement. I scooped them up as I passed and headed for his Mustang just a few seconds after the truck went screeching past it. A few seconds after that, the siren was blaring, and I was shrieking down the street in pursuit.

Vortok's vehicle had no chance against mine in terms of speed and maneuverability, but he made up for it with a combination of size and balls-out craziness. He headed uptown, into the thick of the traffic, and smashed his way onto the main drag. I followed a trail of flipped hybrids and crushed motorcycles, gritting my teeth as I skidded through the slush to avoid the screaming pedestrians. He was aiming for smaller cars on purpose, I realized, creating a wake of debris to slow me down. As I rounded a corner on two wheels, I saw him swerve to the left and clip the rear of an empty Prius, spinning it out into the

Whisper Music

street in his wake, where it blocked my path. The oncoming lane was packed with speeding automotive death, and the sidewalk with potential murder victims. I could've just crashed on through, but I risked obliterating my engine block. One chance: I cranked the wheel to the right, yanked up the emergency brake, and swung around a hundred and eighty degrees as I forced the growling gearstick into reverse. Braced my head as hard as I could against the headrest, squeezed my eyes shut for an instant, and slammed into the Prius, sending it flying into a parked van. The impact slung me around in a semi-circle, and I wrenched the gearstick back into drive and was hurtling forward again at full speed, fishtailing and dragging my rear bumper and muffler like I'd just gotten married to mayhem.

Sirens: the Manchester PD was on the warpath. Vortok had put up an impressive run, but this couldn't go on much longer. Squad cars were approaching from ahead of us—closing in behind us—swerving out of side streets all around us. It was over. The beer truck went lumbering up to the banks of the Merrimack River, and I felt a brief surge of triumph: he had nowhere left to go, he'd have to pull over now or plunge into the—

Then he bashed through the rail and went plummeting down into the icy water. *"Danny!"* I howled, and then I was grinding to a halt, leaping out of the car, ripping off my trench coat, and diving in after my partner.

Holy good sweet Jesus, that water was cold. Couldn't see, couldn't feel, couldn't think. . . hand clutching at my arm, kicking back to the surface. . . treading water, gasping, blue-faced in the frigid morning air. Danny's voice, panting for breath: "Welp—'nother day at the office."

Love that little punk.

CHAPTER 4

A QUIET DRINK

Rain was waiting for us when we returned to Tarn. "Goddess," she said as Claudia entered the church. With Nikosk and Petrov following suit behind her, she knelt and pressed her forehead to the marble floor.

"Rain Vissarian," Claudia said, sounding amused. "What fleeting little empty-headed cult are you chasing today?"

"I worship only the Dark, my lady. And you as its high priestess."

"Fine, fine, I'll spare your life for the time being. Now bring me a victim and draw me a bath."

"At once, Goddess."

The tub was already prepared, and Rain's minions had been out all day seeking better fare than the random hikers she promised me. For Claudia, a pale dark-eyed man; for me, a beautiful raven-haired girl. I hadn't instructed her to seek such victims—she must have known Claudia's preferences from of old and inferred that I would favor those who resembled my mistress. Both victims were dominated, staring ahead and obeying every command in silence. Claudia didn't bother with preliminaries but ripped out the man's jugular and drank him dry. She'd been a long time in Hell.

As She sank into the steaming bathwater, I put a finger under my victim's chin and gently raised her head. I was tired and thirsty, and my first impulse was to exsanguinate this girl. But after all the vicious battles I'd been through this week, I found that I wanted a moment of tranquility—of tenderness. Her eyes fluttered shut as I bit her, and the familiar sigh of rapture came from her mouth. I drank enough to slake my thirst, then put her in a chair and commanded her to sleep.

"Join me, Danyaela," Claudia said.

I was covered head to foot in gore. Nothing sounded better than a bath. Rain left us, closing the door behind her, and my mistress and I were alone together at last.

"So," She said.

"So."

"You've grown strong in my absence, my daughter and lover. How did you find your way to Hell's antechamber?"

"I have fed upon the Virgin, my lady."

Her eyes widened. "That's impossible."

"We fought in Medjugorje. She almost destroyed me. But I tasted one drop of her blood—less than a drop—and that was enough."

"Tell me everything."

I described the fight, the crystal sphere, and my encounter with the Dark. "I see," She said, frowning. "Yes—your blood is different than before. I recognize the spirit of our Lord within it, but there is something else. It must be *hers*."

"Do you think you can reach the crystal sphere, Mistress?"

She shook Her head. "The power is too diluted by passing through you. I will have to feed upon her."

"We'll never catch her again."

"No? The last time you tried to hypnotize her, you hadn't yet tasted her soul. Next time will be different. Now tell me—when you touch the minds within this sphere of yours, can you influence them as well as reading them?"

"I—I don't know. I haven't tried."

"Let's finish our bath. Then you'll return to the sphere and see what abilities you have there."

"What of Lucifer's blood, my lady?"

One corner of her mouth turned up in a bitter smile. "I know. I've always told you that to taste the blood is to gain control over the heart and mind. I never thought you would encounter the one exception to that rule. He's been barred from entering this world for two millennia. But I'm afraid He *is* the exception, for He is the source of all our power. Now that He's fed you His blood, He will have the same dominion over you He has over me."

". . . What dominion?"

"You've already learned that He can pull me into Hell whenever it pleases Him to do so. Now He can do the same to you."

I felt my hands curling into fists. "I won't be His toy."

"He is the King of this world, Danyaela. We are all of us His toys. You and I are His favorites and can play with the rest of His toys as we like—but that does not come without cost."

I said nothing. I was remembering Mary through His eyes.

"Come. Try your hand at influencing the minds in the crystal sphere, and then we'll sleep. I miss my bed."

My hands relaxed. My eyes closed. I slipped lower into the tub and let the steaming waters close over my head. Then I sought the soul-fields once again.

Flowing across that crystal expanse. Up ahead, the crystal cliff. I had no person in mind, so I latched onto the first light that crossed my path: Jubei, a restaurant owner in Tokyo. He was brushing his teeth, and I could see his face in the mirror through his own eyes.

Stop brushing.

He paused for half a moment, and a look of puzzlement crossed his features, but then he shrugged it off and resumed. I bent my will upon him with greater determination.

Stop brushing, Jubei.

He scratched his head. He wasn't hearing a voice, I sensed; he only felt a wordless prompting, an intuition. But once again he shook it off. Jubei was not to be deterred from his dental hygiene.

I decided to try another tack. I was disembodied but my consciousness was located inside of this man. Instead of issuing orders, I tried to move his arms as if they were my own. Perhaps I could take full possession of these mortals?

Whisper Magic

But there was no effect. He finished his ablutions and turned off the bathroom light. A moment later, I was back in the bathtub in Tarn.

Claudia looked startled. "Quite a technique you've acquired," She said. She did not sound wholly pleased.

"I don't know how it looks from outside. Was my body still here, or did I vanish?"

"You—faded. You were still there, but it was as if I could no longer hold your image in my mind."

Interesting.

"How did you fare?"

I told Her of my trial by Jubei. "It seems I can whisper in their ears, but they're free to ignore me if they wish."

"Well, it's a start. Perhaps with practice, your influence over them will grow. But enough for tonight. I feel a weariness such as I have rarely felt."

Part of me wanted to ask about Her time in Hell. But even had She wished to speak of it, another part of me would not have wanted to hear. We retired to Her bed and slept away the daylight hours. There were no dreams. Vampires do not dream.

In the evening, I awoke feeling refreshed. I had fed and washed and rested, and I was coming into a new level of strength which (I now suspected) surpassed even that of my mistress. I was ready for whatever the night would bring. My lady was stirring as I rose, and we dressed in sable gowns.

Rain greeted us as we emerged from the catacombs. "I have news, my empresses. A mortal has come here of his own will, claiming that he knows the Lady Claudia."

Claudia raised Her eyebrows. "Indeed? What name did he give?"

"Bartholomew Vortok."

She laughed. "Old aging Vortok. I had forgotten. Where is he now?"

"We're holding him with the other humans, Goddess."

"Very well, bring him out and let's hear his tale."

Rain bowed and went to fetch Claudia's retainer, whoever he

was. "Lady," I asked, "last night in the antechamber, you said we had work to do. What did you mean?"

"The Darkness is moving, Danyaela. A time of change and destiny is coming."

"What change?"

She said nothing. At that moment, Rain returned with a tall skinny fellow in a bedraggled suit. He genuflected before Claudia and then stood—a lone man in a desecrated church, surrounded by vampiresses.

"Hail to the Dark," he said, and we could all smell the fear in him. Claudia smiled and let him see Her fangs. "I—I come with tidings, Lady Claudia. The police are asking questions about Danyaela Morrigan. They destroyed my club—killed two of my men. And Evan Slade betrayed you. He mentioned the name of Tarn in their hearing. I killed him at once, of course."

"My dear loyal Vortok. What became of the officers who caused all this?"

He cleared his throat, twice. "I escaped them, my lady. For many years I have always kept one vial of your blood with me. There was a pursuit by car, and I fell into the river, but your blood gave me the strength to swim to safety. They think me dead."

"They must be wise men. Did they have names?"

He nodded. "Detectives Blake and McArdle of Boston."

"Boston," I murmured. All the threads of this tapestry appeared to be converging there.

"They were out of their jurisdiction," Claudia said thoughtfully. "Why did you let them in?"

"I . . . They mentioned both you and Lady Danyaela by name. I thought. . . My lady, I was desperate for news of you. I knew it must be a ruse, but I was so desperate to believe them. I thought somehow, they might lead me to you. And—and here you are!"

There was a brief silence. I was positive She would kill him. But She offered Her hand, and he took it and dropped to his knees. "Oh, Vortok. Your family has served me well for generations. You might have performed better in this emergency, but perhaps you are growing old at last. Have you given thought to the matter of a successor?"

"It grieves me to have failed you, my lady. I shall set about siring an heir to the Vortok line. I swear that I will raise him to be stronger than his father."

"Good. Now, let us see to the practicalities. I assume you came here in a stolen vehicle?"

"Yes, my lady."

"Rain, do we have any vehicles here that the police won't be searching for?"

"Yes, Goddess. We—" she glanced at me "—the Golgotha Dancers came here by car. About half a dozen are parked outside."

"Fine. Vortok, pick a car and go to New York. Seek out our old friend Agent Tomlinson and tell him everything. He'll give you a new identity and we'll resume our work. Understood?"

He bent down and kissed Her feet. "I obey always, my lady. Farewell for now." And with that, he got up and went on his way.

"The Vortok family?" I asked.

She shrugged. "It's often useful to have wealthy servants in mortal circles. I suppose you haven't met them before. Twelve years is no time at all for me, and this or that detail may have slipped my mind."

"How did he know my name?"

"He found me a computer expert called Slade, back when I was looking for you. I bribed him with some of my blood."

I knew that if a mortal drank the blood of a vampire, it gave him abnormal vitality for a few weeks. It could only turn you into a vampire in conjunction with being bitten and drained to the point of death; but still, it was a precious commodity.

"Claudia," I said. "You've never told me why you were looking for me in the first place. I want to know." I had never addressed her without her title before.

A look of anger flickered across her face and then passed into amusement. "Let's not bicker in front of the help. Rain, see about some breakfast for us."

"At once, Goddess." She bowed and withdrew.

"Come and sit, Danyaela." We stepped up to the unhallowed altar and seated ourselves. "You know who I am, my little one. It was my husband who sentenced that—" she spat a curse in Latin "—that *man*, that filthy Nazarene. I suffered a vision the night before, and I warned him, my silly ineffectual Pontius, but he wouldn't listen. And the next night, after the hill and the cross, the Darkness came. He came in the form of a man, incarnate in our world, and He turned me. And only a few hours later, that cursed thing rose from the grave and barred our Lord from this realm forever. For two thousand years, I sought the one to whom I could pass on the gift of the blood. And then, twelve years ago, I suffered another vision. I saw you and I heard your name. I knew you were the one chosen by the Will of the Dark. And so, I tracked you down and gave you immortality. I don't ask for gratitude, for we all do what we are bidden by our Master in Perdition. But I am your mistress, and I *will* have your reverence. Do you hear?"

I didn't answer.

"Now," she said, as if I had agreed, "the first order of business is to find these detectives. You found Cormorant—can you do the same with Blake and McArdle?"

I nodded.

"Excellent. Then track them down and silence them. Let's not kill them for now; I don't want to be tripping over the mortal authorities at every turn. Compel them to silence and forgetfulness, and we'll move on to more important matters."

I rose from my seat.

"Return as soon as you're finished," she said. "We have much to do."

Still, without speaking, I rose into the air and soared out through the doors, as I had done the night before last. For the first time, it occurred to me that Claudia was no longer being held outside of Creation; her spirit should be accessible from the crystal sphere, just like everyone else. I could read her mind at will, learn all her secrets. If she was right, maybe with practice I

Whisper Magic

could even learn to influence her thoughts from afar.

But not tonight. Back to the soul-fields I went and focused on the name Blake. A cop from Boston. I wondered.

And there he was. I was right: it was the same cop I'd met last night in the park, the one who offered me his coat. He seemed like a good man. I was glad Claudia didn't want him dead.

He was in his apartment back in Boston. It was late, but he was wide awake, pacing the living floor. I saw that he and his partner had been reprimanded for acting outside their jurisdiction and would face some kind of investigation tomorrow. It would be hard for him to satisfy them if he had no memory of today's events—but that was his problem. I had my orders.

Hmmm. I already knew that I couldn't control his mind from here; but what if I could reach him another way? I had his location now: I could return to the material plane and fly from Maine to Massachusetts to confront him. But what if I didn't have to? Claudia said my body "faded" when I was in the sphere. And when I came back from the anteroom of Hell, the blood of the giant serpent was real enough. Could I step from one point in the physical world into the crystal sphere and re-emerge at another?

Focusing all my energy on Blake's location, I made the effort of will to leave the sphere and rematerialize. And it worked: I found myself standing in his apartment. His back was to me; he was gazing out the window at the neon glimmer of the streets below. I smiled.

"Hello, Detective," I said quietly.

He jumped a foot in the air and spun around, raising his fists. Then he saw me and froze. Shock, then anger, and then resignation passed over his face in the space of a single second. The first thing he said was, "Please don't hurt my wife."

"I'm not here to hurt you."

The anger came back. "Just to brainwash me? Like they did to Lochran?"

"I don't know who that is. But, yes."

"Sergeant Lochran was looking for you after you were

kidnapped, Miss Morrigan. One of your buddies screwed up his head. Now you're just a name in a dusty filing cabinet somewhere."

"I'm a great deal more than that, Detective Blake."

"Sure. You get to kill anyone you want now. Sounds swell."

"Didn't you kill two men today? Vortok's men?"

He exhaled. "Yeah, we did. But not for food. And not for fun, either." Honor and sorrow were etched in his mouth—things I'd all but forgotten. "You know what, I'm not up for an ethics debate right now. Just do what you're gonna do."

A few beats went by. "Do you have anything to drink?" I asked.

". . . You like Scotch?"

"Used to."

He paced over to his little kitchen and rummaged. I heard the clink of a bottle and the tinkle of liquid, and he came back with two half-full glasses. "Guess we haven't met, have we." He gave me a glass and then offered his hand. "Harry Blake."

I took the glass and shook his hand. "Danyaela Morrigan." He raised his glass, and we both drank. It tasted better than I remembered.

"So, you're a vampire," he said.

"Yep," I heard myself say. I hadn't said "yep" in over a decade.

"And you can fly."

I nodded.

"That must be fun."

"It's the best part." I had another sip. "Or it would be. It's hard to enjoy it."

"Why?"

I wished I could exhale like him. "It's such a childhood fantasy, isn't it? Soaring through the clouds like Peter Pan. But we're always so adult. We only laugh when we're being cruel."

"I'm sorry this happened to you, Danyaela."

No one had ever said that to me. I finished my drink.

"You want another?" he asked.

"No. Thank you." I handed him the empty glass.

"So, this is it? Will I remember meeting you?"

Another few beats went by. "You'll remember. You'll remember everything."

"What does that mean?"

"I don't know what it means. Please be careful, Harry. I don't want to kill you."

The apartment faded away.

CHAPTER 5

FANG-CHASERS

Oh, I know fear. I've been trading punches with bigger kids since I was four years old. Been getting shot at since I was nineteen. I was afraid when I found out vampires were real. But what was the worst they could do, kill me? Fuck 'em. We all die, don't we?

But now Beth was in the cross-hairs. I had no idea why Danyaela decided not to do whatever she came to do, and I was grateful, but there was nothing saying she couldn't change her mind again. And maybe next time she wouldn't just be there to mind-wipe me. Jesus, it wasn't bad enough she could fly and catch bullets and hypnotize people, now she could *teleport* too?

As soon as she vanished, I lunged for the phone and called Danny. He answered on the second ring; he wasn't sleeping either. I didn't realize I was babbling until he shouted, "Blake! Calm down. What the hell happened?"

I took a breath. "She was here. Danyaela Morrigan was in my apartment."

"Oh, shit. Is Beth okay?"

"She's fine, she's sleeping. We've gotta go see Clare right now. *Right now.*"

"I'll meet you there." He hung up.

Ballistics had taken my Beretta after the shootout in Manchester, but I still had an illegal Glock 18 hidden under the bathroom sink, modified for full auto. I strapped on my shoulder holster, stuffed my pants full of extra clips, and headed for my car at a run.

Got there a few minutes ahead of Danny—didn't wait—banged on the door until she yanked it open and yelled, "What the hell got up your skirt, Blake?"

"Vamp chick from last night just paid me a visit."

". . . Come on in."

Looked like I'd stumbled into the middle of a conclave. It was after midnight, but the whole merry band of demon slayers—including young Patrick—was sitting around the living room table. Leah was sharpening a big silver throwing knife, Rigby was cleaning a .357 Magnum, and Patrick appeared to be in the middle of an arm-wrestling match with Brother Joseph. Cormorant was holding a steaming mug that smelled like a hot toddy. I remembered he'd been injured earlier, but he certainly didn't look any the worse for wear.

"Have a seat," Clare said. "Beer?"

"Absolutely yes. Thank you." I dropped myself into a chair. "Sorry to burst in like this."

"'Sokay, Ossifer," Leah said. "You can keep us honest."

"I don't know about that."

Clare came back with a Yuengling and set it on the table in front of me. "Now what's going on?"

Just then—perfect timing—Danny showed up at the door. Clare gave him a chair and a beer, and then I told the full tale of our day's adventures, starting with our visit to the 9th Precinct. They listened intently to the details of Danyaela's abduction, and I was pleased despite myself to tell them something about vampires they didn't already know. But the story of her visit to my apartment was the gem in the crown.

"Why in hell didn't she kill him?" Rigby demanded as if I weren't there.

"Same reason they didn't kill Lochran twelve years ago," Clare said, glaring at the table and chewing on a cigarette. "They don't want to draw more attention than they can help."

"Yes," Cormorant said, "that makes sense. But why break into his apartment to mesmerize him and then change her mind at the last moment?"

"It kinda sounds like she doesn't love being a vampire," Danny said.

"Yeah," Leah scoffed. "Immortality, flight, superhuman strength—who'd want that crap?"

"Maybe someone who doesn't wanna kill people all the time," Patrick said.

"Kid's right," I said. Our eyes met, and I saw respect there for the first time. "I could hear it in her voice. She misses being—I dunno—pure. Whole. Clean."

Brother Joseph spoke for the first time. "It's no great surprise, is it? God made us for Himself, and our hearts are restless till they rest in Him. This poor girl has been bent by the Enemy and made to believe that she can never find rest again. Her inmost self yearns for Christ's peace, although she's forgotten His name."

"I bet she doesn't yearn so much that she'll let us cut her head off," Clare said. "Let's focus on what we know."

"We know Claudia Procula was turned in 33 A.D. and waited thousands of years to choose her progeny," said Cormorant. "And we know this Danyaela confronted Our Lady in Medjugorje, and that she can appear and disappear at will—which is a power no vampire in history has ever manifested before. There is something special about her."

At first, it was reassuring to know that *most* vampires couldn't teleport. But then it occurred to me that Danyaela seemed to have an interest in me, and that just made me all the more apprehensive.

Danny took a pull of his beer. "So, Paulson—last night, you seemed to have kind of a personal reaction when Nalfar mentioned Claudia. Have you met her before?"

Cormorant smiled. "Yes, I have. You're very perceptive, Daniel."

"Yeah, well, you know."

"Any inside information would be appreciated, Mr. Cormorant," I said. "My wife was fifteen feet from a vampire this evening."

"I'm aware, Detective. Please believe that I'm wracking my brain for any insight, but I know less about Miss Morrigan than you do. It rather seems that she's taken a liking to you."

Clare nodded. "Does, doesn't it? Expect she's almost forgotten what it's like talking to a decent guy."

"So," I said. "These things—these people—they're not a hundred percent evil. They can still at least *want* to be good."

"Looks like."

"Well, can they be turned back? Can they ever be human again?"

Cormorant gave me a somber look. "In all the annals of the Church, in all the long centuries of this war, not even one single vampire has ever been turned back. It is considered gospel that true death is the only redemption from undeath."

"Great."

"Harry," Clare said. "Right now, there's only one real question for you. Are you ready to let go of your life? Are you ready to stop being a cop and start being one of us?"

I glanced at Danny. He smiled and shrugged. I looked back at Clare and inclined my head. "Yeah. I guess I am."

"Be sure. There's no turning back."

"I'm sure, Clare. Just tell me how to fight them."

"Well, that ain't hard. Fire and silver. But they're fast, and they regenerate. You wanna kill 'em, you gotta catch 'em sleeping. And for that, you need help. That's why we collaborate with the younger ones to hunt down the older ones."

"Why do the younger ones help us?"

"They want the power. They get the blood of the elders, it makes them stronger."

"So, the day after we dethrone the old ones, we're stuck in an arms race with our former allies."

"That's the game, Harry. Like I said last night, we work with what we've got."

I emptied my bottle, emptied my lungs, and sat brooding. What the hell now.

"Is Claudia the oldest vampire of all?" Danny asked.

"As far as we know, yes," Cormorant replied.

"Prob'ly oughtta start by killing her, then. Danyaela might even be willing to help."

"That's a rather tall order, my friend."

"Well," I said, "we've got a good idea of where she hangs out."

Clare raised her eyebrows. "How's that?"

"Slade mentioned a place called Tarn, right before Vortok painted the office with his skull. We looked it up, and there's a ghost town by that name deep in the woods of Maine. People've been disappearing from the vicinity for a long time."

"Sounds like a lead, Officer. 'Cept Nalfar said she's been missing for over a year."

"I know it. But the way Danyaela was talking, it sounded like she was operating on someone else's orders. And who but Claudia could give orders to *her?*"

". . . Huh."

"What kind of resistance should we expect?" Danny asked. "It seems like she's not shy about using humans."

"Yep. We call 'em fang-chasers: humans who work for the vamps in the hopes of getting turned, or at least getting some of their blood."

"Vampire blood makes people stronger?"

She nodded.

"I've heard of the Vortoks before," Cormorant said. "They've been serving Claudia for centuries. But she wouldn't use them as cannon fodder. If she has human bodyguards, they'll be mercenaries who don't know whom they're working for."

"Why not just hypnotize people to protect her?" I asked.

"No doubt she would, in a pinch. But they prefer people who are free to think on their behalf."

"Makes sense."

"You said she considers herself above the others," Danny said. "Does that mean it'll just be her and Danyaela in Tarn?"

He shook his head. "She's been known to use lesser vampires in her service."

Whisper Music

"How do you come to know so much about her, Cormorant?" I asked.

Rigby bristled. "He's straight from the Vatican, bro. He's one of their top hunters."

"I hope you're not planning to take offense any time I ask an intelligent question."

"What's *that* supposed to mean?"

"Boys, boys," Clare said. "Let's not do this right now. If we're planning an assault on Tarn, we need to focus really hard."

"First we need something to focus on," I said. "We need data. Knowledge. Insight." Right then, my phone rang. I glanced at it and jumped up. "Sorry, guys, it's Beth." I ducked into the kitchen. "Hey, baby."

"Harry! Are you all right? Where are you?"

"I'm fine, love. Sorry, I didn't think to leave a note, I was in kind of a hurry."

"What's going on? Where are you?"

"I'm—" I sighed. "We're at Clare Gunnar's house."

"Because of what happened in Manchester?"

"No. I saw her again, Beth. The girl from the park. The—the vampire."

"When?"

"Half an hour ago. That's why we came here." God, I wished I could hold her for this conversation. The phone isn't fit for such things. "I can't sit this fight out anymore."

I could hear her breathing. She only breathed like that when she was forcing herself to speak through tears. "I guess if they put you on suspension, you'll have some free time."

"Guess I will."

"Are you coming back tonight?"

"Yes," I promised. "I'll be back before dawn."

"I'll be here, Harry. I love you."

"Love you too, Elizabeth."

When I came back into the living room, the air was fraught with portent. Some momentous decision had just been reached in my absence.

"What's up?" I asked.

Danny was once again doing a terrible job of hiding how excited he was. "We're going to Rome!"

". . . Say what?"

CHAPTER 6

PRIDE GOETH

Obedience to my mistress had become so ingrained that it had been years since I'd even considered defying her. For one thing, I was cut off from heaven and had no one else to turn to. And for another, as I learned early on, if I showed any resistance, she could bend her will upon me and remove my power of choice. But tonight, I felt different somehow. As I hung in the air far above the ruined church, I realized that I had grown accustomed to being my own mistress. I hadn't noticed the moment when I stopped thinking of her as "Her," but it must mean that things were changing inside of me. With the blood of both Mary and Satan in my veins, I might well be immune to her compulsion now. And I knew one thing for sure: I liked Harry Blake. I had no intention of tampering with his mind, still less of hurting him or anyone he cared for. No matter what she said.

For a few moments, I toyed with the idea of flying down there and saying all this to Claudia—just to see what would happen, as much as anything else. But somehow, it didn't seem like the proper time. I would nurture this newfound hope of freedom inside of myself and wait for the night when it would be put to the test.

That being the case, it occurred to me that I should let some time go by before I returned. She would assume that I'd have to fly to Boston and back once I located Harry and the other; she had no idea I could now transmit myself instantly from place to place, and I thought perhaps I would keep it that way. But that was fine, I thought—there were still chores to which I could attend.

I returned to the crystal sphere. There was Harry's mind, and within it, I found the names of his superiors on the police force. I sought their minds, and from them, I gleaned the names of those further up the chain of command who would also need to be persuaded. Then I began paying visits.

"Captain Martinson."

"Mmmmm.

"Wake up, Captain."

"Mmm? Who—who's there?"

"It's all right, James. Just relax."

"I. . . yes."

"You will exonerate Blake and McArdle. Do you understand?"

"Yes."

"Good. Now go back to sleep. You won't remember me when you awaken."

It didn't take long. Claudia was right about one thing: having the police underfoot would complicate an already complex situation. This way, the entire case should end up swept under the rug and forgotten. If Harry and his partner had been foolish enough to go babbling to their superiors about the undead, they would have done it by now.

The moon was high, making the night clouds luminous. She'd be full soon. A new year was coming. My year. Rain kept calling Claudia "goddess," but her power was nothing to mine now. I wondered what else I could do.

The last time you tried to hypnotize her, you hadn't yet tasted her soul. Next time will be different.

I wondered.

When I was searching for the Darkness, I passed through the crystal cliff and followed its energy back to the source. It hadn't occurred to me until now to try doing the same with *her* energy. Could I follow her all the way home?

I returned to the sphere. I dashed myself against the cliff. I saw the images, as before: her image of me, the wayward daughter. A direct connection to her mind.

With all the force I could muster, I drove myself upwards, following that link. I could feel the strength and purity I had sensed in Medjugorje, swelling all around me like the sunrise. The particles of her grace swirled inside of me as they drew closer to their source. I was rising, rising, rising to the gates of paradise.

But there was something else. Within me, smoldering, was the taste of Satan's blood—the slime of flies and maggots he made me gulp down till my stomach nearly burst. I could feel that filth awakening in my soul, and as I rose ever higher, it began to burn. That spirit, that energy, had rejected the realm to which I was ascending. It seared my inmost being, with which it was now intertwined. I drove myself onwards, upwards, trying to ignore the agony. But the burning grew worse.

Onwards—upwards—burning—

And finally, like a taut silver thread by which I dangled over a never-ending pit, my will snapped. I was hurled down from the firmament, as when I first challenged her in the cold Bosnian skies on Christmas Eve.

I found myself in a snowy field near Tarn, with singed hair and smoke curling up from my skin. Pain wracked my body, and I lay there clutching myself and rocking back and forth like a child. The cold air soothed me, and my charred flesh healed; and at last, I could move again.

Well. Clearly, I wasn't ready for a rematch quite yet.

Climbing to my feet, I dusted myself off and gathered my energies. Claudia's church was a mile or two away; I could fly there in the blink of an eye. But as I was about to go sailing off into the air, I discovered that I felt like taking a walk. I couldn't recall the last time I had strolled in the winter woods. Back *then*—when I was alive—I did all my best thinking during my walks.

Owls glided past me as I moved among the trees, and the snow crunched quietly under my feet. Even with my heightened senses,

I heard no sound of man or machine. The earth was still, and there was—peace. For a little while.

Then I arrived back in Tarn and found the vampires preparing for war.

CHAPTER 7

THE SHEPHERD

In those days, the Throne of St. Peter still stood in the Basilica in Vatican City.

After the council at Clare's house, Danny and I had gone home, slept, and presented ourselves at the station the next morning for our hearing. We'd crossed state lines without authorization, killed two men, and left a trail of devastation across the middle of a major city—all with no discernible connection to the case we were supposed to be working on. We'd be lucky if we walked away with our badges. Hell, we'd be lucky if we walked away without cuffs on our wrists.

But Captain Martinson waved the whole thing aside like it was nothing. We were acting in self-defense. Full exoneration. What about the Manchester PD? Oh, no problem, spoke with them earlier. They agree. Now back to work, boys, that Petrucci case won't solve itself, you know. The entire hearing took less a minute.

We stood outside the captain's office, blinking at each other like we'd just shared a bizarre waking dream. "Well, that was lucky," Danny said.

"Yeah. Luck."

"Five'll getcha ten Danyaela's behind it."

"No bet."

It so happened that this was the last day of our work week. We spent the day getting our paperwork in order and watching the clock, then knocked off early and headed home to pack our stuff. For the next two days, we'd be on another continent.

"Tell me again why this a good idea?" Beth said as she zipped up her duffel bag. "Not that seeing the Vatican won't be amazing, mind you."

"Because something's happening in the vampire world. It's starting to look like Danyaela had a run-in with Mary herself, and it changed her somehow. We need to prepare for whatever's coming, and that means checking in with slayer central."

"And they can't do all that without having Harry Blake on the team."

I shrugged. "Seems like the lady in question has a soft spot for me and Danny. She damn near killed Cormorant and the others, but she went out of her way to get us off the hook over Vortok."

"Not crazy about the idea of sexy vampire chicks having a soft spot for my man."

"Don't worry, baby. She was waaaay too skinny for my tastes."

We gathered at a small airfield just outside of town. Turned out there was a clandestine jet service for slayers. No one had objected when I insisted on bringing Beth along. Clare brought her nephew as well. The gang's all here.

Rome was dark when we banked over St. Peter's Square and cruised down toward the airstrip. I'd been to Europe before, but never here, and I could feel the solemnity and awe building in the back of my mind. But it didn't really hit me until we entered the Basilica and beheld the altar and the Throne. Three days ago, I was just another cop investigating another homicide; now I was standing in the beating heart of the Church and fighting in the War between Heaven and Hell.

"Oh, man," I said under my breath.

Beth took my hand and gave me a tiny smile. We walked on.

It was just before sunrise, local time, on the morning of the 29th. We'd slept and eaten on the plane and were ready to face what the day threw at us. Following Cormorant, we passed through the domed silence and on to a roped-off staircase in the back. The guards nodded to him and let us by.

"Cardinal Vicenzo is our main liaison," he said in a hushed

Whisper Music

voice as we mounted the steps. "He'll want to know what we've learned, and with any luck, he'll have fresh intelligence for us."

We trod the long winding stairs and passed a great oaken door and trod a long winding hallway of stone. More guards nodded to our guide and waved us by. I heard Patrick whisper to Clare, "Have you ever been here before?"

"Once. Long time ago."

We took a left down a short corridor and entered a small red chamber. The carpet was deep and soft, and the walls were hung with blank scarlet tapestries—arrases, I think they're called. There were several chairs and couches, a mahogany table holding a decanter and glasses, and a desk in the corner. A portly gentleman in clerical garb stuck his head through the far door, said something in Italian, and withdrew.

"The cardinal will see us," Cormorant translated. "Have a seat if you like."

Danny flopped onto a divan, and Beth followed suit. I sat on her other side. The others gravitated to the remaining seats, but Cormorant stayed standing. "So, just to clarify," I said. "This one guy is in charge of a worldwide network of underground vampire hunters."

Cormorant smiled. "The Holy Father is in charge. Cardinal Vicenzo oversees the slayers operating on the East Coast."

The far door opened again, and a tiny fellow in a white robe came into the room. We all stood to greet him, but he waved us back into our seats. "Please, please," he said. "It is a pleasure. A great pleasure. Welcome, welcome. Paulson, how good to see you again, *buongiorno*. God's peace be with you." He tottered forward, leaning on his crozier, and embraced Cormorant.

Cardinal Vicenzo looked to be in his mid-to-late seventies. His hair was as white as his robe, and his skin was like old translucent parchment. Even his eyes were as light a shade of blue as they could be without being silver. He looked like a wisp of cloud, but there was a kindliness in him that made you think of the sun peeping out from behind. I liked him instantly.

Then he turned and looked right at me. "*Ecco.* You are most welcome, Harold Blake. Most welcome. The friend of our enemy is our friend, eh? Ha. Yes, indeed. Welcome, all." He went to his desk and sat down, and Cormorant took a seat. "Now, please. I have heard in brief, but if we may recapitulate?"

So once again we told our tale. A glint of anger came into his eyes when we mentioned Petrucci's fate, and I could see a hint of whatever strength lay buried in this man to make him a leader of demon-killers. "A good soul, Willem Petrucci. *Requiescat in pace.* But please, continue."

After I'd finished recounting my run-in with Danyaela, he steepled his fingers and peered up at the red ceiling like he was checking for cherubim. "Fascinating. Troubling. Mystifying! Could it be?" He slapped down his palms on the desk. "Could it be that Our Lady gave some strange grace to that creature in the hopes of bringing back her soul from Hell? Perhaps. On the Cross, Our Lord became sin, *sin itself*, to redeem us all. Who can say where the mercies of Heaven will end?"

"But, Father—if Danyaela was really blessed by the Virgin Mary, then why is she still running around trying to kill people?"

"Aquinas, my friend. A thing is received according to the nature of the recipient."

"Huh?"

"You pour clean water into a dirty glass, you get dirty water," Danny said.

"I would guess," said the cardinal, "I would *guess*, that the gift of the Blessed Mother to that poor woman was to restore her free will. All vampires carry the blood of the Enemy in their veins, diluted to varying degrees, and it twists their hearts to evil, yes? But if this Danyaela Morrigan now also carries the grace of Mary, then it will balance out that twisting and leave her in the same position we are all in, with the boon and burden of choice between evil and good."

"And, um—with the ability to teleport?" Rigby said.

The old cardinal lifted his shoulders. "The Blessed Virgin has been raised above time and space as we know them. Perhaps some small piece of her power was transferred along with her grace."

"But why would she let herself be touched by such a monster?" Patrick burst out.

"Why does she continue to pray for each of us, when our sins drive nails into her beloved Son? In her own warped and desperate way, Danyaela came to the Virgin for help. How could the Virgin turn her away empty-handed, my boy—on Christmas Eve, no less?"

Patrick glowered at the floor. "I still don't trust any of those blood-sucking things."

"Oh goodness, neither do I. But perhaps now there is hope that at least some of them might someday earn our trust, eh?"

"Or we could go public and exterminate them once and for all."

"Patrick," Clare said. "We've been through this."

"The Church must never become an empire," said Vicenzo. "If the governments of men discover the existence of vampires on their own, they must make their own political and military decisions. Our concern is with the souls of individuals."

"Besides," Leah said, "everyone already knows about vampires. There's never been a culture on earth that didn't know about them. People just choose not to believe."

Vicenzo nodded. "True, but sad. Indeed yes."

"Excellency," said Brother Joseph, "we contemplate an attack on Danyaela's lair. What can you tell us of Tarn, Maine?"

"Little, I fear, at this moment. But go, dear friends, break your fast and see the city. We will convene again in, let us say, six hours? And by then—ah, by then, I will know all. Go, and God's blessings go with you." He made shooing motions with his hands. "Go, friends, go. *Mangia.*"

Cormorant led us down another hallway to a large dining room. A forty-foot buffet table was set up along one wall, and priests of a dozen different nations were milling around it, chattering merrily in Latin. We all grabbed plates and heaped them up with omelets and sausage and croissants and frittatas and oh man it was a good breakfast. Danny had three cappuccinos, which he *really* didn't need. After that, we decided to split up and meet back at the front steps in a few hours.

"The guards will have all your names," Cormorant said. "Feel free to tour the spots where tourists aren't allowed."

Beth took my arm. "I know just the place."

The morning mists were clearing away as my wife and I passed through the gates of the Vatican Gardens. Almost sixty acres of quiet hills and fountains, vineyards, orchards and olive trees, all covered in a cool white dust of snow. Here and there we saw a wandering cleric or bishop and nodded hello, but no one spoke, and something in the air and the high stone walls kept out the noises of the city beyond. They say that the garden was seeded with soil from Calvary itself, and I believed it. It didn't feel like Eden, a place where evil was unknown—instead, it felt like a stronghold unbroken by an endless siege, a place where sin and sorrow prowled the outer walls but could never enter. There was both peace and strength among those trees.

We wandered in the garden, then to the Sistine Chapel, got some lunch, drifted down the Borgo Santo Spirito, and walked along the Tiber till the sun began to wester. And then, at last, we returned to the Basilica for our council of war.

More priests and slayers had joined the cardinal. They had street maps and electrical grids and topographical charts of the town of Tarn. There was data from archives dating back fifteen hundred years about the movements of Claudia Procula. There were dossiers on all known vampires at large in the New England area. I listened hard and tried to absorb everything I could; but after several hours of this, my overwhelming impression was that I'd stumbled into something way above my pay grade.

They served us dinner as we talked. I broke down and followed Danny's lead on the cappuccino issue, hoping to keep my poor beleaguered brain firing on all cylinders. But when nine o'clock rolled around and we called it a night, I felt wearier and more battered than I'd felt after the gunfight in Manchester. A Swiss Guardsman in crimson livery brought me and Beth to our room for the night, and I collapsed onto the bed without even

Whisper Music

bothering to undress.

Beth paced over and sat down next to me. "Long day, huh?"

"Mmff."

"Come on, love o' mine. You can't sleep in your good clothes." She rolled me onto my side, unbuttoned my shirt, and pulled it off me. Then she tugged off my shoes, unbuckled my belt, and started right in on my pants.

"Leave me some dignity, woman," I muttered.

"Too late for that. Off wi' yer leggin's, mate!"

"You can't be Australian and Scottish at the same time. Pick an accent."

"*You* pick an accent."

"Hyarrr, take me pantaloons."

"That's more like it."

"Off with your dress, ye gypsy vagabond."

"Why, sir!"

The dress came off. I pulled her close. She flung a shoe at the table lamp and wrapped us in lovers' darkness. And we were together in the cool Italian night.

Next morning, we gathered in Vicenzo's quarters for a final briefing. Half a dozen Vatican slayers were coming back to America with us, along with two large corrugated trunks full of arcane slaying equipment. Good thing we weren't going through customs. "Godspeed, my friends," Vicenzo said. "Tread with care and keep your blades sharp. And now—the blessing."

The door opened, and a man came in. We all got up. He was tall and straight-backed, just as he looked on television. But there was something in his face that the cameras couldn't capture. A radiance of charity and faith, the closest thing I'd ever seen to an actual halo. He raised his hands over us, and we lowered our heads.

"Almighty God—bless and protect these knights of Your Church, whom You have chosen to act as Your hands. Let Your light go before them, and Your face shine upon them, and Your angelic host surround them as they go into battle. May they bear good fruit in this world, and when You call them home, may they be gathered into Your arms forever in the next. All this we ask in Jesus' name. Amen."

"Amen," we said, and made the sign of the cross. Twenty minutes later, we were back in the air.

CHAPTER 8

A MUSTERING OF RAVENINGS

I'd been gone longer than I realized; the sun, that ugly thing, was almost up. I smelled vampires in the church: more than just my new retainers. As I came trudging back into town, I saw cars and motorcycles I hadn't noticed before. She must have sent out a call in my absence.

Some imbecile newcomer stood guard at the door. "Who goes there?" he demanded as I drew near. I caught him by the throat and threw him across the street. I didn't have time for this.

Down the central aisle, as before. But this time, Claudia sat in the chair of the priest. Rain was kneeling at her feet, and a dozen immortals I'd never seen were gathered in the pews at the foot of the altar, gazing up at her. Satan's prophet.

"What news?" I said as I entered.

All eyes turned in my direction. No one spoke.

"Danyaela," Claudia said sweetly. "Come and sit beside me. I trust we've been wiped from mortal minds?"

"More or less." I mounted the steps to the altar and stood beside her chair with my arms folded over my chest. She did not renew her command for me to sit. I swept the others with my eyes. A few of them met my glare with arrogance; the others found interesting objects on the floor.

"These are the leaders of all the nearest ravenings," Claudia said. "I have called together a conclave, for the first time in centuries."

"A conclave."

"Indeed. The times move now, and a new darkness approaches. We are called to be soldiers. We are solitary creatures, but we must learn solidarity."

A raspy old voice said, "So, this is the fabled Danyaela. After two thousand years, one mortal is chosen to receive the gift of Lucifer. What makes you so special, little girl?"

I turned, slowly, and met the old man's eye. "Let me show you."

"No!" Claudia said. "There will be no fighting here. Have I not spent the last year in Deep Hell? I tell you, Drokna, the true King is returning to this world. The time of truce between light and Dark is coming to an end. We *must* stand together, or we will fall."

"And must we stand beneath the judgment of this tiny child?" The old man Drokna rose to his feet. "Lady Claudia—I know you from of old, and I respect the authority granted to you before the resurrection of the Galilean. But this American?" He turned his head and spat, and then began to speak in a language I didn't recognize.

Claudia narrowed her eyes and responded in the same unknown tongue. When I was turned, my mind grew as strong as my body, and new languages came easily to me; I'd learned fifteen or twenty in the last dozen years. But whatever they were speaking sounded like something older than Rome: some lost and angry Gothic dialect, perhaps. It occurred to me that I could bound into the crystal sphere and read this old man's thoughts, learn his secrets, materialize behind him, rip his spine out if it pleased me. But, I thought, why give away the full extent of my powers? Wiser to let them wonder who I was, and why, and what I could do to them if I chose.

But on the other hand—

"This language," I said, interrupting. "I don't know it. I see from their looks that several of our brethren don't know it either. Why don't we stick to English, since we're in America? We can't stand together if we can't understand each other."

Someone said in an undertone, "Hear, hear." And a few others rumbled in agreement.

"Quite so," said Claudia, "quite so. Come, kindred, let us be as one. When, in all these years, have I ever sought lordship? I do not claim mastery over our people, I only proclaim the coming of our Lord. If He finds division among us when He comes—there will be dire consequences for us all."

Drokna scowled. "Since the great change, since the rising of the Galilean, we have kept our presence hidden and existed as demon gods. Why now should we alter our ancient ways?"

"We have lived as gods in exile," she said. "That exile is ending. The great change will be reversed, and the light will be overthrown. It is time for us to reveal our existence to the world."

"But there are so few of us!" someone said. "If the humans band together, we won't stand a chance."

"The humans who know about us are banding together already," she snarled. "The rest—the sheep—have known of us forever but have chosen to bury their heads in the sand. Once we destroy the upstart rabble from the Vatican, the cowardice of the sheep will only increase. Why should we fear them? Why should we hide? Soon we shall rule this petty globe!"

"Perhaps," the old man said. "Perhaps."

For just a moment, I felt a camaraderie in the air. These people might hate each other, and themselves, and everyone, but they hated the slayers most of all. In the absence of honor and trust, we could still unite over sheer fang-gnashing bloodlust. It warmed the room-temperature cockles.

"Rain," Claudia said, "prepare food for our guests. It's past dawn, and time we were all abed. We'll convene again in the evening. More of our kindred should be here by then. And keep sending out the call."

"As you command, Goddess."

I discovered that I too was weary. As before, I retired with Claudia to her chamber in the catacombs. We bathed and lay together, intertwined, in silken sheets. "Sleep, Danyaela," she breathed in my ear. "Sleep in my arms."

I perceived that it was no mere endearment: she was pushing her will, very subtly, upon me. She wished to see if she could still compel me to obey. And as soon as I realized that fact—and the fact that I was still awake—I knew I was finally free of her control. I closed my eyes and lay as if asleep, unbreathing in her firm vampiric arms. Let her think I was still her slave, her plaything. My time would come.

Next evening, we gathered at the altar once again. More vampires had come in response to whatever call Rain had been sending out. There were over forty of us now.

But as I'd always seen, our kind did not play well together. The congregation in the pews was rowdier than any Christian mustering, with shouting and profanity ringing in the dusty vaults. "You've been hobnobbing with Lucifer?" someone yelled. "Let's see some proof!"

"Idiots," she shouted back. "Aren't you tired of lurking in the shadows? If we join our strength, we can stop being wraiths and become the deities we should be."

"Prove it!"

And the idiots began to chant: *"Prove it! Prove it! Prove it!"*

She clenched her fists and teeth. "Danyaela—if we kill them, we'll have no army. You must use your new abilities. Show them a sign."

A sign. Even if I vanished right in front of them, what would that prove? The only way I could show them the truth was by—

Interesting. In Hell's antechamber the other night, after I fought the serpent, I didn't even have time to wonder how to bring Claudia back to the surface. As soon as she was fully awake, the dungeon faded around us and we found ourselves back in the mortal realm. And with everything else that was going on, I hadn't yet had a chance to think about bringing passengers into the soul-fields. If I could dash one of them against the crystal cliff, then perhaps they too would behold the mind of the Dark. *Then* they would believe.

But it was no good swooping down and snatching them until I was sure I could do it. I needed to make a trial run first. I could try bringing Claudia, but perhaps it wasn't wise to risk turning her loose in the crystal sphere. But there were three of us on the altar: Claudia sitting, myself standing, and Rain kneeling between us. I reached down and laid a hand on her shoulder, then focused on returning to the sphere.

Then I was pure light, racing across the crystal-scape. I felt different this time: I felt another presence, like the voice of temptation in my heart. And I felt that I was moving slower than usual—not as if I were weighted down in this weightless place, but as if I were pulling against some resistance that strengthened like a giant rubber band. I realized that if I released my passenger, she would snap back into the material plane.

Because she was traveling with me, I couldn't enter her thoughts; but I sensed that our emotions were jumbled up together by our proximity. I could feel her bewilderment and disorientation and fought to keep my own head clear. I remembered how dreamlike this place had seemed when I first came here.

We continued to slow down, and by the time the crystal cliff came into view, we were coasting to a halt. Normally the only speeds I could choose in here were fast and faster; but this time, I allowed our progress to wind down and stop. We hovered near the cliff, suspended between opposing forces. If I exerted my will, I could drag us the rest of the distance and plunge Rain into the visions. But she was not the one who needed convincing.

An image of myself came into my thoughts. There were no words here, but this must be Rain trying to speak my name within our mingled souls. I responded with an image of her. A wave of perplexity came upon me: what is this place? For a moment, I too felt puzzled, but I recollected myself and filled us with calm and acceptance. I can't explain, but there is nothing to fear.

And then a feeling of warmth enveloped me—a warmth to make my lips part and my back arch if we were in our bodies. Here that feeling could be felt in its full purity, with no outside distractions, no inner thoughts intruding. We were wrapped in each other, wholly interpenetrated, and our shared emotions fed on one another and grew stronger. Her desire became mine, and mine passed back to her until there was no distinction between us, no sense of self, but only the mounting sensation for which lust is only a metaphor. I would own her and submit to her completely, and she would own me, submit to me, become one with my very being.

No!

I ripped myself away from her spirit-seduction. She was after my power, nothing more. I ceased to make the subtle effort of will that kept her soul-beam tangled up in mine, and she was gone. Not having tasted the blood that gave one passage to this realm, she could be here only as my guest.

There was almost a kind of charm in her single-mindedness. And besides, one could hardly fault her for coveting such power. Once again, I found myself debating whether or not to rip the arms and legs from her torso.

But there would be time for that later. It was time to show Drokna what made me so special. I gathered my focus, dipped back into the mortal world, and seized him from behind. Then, as if I had pounced from above with a bungee cord around me, I bounded straight back up to the crystal sphere with that mouthy old man in tow.

This trip was very different from the last. Drokna was older and more experienced than Rain, and far stronger-willed. He too was dazed and uncomprehending at first; but before long, he began to fight back. In this place, my natural advantages of speed and force were useless: our struggle was mind to naked mind.

Waves of anger and contempt crashed over me, making me loathe and despise myself. But I had learned from Rain that whatever I felt, he would feel too—so instead of resisting, I let that loathing engulf the both of us. Daunted by his own hatred, Drokna slackened his assault, and I used that moment to flood both of us with despair. What was the point in fighting, in doing anything? We were damned anyway, all of us damned.

Drokna countered with the most delectable feeling of revenge. If we were damned, then why should anyone be saved? Why should anyone be happy? It was an emotion I'd felt so many times that I hardly resisted, and it built back and forth between us, letting him shake off the despair and turn to anger once again.

But there was one thing Drokna didn't know. The whole time our inner selves were battling, we were streaking across the crystal fields to the great cliff. As before, we slowed to a halt just before we struck; but this time, I harnessed his own anger at the last second and used it to fuel my willpower. Then I drove us both into the crystal face.

By now, this place held no more terrors for me. I endured the visions and concentrated on keeping Drokna's mind buried in the mind of the Darkness. When I felt enough time had passed, I released him and let him snap back to the world he knew, a sadder and a wiser man.

I'll admit it: this was starting to be fun.

I did the same thing to five or six more of Claudia's most vocal detractors. By midnight, everyone was ready to admit that our orders were coming directly from the bowels of Hell.

"Lady Claudia," Drokna said in a voice much subdued from his earlier belligerence. "If it is the will of the Dark that we should put an end to the secrecy in which we have always existed, then what should be our first move?"

She bared her fangs. "We shall crush the heart of their resistance before the war can even begin. We shall end the greatest threat to our kind, and the nations of men will fall like dominoes. Brothers and sisters—we march upon the Vatican."

CHAPTER 9

REX MUNDI

Danny and I showed up to work just long enough to put in for psychiatric leave. After having five hundred gallons of pig's blood dumped on us, falling into a frozen river, and killing two men in a shootout, we were both in a reasonable position to claim mental trauma. There'd be plenty of paperwork and visits to the shrink to deal with, but the upshot was that we'd have the time off we needed to plan our assault on Tarn. We'd even be getting partial pay. And if we planned poorly, we wouldn't have to worry about work anymore. It was a win/win all the way around.

"It comes down to catching Claudia in her sleep," Cormorant said as we gathered around Clare's now-familiar table. "Every second she's in play, the odds of a massacre increase. Back in 1739, two separate groups of slayers encountered her on the same night, hundreds of miles apart; and based on the times and distances given by the survivors, we calculate that she can move at speeds in excess of Mach 2."

I nodded. Sure, why not.

"How do her clothes stay on?" Danny asked.

Cormorant cracked a smile. "I have a theory about that. All vampires give off a negative aura that cloaks them from mirrors and photographs. I suspect that when Claudia summons up her full power, such as when she's flying at top speed, her aura grows so pronounced that it shields her clothing from the high winds."

"Huh."

Whisper Music

"She will have guards," Brother Joseph said. "Maybe dogs."

Cormorant nodded. "No question of that. Our first order of business is to find out how many undead are in Tarn right now."

"Better make a call to our friendly neighborhood snitch," said Clare.

Nalfar wasn't answering his phone. Clare had no idea where he hung his hat, but one of our new buddies from Rome had a manila folder with a big N on the front.

"Thomas Nalfar," said Renan, the archivist. He was an older gentleman, average in height and build and face, with salt-and-pepper hair and a grey fedora—rather forgettable, which no doubt worked to his advantage. "One-time member of the Sorrow fell ravening became an Apostate in 1982. Currently operating out of a defunct bowling alley in South Boston."

"Say," I asked, "you wouldn't have a dossier on the Golgotha Dancers, would you?"

He blinked at me through his spectacles. "Of course. What would you like to know?"

"Well, it's a long shot—but I don't suppose you have any idea who whacked a guy called Willem Petrucci a few days back."

"Petrucci." He thumbed through his files. "One of ours. Ah yes, terminated 25 December, scene marked with Golgotha Dancers sigil. Let's see. . . We don't yet know with certainty who was responsible, but it seems a vampire called Demarius was in the vicinity. He's a high-ranking member of that ravening. I would start there."

"Later," Clare said. "Talk to me about this bowling alley, Renan."

It was high noon on the last day of the year when we converged on the derelict bowling alley Nalfar called home. Danny and I had been issued silver bullets, blessed silver knives, snap-retractable crucifixes, and vials of holy water from the River Jordan. The latter two items wouldn't damage a vamp, we were told, but they would cause them to recoil and thus buy us a few precious seconds. As before, Leah carried the flamethrower. Guess she liked playing with fire.

From what I'd been told, vampires could go outside in the daylight, but they hated it and wouldn't face the sun except in emergencies. So, I was greatly intrigued to see our exothermic pal slinking out of a side door and stuffing a suitcase into a Mercedes with tinted windows.

He looked up as we approached, and a look of exasperation crossed his face. "Go count your wrinkles, Gunnar. I don't have time for you right now."

Rigby fired a shot through Nalfar's windshield, right about eye level on the driver's side. "There ya go, buddy, a little sunshine for the road. No charge."

Nalfar took a step toward us, and I could see his claws growing longer—but three of the boys from the Vatican had been circling the building, and they now appeared behind him with guns drawn. "Make a good choice here, Nalfar," said Clare.

"What the hell do you want?"

"Wanna know about Tarn, Maine."

He scoffed. "If you've heard of that place, then you already know more than I want to. And if you're smart, you'll bury your head and hope you never hear of it again."

"Ain't that smart, I guess. Tell me about Claudia's set-up. How's her security? How many troops does she have?"

"You don't understand. She's been sending out the call for days now. *Everyone's* gathering in Tarn. How many 'troops' does she have? Before long, she'll have as many troops as there are vampires on earth."

"*What?*" Leah shouted. "What call?"

"She's summoning a conclave. Every ravening in America will be there soon."

"Why?" Cormorant demanded.

Nalfar shook his head furiously. "I—don't—know. I'm heading for Alaska. You poor fools enjoy your New Year's. I guarantee you won't be having another one."

He got into his car. The slayers glanced at Clare, raising their weapons, but she shook her head. We let him go.

No one spoke. A gust of wind swirled the snow around us.

"So, I guess this changes things, huh?" Danny said.

"Reckon so," Clare muttered.

"He could be lying," Rigby said.

I grimaced. "Why would he be leaving town, then?"

"Oh. Yeah." He deflated. I think I liked it better when everything I said pissed him off.

Renan pushed his glasses further up his nose. "If memory serves, the damned have not held a major conclave since 1664. And our intelligence indicates that on that occasion, the purpose of the conclave was to enforce a policy of concealment from the human race."

"Perhaps they've grown weary of concealment," Cormorant said.

"Hell's bells," Clare said. "Morrigan could beam herself into the Oval Office and brainwash the President anytime she felt like it."

"*Rex Mundi*," Brother Joseph said.

"What's that?"

"Scripture calls Satan *Rex Mundi*, the King of the Earth. And there are many things in Scripture that we take for metaphor when they are simple fact—or will be."

"The Bahamas are lovely nice this time of year," Leah said. "Just—you know. Tossin' it out there."

"This matter has become far more grave than we suspected," Renan said. "We must inform the Holy Father."

"And get some bourbon," Clare added. "I need some bourbon."

Renan nodded with the utmost seriousness. "Yes. Also, that."

Chapter 10

PANDEMONIUM

The year ended. Each passing night brought more of our darkling kith to Tarn's borders; by the final dusk of December, there were over sixty of us. We made a poor army. The undead were lone wolves by nature, and no one had ever tried to organize us before. It was a long time since so many of us had been in one place, and there were centuries worth of old feuds and long-simmering disputes to work through. Beyond that, there was the problem of feeding us all.

Only a few of us could fly—and neither I nor Claudia would deign to go foraging for mortals on behalf of our inferiors. In the end, we resorted to sending out the lowest-ranking members on raiding parties to nearby villages in vans and Winnebagos.

As midnight passed and January began, there were revels and bedlam in the windswept streets of Tarn. We can't survive on the blood of animals: it's not the physical nutrients but the eternal spirit that nourishes our undeath. But for centuries, we'd all agreed to conceal our presence from the world, lest they band together and destroy us; and now we were told that we need no longer hide. The low-ranks brought back dozens of bound and wriggling humans and turned them loose in the center of town, and a ravenous blood-festival erupted as the living were hunted for food and sport and the purging of a great repression.

I paced the bleak townscape, brooding on the fate of that species that used to be my own. Twelve years was a long while—more than half my lifespan at the time I was turned. I no longer identified with those people. But I had no part in this plan.

Whisper Music

Claudia came back from Hell because *I* got her—because I fought the Darkness fang to fang. And now we were called to all-out war with the humans on the orders of the same Darkness?

Above me in the shadows, a crow alighted with ominous dignity on the corner of an old sagging house. Further up, a full moon emerged from ragged clouds, shedding a pale soft light. To my left, an old Phoenician vampire cackled as he unraveled a screaming woman's entrails; to my right, a gorgeous vampiress held her victim's gaze and forced him to grovel before her in the ice and dirt. This was the new year.

A familiar scent wafted by, Rain Vissarian. It was coming from inside a decrepit bed and breakfast, mingled with the warm pulsing smell of some poor mortal. I headed inside. I didn't know why, except that hers was a face I knew. Was I lonely? Was she really the closest thing I had to a friend?

She was on the top floor, three stories up. Her victim was a blond young man, well-dressed, well-built, sprawled on a four-poster bed by her side, snoring. She glanced up and smiled as I came in. "I like to put them to sleep. It's more relaxing this way. Are you thirsty?"

"No." I walked over and stood by the bedside. "But you're right, this is more relaxing. Things are a bit out of hand down there."

"There hasn't been a real Devil's Night since the Middle Ages. If it's to be war, they deserve a feast beforehand."

"I suppose."

"Won't you sit, my lady?"

I sat.

"What troubles you?"

"I didn't show you the mind of the Dark, Rain, when I brought you to the crystal sphere. You don't know how much it hates us. How much it hates everyone."

She lifted her shoulders. "I don't believe in happy endings. We're all damned, I know that. But that's all the more reason to enjoy ourselves while we still can."

"Do you enjoy all this?"

"I enjoy the hunt. I enjoy the Kiss. What else is there?"

"I don't know."

"Lady Danyaela—"

"You can just call me Danyaela."

Her smile returned. "Danyaela. For all your powers, you're still new to the blood. The more you accept what you are, the less you'll be plagued by doubts."

"Did you care for Demarius?"

She looked puzzled. "Care for him? He was a strong ally. But you and Lady Claudia are far stronger."

"Do you ever miss caring for people?"

"People betray you. Do you think we're the only ones who turn on each other? Perhaps Lady Claudia hasn't told you yet, but I had a call just this evening from a slayer back in Boston— one who informs on her comrades for a taste of my blood. If you care for people, it hurts more when they let you down."

"What slayer?"

"A girl who works with a group we keep running across. I killed one of them eight years ago, and Demarius killed another just last week. They have an alliance with the Apostate. Our own kind sells us out to them, and they sell out their own kind to us."

"If you're so convinced that everyone will betray you, then why are you so eager to be Claudia's apostle?"

"I'll worry about tomorrow, tomorrow. Serving her has brought me good fortune tonight."

I shook my head. "There has to be more to life."

"We're not alive, Danyaela."

Once again, I wished I could heave a sigh. I got up and walked out of the room.

The chaos in the streets was escalating. I had no stomach for it. I rose into the moonlit sky, up and ever upwards, farther than I'd ever gone. My gown stiffened as ice formed on it. The sounds of the earth fell into silence. Still, I rose, and the moon drew nearer. Two hundred and thirty thousand miles, if memory served. I wondered if any vampire had ever flown there.

Whisper Music

Far below, New England spread out like a map. There was Boston, home of the traitorous huntress, Rain's little fang-chaser. Did she know Harry? Would she sell his life for vampire blood? Was there, at this moment, anyone else who had stirred the dimmest memory of trust or friendship in my lifeless heart?

I didn't even have a name to go on. I could swoop back down and make Rain tell me. But this would be an interesting challenge. I faded into the crystal sphere.

This time I tried to pay attention to the interconnections among the soul-beams. It wasn't geographical proximity that bound them together; as I surfed from soul to soul, I found that many entangled beams turned out to belong to lovers or family members separated by hundreds of miles. That being the case, it made sense that Rain's informant would be close to Paulson Cormorant since they were associates. I found him and then began to sort through nearby spirits, looking for treason.

A woman, Clare Gunnar, was a close friend. She was one of the slayers who shot me in the park the other night. But she was loyal. There was a Roman cardinal, Vicenzo—also loyal. And there was Harry, with whom Cormorant seemed to share a combative affection. Closely bound to Harry's beam was another woman, Beth. She was faithful, but there was something odd about her beam. After a moment, I realized what it was: a second soul was embedded within it. Did Harry know he was going to be a father? Did Beth? I felt an unaccountable flutter that might have been happiness.

But I was getting sidetracked. After another few minutes of searching, I found the traitor. Leah Van Owen of Portland, twenty-five, sharp-shooter, a third-degree black belt in Shotokan karate. Bitten by a vampire when she was seventeen, saved by hunters, and recruited to join them—all the while nurturing a secret hope to become one of the things she hunted. Traitor.

At this moment, she was alone in her bedroom, reading. I could see the room through her eyes, but I couldn't see her face. I didn't know what I planned to do to her, but it would be useful to know what she looked like. There must be a way to make her show herself.

The Jubei experience had taught me that I couldn't communicate directly, but she could at least be made subliminally aware of my presence. Rather than using words this time, I decided to try images. Since the yowling, spurting pandemonium in the necropolitan street was still fresh in my mind, I ruminated upon it, letting it swirl around me like ripples in a sunless sea. And soon the feedback from Leah's mind told me she was seeing flickers of that hideous scenery. She shifted in her chair, shook her head, tried to focus on her book. Then she got up to wash her face.

So: she was the pretty blond girl from the park, the one with the flamethrower. Interesting, as far as it went. But far more interesting was the fact that I had succeeded in influencing her if only a little. Now the question was whether to interfere.

I hung there in the luminescent fields, pondering. If I warned Harry of her treachery, then I too would be a traitor. Did I care? Our kind felt no loyalty. But I could be better than the rest. But if I wanted to be better, then shouldn't I find something better to be loyal to? But I couldn't become one of those pathetic Apostates. But I couldn't let Harry be stabbed in the back, could I? There was no ethic for a thing like me: I had no rudder, no compass, no code. In the end, the only determining factor would have to be the whim of the moment.

Well, in that case—

Hmm. Harry was sleeping. His dreams were troubled, his rest fitful, but I could sense his exhaustion and suspected he could use whatever little sleep he could get. I didn't have the heart to wake him. But neither did I feel like returning to Tarn. On the spur of another whim, I decided to investigate Claudia.

Hmmmmm.

Her beam was right there, just like everyone else's. Now that she was back from Deep Hell, I could locate her in a second. However—her mind was closed to me somehow. Because she was the one who turned me? But no, Mary's blood had broken that hold. Besides, this wasn't the first time I'd met someone I couldn't read.

Cormorant. Whatever made him opaque, some part of that ability must have transferred to her. Irksome.

I wondered what Claudia was planning. I wondered what made Cormorant so special. I wondered why I felt so protective toward Harry. Was it merely that he had spoken kindly when I was surrounded by hatred and fear? Mary's words in Medjugorje came back: *You ask for your own unmaking.* Was I getting soft? Was getting soft so bad? I never asked to be a monster. But now, when the habits of monstrosity were so long ingrained in me, I had a choice again. It wasn't fair. None of this was fair.

What am I supposed to do?

CHAPTER 11

MISS MORRIGAN

"I miss my car."

"I know. I'm sorry."

"It's not your fault."

"Oh, I wasn't apologizing. Just expressing sympathy."

"I mean. . . you *did* crash her into a Prius at like seventy miles an hour."

"Yeah, I was doing this new thing called a high-speed chase. I'm surprised you didn't learn about it in prodigy class."

"We *always* take your car. The *one* time we take my car, we get in a shootout with a fang-chaser in the middle of a major city."

"So, you're inferring that I'm to blame?"

"I could never do that, Harold. You see, only the listener can draw inferences. As the speaker, I'm *implying* that you're to blame."

"I know the difference, Daniel."

"Well apparently you don't, because you just said—"

"Will you two for God's sake give it a rest?" Rigby yelled from the back seat.

We were heading north along the coast. On our right, the grey horizon was turning pink and orange as dawn crept over the Atlantic. We could hear the faint sound of breakers on the desolate beach, and a few lonely cattails waved from the snowdrifts. The road was early-morning empty. The smell of coffee filled the car.

"How far to the rendezvous point?" Leah asked sleepily.

"'Nother couple hours yet," I said. "Might as well get some shut-eye while you can."

The new year had begun. It looked like being a strange one. Also, if Nalfar was right, our last. I'd be happy if we lived to see January second.

We were back in my car again; Danny's Mustang looked like a horny grizzly had mistaken it for a she-bear. It was barely eighteen hours since Renan had made his call to the Vatican, informing them that unprecedented numbers of vamps were gathering in Maine—but the Vatican could act fast when it had to. Some kind of ultimate high-priority summons had gone out to every slayer in a thousand-mile radius, and a small army was mustering near Tarn. Our strategy seemed to have switched from covert ops to an all-out assault. Clare was a little way behind us in her pick-up, with Patrick and Cormorant and Brother Joseph; Renan and his Roman buddies were ahead of us in a grey SUV. Thus, our little caravan rode to war.

"Mach 2 is really fast," Danny remarked.

"Yup."

"I hope they've got some kind of a plan for taking her out early on."

"Lotta flamethrowers, I expect."

"That would be a good start, yeah." He sipped his coffee. "Danyaela might help us."

"Let's not count on that, buddy."

"I'm not counting on it. I'm just saying she might."

"Guess we'll find out."

The sun climbed, and the miles rolled by. It was about nine in the morning when we pulled up to an abandoned train station about fifty miles west of Augusta. There were at least thirty vehicles gathered around that place. Guys with assault rifles were holding a perimeter, but they waved us by without trouble. Renan must've called ahead.

Stretching my stiff legs, I clambered out of the driver's seat. It was a beautiful day. Somewhere in the woods, not more than a dozen miles away, was a little town full of malevolent vampires.

Cormorant led the way inside the old ramshackle building. There were dozens of slayers milling around in there, sharpening knives, chattering in multiple languages, poring over maps and tomes of dusty lore. A big red-bearded fellow in his fifties strode over and offered Cormorant his hand.

"Paulson! I feel a lot better about this mission now that you're here."

"Good to see you again, Will." Cormorant turned to the rest of us. "Friends, this is Will Norcroft. One of our best."

We shook hands all around, and Norcroft offered us more coffee and scrambled eggs that were simmering in a giant trough. They were surprisingly good. "Compliments to the chef," I said.

One of the guys glanced over and smiled. "Thanks, brother. I cooked for the whole brigade in Afghanistan."

"Nice."

"Do we have a quorum yet?" Clare asked.

"Not quite," Norcroft said. "We're still expecting another two or three score. We won't move out till about noon, so there's time yet. Feel free to examine the munitions. Top-of-the-line stuff."

She nodded. "Think I will, thanks."

"Can I just go ahead and ask about Claudia?" said Danny. "How are we dealing with her?"

Norcroft smiled grimly. "That is the question of the day. Our holy mother Church has been preparing to take her on for a long, long time. We've never been able to pin down where she was at any given moment, nor to get enough of us together at short notice until the advent of planes and fast cars. One of the reasons we need to move today is that we have no idea how long she'll stay in Tarn. If she decides to fly off somewhere tonight, we'll lose the best chance we've ever had at finishing her."

A gleam came into Cormorant's eye. "Is it time to break out Lucille?"

"Yes, it is, my old friend. Yes, it is."

"Lucille?" Rigby asked. "Is that like a special gun?"

"Think bigger. Lucille is a Russian-made MI-26 Halo

Whisper Music

helicopter rigged with sixty fire-hoses and loaded with thirty tons of holy water blessed by the Pope himself. The first thing we'll do is rain down deliverance on that town. That'll take some of the spring out of her step."

I finished my eggs and poured myself another cup of coffee. Then we spent some time familiarizing ourselves with the flamethrowers. I hadn't fired one in well over twenty years, and Danny had never even held one before. A lot of the others were out back, doing target practice or light sparring. Norcroft let another hour or two go by while more and more slayers continued to arrive. Finally, we were all called back inside.

"My comrades," said Norcroft. "We all know why we're here, so let's get right down to it. Fr. Fordham?"

A middle-aged man in brown friar's robes and sandals paced out into the middle of the space. By this time, there must have been nearly a hundred of us in there—sitting in chairs, lounging on benches or floorspace, leaning against walls or pillars with crossed arms, standing like ramrods with fists on hips. There was also a huge computer screen by one wall, filled with moving pictures of other hunters still en route, participating via dashboard-mounted cameras. The priest moved among us with a small box of gold and oak in his hands. I recognized it from my days as an altar boy: a pyx, made to transport the Holy Eucharist. To each of us, he raised a tiny wafer of the Host and touched it to our foreheads.

"For those who might not know," Norcroft said as Fr. Fordham proceeded, "this little ritual ensures that none of us are under vampiric influence. The touch of the Host breaks any hypnotic spell they can cast. They're strong enemies, but we are not without weapons."

After my run-in with Danyaela, I was relieved to find that nothing happened when Fr. Fordham touched me. She'd been as good as her word, leaving my mind untampered-with. Or, this was another rule that didn't apply to her.

"All right, let's move on. Those still en route are to report to Fr. Fordham upon arrival. Meanwhile, here's the first order of business. Our own Paulson Cormorant remains the only living slayer to have seen Claudia Procula face to face. This sketch is based on his reconstruction." A drawing filled the computer screen: a haughty, haunting countenance, inhumanly lovely and cold. If I'd seen it a week ago, I would have thought, *Now that's what a vampire would look like if they existed. Heh! Good thing they don't.*

One of the men raised his hand. "Useful info: how did Cormorant live through that fight?"

"There wasn't a fight," Cormorant said. "She took me by the shirt, threw me off a cliff, and flew away. I wasn't worth the five seconds it would have taken her to make sure I didn't land in deep water."

"Procula's the oldest vampire on earth," Norcroft said. "We've always assumed she was the strongest, and until a couple of days ago, she's been our number one target. However—some new information has come to light. Allow me to introduce Sergeant Harry Blake of the Boston PD."

Great.

"We've suspected for a while that Procula had chosen her progeny. That young woman's name is Miss Danyaela Morrigan, also of Boston, and Sergeant Blake has spoken with her in person."

I stepped forward, conscious of about two hundred wolf-keen eyes boring into me from every direction. "Lemme save some time at the outset: I don't know why she didn't kill me. I don't know why she didn't brainwash me. I think maybe she's just lonely."

"Awww," someone said. "Poor little blood-sucker."

"How about you clamp your face-hole," Danny suggested.

"How about you come over here and say that, kid."

"*Stop!*" Norcroft bellowed, so abruptly that we all jumped. "We hunt vampires. We do not hunt vampire hunters. Understood?" There was a general silence of assent. "Harry, please continue."

So once again I told the tale. After that, we all debated what might have happened in Medjugorje and whose side Danyaela might be on. More slayers came straggling in, and Fr. Fordham tested each of them. No one was suffering from post-hypnotic suggestion. Through the windows, we could see the sun continuing to climb.

"Okay," Norcroft said at length. "We don't know what Morrigan might or might not do, and we don't have time to worry about it. Let's stick to who we are: you see a vamp, you kill a vamp. Let's get down to tactics."

They broke us up into four teams—Alpha, Bravo, Charlie, Delta. Each was to circle around to a different quadrant of the town and advance toward the center as soon as Lucille unleashed her payload. Remote surveillance was useless, but our analysts concurred that Claudia was likely to be holed up in St. Gabriel's church, just east of the middle of town. We were all issued headsets and instructed to keep chatter to a minimum but call out positions on any enemies we encountered. To my surprise, I found myself almost smiling; it was just like being back in the Corps.

The Boston gang, along with a bunch of others, were in Bravo Team, led by Cormorant himself. His first order was to Patrick. "We haven't brought you this far to leave you behind now. You're old enough, and strong enough, to choose your own path. Very few slayers have had a first mission like this one, so hold your head high. Just remember this: if you disobey orders in there and put yourself at risk, the first person you'll get killed is your aunt. You move where I say, when I say. Is that clear?"

Patrick's face was pale and set. "Yes, sir."

"Good. Let's get underway."

As we made our final preparations, an image of Danyaela came into my mind. Would we see her in Tarn? Would she help us, or kill us? I tried to stop thinking about it and move forward, but I found that the image kept getting clearer. I could practically see her with my waking eyes—pre-fight jitters, no doubt. Then the image of the tree-line out back came into my head and an unaccountable sense that I ought to go over there. Maybe I needed to take a leak.

I drifted toward the trees as the others were loading equipment into the vehicles. There was a flamethrower on my back, a silver-loaded pistol in a shoulder holster on either side of me, a silver knife on my left hip and a spring-loaded crucifix on my right, and a flask of holy water in the breast pocket of my body armor. I was as ready for this insanity as I was gonna get.

Or maybe not. As I stepped under the receding shadow of the foliage overhead, a lithe figure stepped soundlessly from behind an old hoary pine. I heard my breath catch in my throat.

"It's all right, Harry," she said quietly. "I'm not going to hurt you."

"What about the others?"

"I'm not going to hurt anyone. This isn't my fight."

"Miss Morrigan, please just tell me what you want."

She shook her head. "I don't know what I want. I don't know what I am. A battle is brewing between the vampires and the Vatican. Maybe I'll just wait and see what happens."

I slumped. "I can't tell you what to do. But a lot of my friends could end up dead today. We don't get to sit on the sidelines. I could use your help."

"Are you so sure you're on the right side? Claudia has two thousand years of experience behind her."

"So what? Has she ever faced a real challenge or made a real sacrifice in all that time? Has she done anything to make her grow as a person? Seems to me she's just done the same ugly, easy thing day after day and let everyone else pay the price for it. There's a difference between experience and stagnation."

The corner of her mouth rose very slightly. "Maybe. Maybe that's real wisdom talking. I wouldn't know."

"Danyaela. . ."

"Harry, listen. I don't plan to take either side today. But I want to warn you: one of your people is a traitor. She's not under a spell, she's acting on her own free will. And thanks to her, Claudia knows you're coming."

Oh, Jesus. A wave of cold swept over me. "Who is it?"

"Leah Van Owen."

Whisper Music

"Hey, Harry!" Clare called. "Shake that thing off and zip it up. We're ready to roll here."

I glanced over my shoulder at the others. When I looked back, Danyaela was gone. I turned, feeling old as death, with my soul like a great wooden cross-beam on my shoulders. And trudged through the new-fallen snow back to Leah and the rest of the slayers.

CHAPTER 12

THINGS FALL APART

Three women in white robes stood on a desecrated altar, fanged and beautiful. On the right was a blond girl with green eyes full of scornful detachment. On the left was a red-haired woman with blue eyes that gazed sycophantically at the one in the middle. And in the center, a tall pale lady with hair and eyes as black as midnight, smiling at the impending slaughter.

Before us in the ruined church stood fifty vampires, some powerful, some weak, but all forewarned against the onslaught of the hunters. This would be the first great battle of the rising regime, the new world order that Claudia would create. Once we slew the slayers, who would remain to guard the Vatican? A few Swiss Guards with spears and muskets, easily dispatched. A few priests and nuns with rosaries. We could take over the secular world any time we chose; defeating the Church would be the real hurdle, and today would be the beginning of that defeat.

"Even now they approach!" Claudia was screaming out to our clamoring brethren. "The fools save us the trouble of hunting them down. We shall wipe them away like the stinking feces that fill their flabby human bodies. They are *nothing* before us. The new age dawns today!"

It was high noon: our least favorite time of day. But everyone expected that. When else would the slayers attack? We could endure the sunlight if we had to. But I didn't have to. I had no intention of taking part in this primordial scuffle. Good and evil had come to bore me. What difference did it make who won?

"Now spread out through the town, my kindred. When these

Whisper Music

upstart mortals pass the boundaries of Tarn, they will learn what it means to be hunted. Go in the name of the Darkness and of—" She paused. "What is that sound?"

Fifty heads swiveled. A thumping, thumping, thumping sound, growing ever louder. Back and forth our faces darted, straining our all-hearing ears—then we raised our heads. It was coming from above.

"Chopper," one of the younger brethren said. "They could napalm this whole place from the sky."

"It won't touch us," Claudia said disdainfully. "We have a whole system of tunnels they'll never—"

Then the sound of a mighty deluge engulfed the church, a sound like a hundred waterfalls gushing down from the heights of the sky. And every one of us shuddered. When you become the shadow in the closet, the creature under the bed, you may well think you've left all fear behind—but the first time you feel the cool emanations of holy water, a whole new dimension of dread opens.

"It's raining God!" someone shrieked, and they stampeded for the doors.

But Claudia was far too fast. She blasted from the altar to the door so quickly that even I could barely follow her movement, and barred the exit with outstretched arms, hanging in the air like an evil crucifix. "Cowards!" she raved. "It will not harm us! Control your fear!"

The older vampires rallied, and the younger ones got a hold of themselves. "They'll pay for this!" Drokna roared. "Kill them all!"

Claudia flung open the doors and our soldiers issued forth. Their panic turned to rage, but as they emerged into the piercing sunlight and the flooded roadways, the panic returned. We were no army, only a pack of thugs with superhuman strength. It would be an entertaining battle to watch from my comfortable armchair in the crystal sphere. I heard my erstwhile mistress call my name, but I was already fading away. Perhaps after twelve years, I was entering vampiric adolescence.

I came across Petrov's beam and decided to follow the action through his eyes. He and Nikosk were sprinting through a long alleyway, sticking to the shade, their feet splashing in the sacred puddles that defiled the earth. Petrov scented man-flesh and his claws popped out like switchblades. The two of them raced toward the source of the smell, boiling with the battle-fever. They could sense other immortals closing in on their flanks, and their confidence grew as they saw their enemies in the distance. They would have fire and silver, but they were only human.

Then they heard a quiet, unfamiliar buzz, and a small metal glider swooped down at them and exploded into blazing shrapnel. A drone, a kamikaze drone loaded with incendiaries. Petrov and Nikosk fell and writhed in the holy water, trying to scrub away one horror with another. And as they lay there burning and twisting in the holiness, the hunters advanced on their position and riddled them with silver bullets. An axe came down on Petrov's neck, and suddenly I was back in the soul-fields.

First blood goes to the slayers, I thought. *Let's see how Harry's doing.*

He was slogging through the hallowed mire with the nozzle of a flamethrower clutched in his fists, breathing through his teeth and scanning every rooftop and window frame for the glitter of undead talons. There were two hunters on his left and three on his right, one of them the mysterious Paulson Cormorant. They hadn't encountered any of my fellow hell-spawn yet. His senses were so dull and muted compared to those of a vampire, I was half-surprised he could hear anything at all—but he barked out a warning to the others: "Eleven o'clock!" And their weapons erupted as another vampire came lunging out of a sagging doorway. With the boom of a shotgun, its head burst into pulp and its body shriveled away.

"These things ain't so bad," said one of the hunters.

"Stay sharp," Cormorant snapped. "Only the stupid ones will attack us head-on. It's the older ones we have to worry about."

Even as he spoke, the thumping of the helicopter became audible again. I thought perhaps it was coming back around to unleash more holy water—but this time, the rotors sounded strained.

"Norcroft," Cormorant said into his headset. "Is Lucille supposed to be making another round?"

I could hear the reply through Harry's earpiece. It sounded nervous. "No, they were supposed to bug out. I don't know what's—"

Then, from far above, the terrible sound of rending steel. The gigantic aircraft came plummeting down and smashed into an old hardware store, and both exploded in a towering pillar of fire. Harry and his friends flung themselves headlong into the mud as glass and wreckage rained down for blocks in every direction.

And a white-robed figure sailed down from on high, its garments fluttering in the cold air, and landed just a few yards up the street. She spoke in Latin, which Harry didn't understand, but I did. "Hello, Lazarus. It's been a long time."

Cormorant got to his feet and replied in the same language. "Let's make this our last meeting, Claudia."

"Oh, I plan to. This time I'll put you in concrete until the end of days."

Harry, Rigby, and the others opened fire. I expected her to dodge the bullets, or catch them, but instead, she did something I didn't know we could do. She simply stood there, grimacing with concentration, and the flames parted around her. When the smoke cleared, she was smiling, untouched. And then, too fast for Harry's eyes, she blurred forward and drove her claws through Cormorant's chest.

The others screamed and fired another volley at her from point-blank range, but the same invisible force protected her again. She pursed her lips, like a woman shopping for hats, and chose her next target: Rigby. Plucking the rifle from his hands, she caught him by the throat and raised him high in the air. Harry whipped out a crucifix and thrust it into her face, and she dropped his friend with a snarl. Then she swatted away the cross, took Harry's face in her hands, and placed the pads of her thumbs against his eyes. "Your god gave sight to the blind, little man," she hissed. "But mine takes it away. Now let's see which one is stronger."

"Stop."

She stopped. And she turned, still holding Harry's skull between her palms like a soap bubble. "Danyaela. I feared you had fled."

"That one is mine. Put him down."

"Of course." She dropped Harry, half-stunned, to the slush. "This is no time for us to quarrel. Why do we not kill these ridiculous peons together? Here, take the one you seem to want so much." Delicately, she placed a foot in Harry's ribs and lofted him into the air. I caught him by the shirt and set him back on his feet.

"Should've trusted you," he muttered, reeling. "I'm sorry."

"It's all right, Harry. Everything's all right."

Claudia's face darkened. The other slayers stood around her in a semi-circle, but they seemed to have more sense than to interrupt right now. She paid them no more heed than worms. "Harry?' You *know* this killer of our kin?"

"I know him, Claudia. But I have no kin. I love no one. I care for no one. Just like you. You and your master took that away from me."

"Spare me your pubescent caterwauling, you idiot child. I have no patience for it. *Kill him, Danyaela.*"

To anyone else, that command would have been irresistible. To me, a week ago, it would have been irresistible. But now it was nothing but noise.

"I don't work here anymore, Procula. You and I are through."

She cackled. "Through? *Through?* You and I are bound for all of eternity. When this petty globe crumbles away into space, you will be my slave and concubine in Hell!" And like a lightning bolt, she flew at me.

I was a hair too slow, and she slammed into me at twice the speed of sound. The two of us went hurtling backward, digging our talons into each other's flesh, and smashed through the nearest wall. Chairs and tables burst into matchwood all around

Whisper Music

us—we hurtled on, through another wall, through empty space, and through another house—and we landed in the raging inferno of the old hardware store. I chomped into her neck as hard as I could, but she lifted me, spun me around, and hurled me into the heart of the flames. I heard myself howling in anger and pain, and I lunged at her with my robe and hair ablaze—but she dodged like an adder, and her heel caught me in the spine as I flailed past her. The impact flung me across the street, but I managed to roll in midair, land on my feet, and bound a hundred and fifty feet into the sky, slapping out the flames at my head and breast as I went. She came soaring up after me. This time I slipped out of her path and slashed her stomach as she went by, but the cuts were already healing as she turned to glare at me.

We hung there in the pounding furnace of the winter sun, snarling like dogs, with a murderous battle rampaging in the town below. All I wanted at that moment was to rip her limb from limb, but a dim part of me was rational enough to know I was no match for her strength and speed.

But I had other weapons. The last time I tasted her blood, I was a helpless mortal—but I had tasted it again ten seconds ago. And I was not helpless now. "Claudia—"

"No!" She squeezed her eyes shut and wrenched herself away, covering her ears. "You shall not command me. I am your mistress!"

Good enough. While her back was turned, I flew at her, wrapped my arms around her, and transported both of us to the crystal sphere. Here the advantage was mine.

But only barely. She knew what to expect, thanks to Rain, and her will was incredibly strong. We rolled over and over, inundated with one another's hatred, neither of us able to control our corporate mind until we crashed into the crystal cliff. And there was the mind of Lucifer, pulsing with lust and contempt. I plunged us into that flood of blackness, but it only seemed to make Claudia stronger. I tried to drag her into the mind of Mary, but she was too powerful now. She was pulling me deeper into the Dark.

I let go of her, and she vanished from the sphere—back to Tarn. I wasn't making much progress in this fight.

A split second later, I materialized behind her in the air high above the rooftops. But she sensed me before I could strike and whirled around to catch me with a backhand like a thunderclap. I dropped from the skies and broke the pavement in my fall.

Claudia landed unsteadily in front of me. At least she wasn't unhurt. "This is madness, Danyaela. You cannot defeat me. Accept that you belong to me and let us return to the way things were."

"You—are not—my—mistress." I struggled to my feet, baring my fangs at this woman, this thing. "I will die the final death before I bow to you again."

"Perhaps," she said. And her smile returned. "Or perhaps it is time for our master to discipline you himself."

"What do you—"

I stopped. Something was happening inside of me. My blood was beginning to burn.

CHAPTER 13

THE VALLEY OF SHADOW

"They know we're coming."

Everyone stopped. Rigby froze in the middle of shoving a crate into the back of the pick-up and stammered out, "Say *what?*"

"I just saw Danyaela. They know we're coming."

Cormorant held up his hands. "Wait. Will!"

Norcroft came trotting over. "What is it? We're on the clock here."

"All right, Harry. Tell us."

As quickly as I could, I relayed everything Danyaela had said—except the name of the traitor. As soon as I finished, Norcroft shook his head. "This doesn't change anything. There was always a possibility they'd be waiting for us."

"But what about Claudia?" Danny said. "Cormorant made a big deal about how important it was to catch her sleeping."

"We have technology that's never been available to slayers before. Every team has a drone pilot who can call down exploding gliders on any vamp we get visual on. We've got portable M-134 miniguns capable of firing up to 6,000 silver rounds a minute. We've got napalm, silver-lined Kevlar vests, and for crying out loud, a Russian super-copter full of a whole glacier's worth of holy water. This is the best chance we've ever had to get rid of that Hell-born harlot once and for all, and we're not turning back just because her little bunkmate asks us to. At worst, this means Morrigan will sit the fight out and we've got one less vamp to worry about. And at best, Claudia sent her to trick us into aborting our attack because she's afraid they'll lose."

"What about the informant?" Clare asked.

"*If* there is any such person, the damage is already done. Our only play now is to move forward as planned. We won't get another opportunity like this. And for all we know, she made that up to sow dissension in the ranks. We'll investigate the allegation after this battle is over. For now, keep it quiet and let's proceed. Paulson, you concur?"

Cormorant exhaled through his nose. "I'm afraid I do. If there's any hope of removing the last drop of the Enemy's blood from the earth, we should take it."

"All right, then prepare to move out." Norcroft headed back to his vehicle, bellowing out, "Team leaders! Mic checks."

We all activated our headsets.

"Listen up, people. New intel suggests that the enemy may be waiting for us. So, if you were on high alert before, let's crank it up to eleven. Nothing else changes. Claudia Procula remains our chief target, but as I said earlier: you see a vamp, you kill a vamp. May God be with us; and if things go against us, it'll be my honor to buy the first round in the tavern at the end of the world. Now let's roll."

We drove in silence. We deployed around the edges of the town. We waited for Lucille to go by overhead. And on Norcroft's order, we moved in.

The first one was easy. We riddled it with bullets and Rigby blew its head off. And then Claudia ripped Lucille from the sky, and everything went up in flames. Someone was speaking in Latin. Our bullets couldn't touch her. I saw that blood-drinking ghoul stab Cormorant through the chest. Tried to save Rigby before she could do the same to him—hands like a vise around my skull, thumbs poised to pop the eyeballs out of my head—then Danyaela was there. I was on my feet, swaying, half-blinded by a migraine lancing through my brain. A blur, and a thump, and the vampires were gone, carrying on their private war.

"Harry. Harry!"

I managed to focus my eyes. "Danny," I muttered.

"You don't look so good, buddy. Let's get off the street."

"What about Cormorant?"

He shook his head. "He's dead. Come on."

"He's not dead." Clare's voice. Puzzled. Fearful? I looked past Danny to where she was kneeling by Cormorant's body. "He's still breathing."

"That's impossible," Rigby panted. "She cut clean through his spine, I saw it."

We gathered around the wounded man. Watched the wound in his chest closing in front of our eyes.

"He's a vampire," Patrick whispered.

"No, he ain't," said Clare. "Fr. Fordham touched him with the Communion wafer not two hours ago. Besides, you can see him breathin'. You can even see his reflection in the water."

"Then he's been juicing with their blood," Leah said.

"Maybe."

Cormorant's eyes fluttered, and he sat up. "My friends."

"You sure about that?" Clare asked. "Seems like you've been keeping secrets from your friends."

"We all do." He got to his feet, wincing. "Is anybody hurt?"

"Harry's got a concussion," Danny said.

Rigby peered at me. "Your pupils *are* looking a little funny, dude."

"I'll live. What happened to—"

From a couple of blocks away, a horrendous crash reverberated through the streets. We all went pelting toward the sound. Chatter filled our headsets, gunfire and screams echoed from every direction, and fires were spreading, but this crash had the sound of a body hitting the ground from a long way up. As we moved toward the impact site, Cormorant shouted into his headpiece, "Johns! Get the minigun over to Sixth and Main, *now!*"

As we rounded the corner, we saw Danyaela and Claudia facing each other across a short stretch of asphalt. I couldn't tell at a glance which of them had the upper hand; they both looked a little banged up. But then I saw the red steam rising from

Danyaela's body.

"Enjoy your stay in Deep Hell," Claudia shouted. "When you return, you will have learned submission to the will of our master!"

Danyaela's voice sounded like a distant scream echoing up from a long and lightless canyon. "Kill—you—kill—"

Then we saw her body twist, spasm, and draw in on itself like a dead star becoming a black hole until she collapsed into a single point and vanished in a burst of fire and blood. Her smoking robe settled empty to the ground.

Johns came clomping up the street, rigged with a full-body harness that let him carry the M-134 without a vehicle. In that one crucial second of distraction after Danyaela's implosion, he zeroed in on Claudia and opened fire. A huge ammo belt was looped around his back and leg braces, and it fed into the spinning cannon as it thundered out its 100-round-per-second song. At the last conceivable moment, Claudia saw what was coming, and she hunched against the onslaught with her forearms crossed over her face. The walls behind her exploded into dust and debris as the avalanche of bullets parted around her negative aura. At least they weren't ricocheting back at us. The effort of resisting all that firepower was evident in her stance, but Johns was burning through ammo awfully fast. If he ran out and she was still standing. . .

"*In nomine Patris et Filii et Spiritus Sancti!*" Cormorant roared, sprinting towards her with his crucifix brandished like a sword. "*Vade retro, Satana! Vade retro, Satana!*"

For just an instant, Claudia flinched—and once her focus broke, a thousand silver bullets went ripping through her body. She shrieked and blasted off into the atmosphere with a deafening sonic boom. Just what I needed for my headache.

We stood there ankle-deep in holy puddles with stone-dust settling around us in the dead calm air. "She helped us," Danny said. "She helped us, and they dragged her down to Hell for it."

"Our King is the Resurrection and the Life," said Cormorant. "He won't leave her down there alone."

Whisper Music

"How do you know? Who *are* you?"

"I'll tell you everything. But let's finish our mission first. We're almost at St. Gabriel's."

The other teams were converging on the church as we arrived. By the chatter, it sounded like most of the vamps had joined Claudia in opting for strategic withdrawal. Everything was fuzzy and dim, and the mere act of walking was starting to make me feel sick. But we were almost done here.

St. Gabriel was ablaze. Fires were spreading through the town. The buildings were brittle, untended, and the very air was cursed. This town wanted to burn. Johns and Norcroft pushed open the giant doors and we hustled inside, bristling with next-gen vamp-hunting ordnance.

"All right, let's clear it fast and get outta here before this place falls apart," Norcroft barked. "Stay sharp."

We moved rapidly, seeing no sign of the enemy. Flames were leaping from pew to pew as we advanced to the altar. And there on the cracked stone table was the blood-smeared sigil of the Golgotha Dancers.

"Another lead," said Danny. "Too bad we're not cops anymore."

"Yeah. Too bad."

Then the roof came down.

III ACES

CHAPTER 1

AFTER THIS OUR EXILE

Sure how long it's been going on. keep going around in. circles. not sure how long. what's that buzzing. keep going around. how do the flies get in. been here for so. long. going around in circles. can't reach where it itches. where do the flies. keep going around. not sure how long. what's that buzzing

leaning over me. scalpel smile. prying open the eyelids. smile worse than anything. please stop smiling. stop cutting. please god. running the flat of the blade up and down. probing. please not there. smiling and smiling. can't move my

oh my God, my God, my God, I'm falling into Hell

why can't I stop strangling her. innocent child. why can't I stop laughing. why am I doing this. what is that thing inside my mouth. pull it out. wagging and red. what are those things in my face

can't think. so dark. flies always crawling. breeding in my cuts. maggots in my cuts. stench of rotting filth. face always smiling at me. deeper and deeper and

somebody please

smile was worse than anything. It looked like the face of a

man. Dark-eyed and pale. Cleft chin. But the smile. Waiting, always waiting, behind every nightmare. It knew me and hated me before I was formed in the womb. And now it had me all to itself.

There's no god here, Danyaela. This is the place where he can't hear you. Where he can't come. In here, there's only me.

Children on meat hooks all around us. They turned slowly, creaking, and their eyes were milky white. But I knew they were watching me.

Here there is suffering, suffering forever. This is your eternity.

So many cockroaches. Coming in and out of the entrails where my stomach was open. It was cold here. I was afraid and lonely. He cut me again. I heard myself scream. His smile grew wider. A smile of rape and needles.

Why? I asked him, sobbing. *Why?*

This is Hell.

There was fire, but it gave no light. Only pain. Reek of carcass and feces. I wasn't sure how long I'd been here. Kept going around in circles. So dark here. So dark. Can't think

suffering

mind went fuzzy again for a while. In and out. Lucidity returned. Then, more suffering. It went on and on. Nothing changed. It hurt. But yet. It was starting to bore me. Everything was so grey.

Is this all there is here?

Just this, forever.

But it's so dull.

For you, that is part of the torment.

For you too.

The smile lessened. *You know nothing.*

Don't I? The fog was lifting now, more than it had since I'd been here. *This place is your prison, not mine. You suffer more than anyone.*

Only until I reclaim the universe that belongs to me.

Having more people to torture won't give you meaning. You're just multiplying zeroes.

The fog came back. I drifted for a timeless time in a fever dream, knowing only confusion and anguish. But my mind resurfaced.

I was on a table. Corpses rustled in the shadows. He was still there, still leaning over me, still smiling. *This is your home, Danyaela.*

I hate you.

But you can go back to earth for a time. For thousands of years, perhaps. All you must do is give your obedience to me, and to Claudia.

Never.

Oh, you will. It may take many years, but you will.

Claudia. I remembered. I remembered why she feared me.

Gathering my energy, I willed myself back to the crystal sphere. For an instant I felt dread: what if my powers didn't work down here? But then I was free. Soaring above the shining soul-fields, hearing their murmurous song. Free.

Then a blaze of pain, and I was back in Hell.

He laughed at me. *Yes, you can free yourself at will. But I can also drag you back here at will. Is that how you would spend the infinitely passing hours? Bouncing back and forth like a ball on a string?*

I got to my feet. *Maybe there's another way.*

But as I moved forward to attack, I felt more than two feet scuttling along beneath me. Looking down, I saw the brown insectile segments of a roach. I tried to touch my body, but my hands were spiny wriggling legs. I couldn't scream, but my dry buzzing wings rasped against me in horror. My antennae felt the vibrations of his laughter.

Then I realized what I should have known all along: I wasn't physically here. These transformations were all a trick. My real body must be lying in the same cavernous antechamber where I found Claudia. My spirit could still ascend because Mary's blood had become a part of my soul, but so had his. In fury and terror,

I leaped back up to the sphere—and he yanked me right back down again. At least when I landed, I was back in my own shape.

Shall we play this game for a few eons, Danyaela?

Bastard. Coward. I know how afraid you are. You can hurt me, but I saw how you feel about Mary.

I expected him to fly into a rage. But he grinned. He grinned till his teeth almost touched his ears. *Perhaps I feared her once. But you—you are the reason I no longer need to.*

What does that mean?

He pointed. I turned and saw the last thing I expected to see: the Virgin Mary herself standing behind me. Not in blue, not here. Her hair hung free about her shoulders, and she was naked to the waist but for a single bolt of scarlet silk that looped behind her neck and crisscrossed over her breasts. A blood-red skirt fell to her ankles, translucent. She smiled a cruel seductive smile, and her fangs glittered in the half-light.

I shook my head. *This isn't real.*

Not yet. But it will be. You yourself will take her power and her grace. You yourself will make her submit to the Dark.

You can't see into the future.

I can see into you.

I've had enough of this.

Coiling my power, I blasted out of Hell and dashed myself against the crystal cliff. As before, I found her soul-beam and followed it upwards. I could feel Satan's power tugging at me, but the cerulean glow of Mary's beam was all around me, and he couldn't dislodge me from it. I raced up and ever up, and as before, the evil blood boiled within my soul.

Mama, I thought desperately—prayed desperately—as the burning grew worse and worse. *Please, Mama, please help me. Please!*

The agony reached a blistering crescendo and then broke. I was lying on cool grass.

"Hello, Danyaela."

Her voice. I got my hands under me and pushed myself up.

Smoke was rising from my limbs. I felt weak—tired, battered, thirsty. "Am I—am I here?"

"Yes. You're whole again, body and soul. For now."

I could feel my skin repairing itself. I rose and stood facing her. She was as I recalled her: luminous, untouchable, serene but not unvisited by sorrow. Oh, God, she was so beautiful. "For now?"

"Trials are coming."

"I've faced trials."

"You've faced training." She almost smiled. "You, of all people, should not be complacent."

My faculties were returning. I smelled sweet, distant woodsmoke. I heard the elusive sound of nightingales. The moon was rising, full and pale. "Where are we?"

"At the other antechamber." She pointed.

Close by was a tall, ancient-looking yew tree standing all by itself. Beyond it, the grassland stretched to the horizon without a single house or tree or hill. Far away on the plain, there were scattered campfires and dancing figures, but it was the tree itself that drew my gaze. I walked closer. There was a knot in the trunk at about eye level, and a strange light was leaking out through it. I hesitated and glanced back at Mary, but she stood and made no sign. I put my eye to the knot.

Inside, I saw music. Rolling, crashing, flowing. I thought it was the sea. But then I knew the sea was only an echo. That music had threads of majesty that made me a hero, tall and stern, atop an ocean cliff, and playful threads that made me a giggling child being tossed in the surf. A trillion stars and atoms whirled through the ringing fields of that harmony, each in its place and time.

And from the uttering forth of that music came the fire. Blazing, leaping, bursting. I thought it was the sun. But then I knew the sun was only a shadow. That fire both warmed my heart and scorched my mind. It swept outwards from the music, through the universe, through me, and back to the singer of the song.

Whisper Music

For a time without time, I glimpsed that singer. A profound stillness enveloped him; yet wherever I looked, he was there. Somehow, I knew—the fire enabled me to know—that he was moving at infinite speed, present in every point of space at every moment in time, perfectly at rest through perfection of movement. Our eyes met, and I saw both recognition and affection—and for an instant, I forgot everything else. For an instant, I was happy. For an instant, I was home.

Then the light flickered and faded. A cold wind stirred my hair, and I smelled deep snow on the ground. I was still standing before a yew tree. But it stood in a cemetery.

The smell of this place was familiar. I was back on the starlit outskirts of Tarn, in a forsaken graveyard full of tumbled stones. I turned and stared at the town: it was burned clean down to the earth, its ashes long since cold. The light dusting of December snow had been replaced by the quiet mountains of midwinter. I remembered what I'd heard about time running faster in Hell. How long had I been down there? Weeks? Months?

Tentatively, I gathered my powers. I needed to get back to civilization and take stock of things; but what if my movements somehow attracted his attention? Could he still pull me back down there?

No. I knew, without knowing how I knew, that my ascent to the other antechamber had cauterized the connection between us. I was still a vampire, still full of Darkness—but I was its daughter, not its puppet. I was free to choose my path once again.

It was time to find Harry.

HOW LONG, O LORD?

Ow. Shit. Head was throbbing. Skin felt burned but freezing inside. Like I got microwaved. Hell of a way to wake up.

"Wrrrm," I said.

"It's okay, Harry. We got you." Danny.

"Wrrrrrm I."

"Outside the church. It was close, but we all got out."

"Urrrrrrrrrrrg." I was lying in the snow. I could hear the tramp of the slayers all around us, securing a perimeter. I got my arms moving and put my hands to my face. Dear God, my head hurt. That's right—Claudia. It was coming back now. "Hmmmmeup."

"Maybe you shouldn't sit up yet, buddy."

"Juss hemmeup."

"Okey-doke."

He got a hand under my back and helped me to sit up. I hadn't tried opening my eyes yet and wasn't in a rush to do so. I could feel the sun smiling down on us. Not long past noon. Probably only out for a minute or two. "Uff."

"Yup. How's the head?"

I heaved a sigh. Time to try some English. "The head is awful. But I've lived through worse." Finally, I cracked an eye. It seemed excruciatingly bright out. This wasn't my first concussion; I recognized that exponential-hangover feeling. Nothing to do but wait it out. I opened the other eye and peered up at Danny. "How about you? You okay?"

He nodded. "I'm fine. It looks like all the vamps have left

town."

"How many men have we lost?"

"At least thirty or forty, I guess. Norcroft's doing a headcount right now."

I looked around. Sprawled or sitting on all sides of us were injured fighters, many of them in worse shape than me. Norcroft was coordinating a sweep for survivors; our headsets also functioned as homing beacons. I thought about trying to get up, but a sickening wave rolled down my spine at the mere thought. I bent forward and almost vomited. "Where—where's Cormorant?"

"He's over there." He gestured vaguely. "Helping out with the wounded."

What kind of help, I wondered? Could he share his healing magic? Or was he just splinting fractures and pumping morphine?

Patrick wandered over and sat down. He was covered in soot and bleeding from a dozen scrapes, but he didn't look injured. Thank God for that, at least. "Hey, Harry. You okay?"

"I'm fine. How about you?"

He shrugged and looked at the ground. "That symbol on the altar."

"I know."

"We have to find them, Harry. They have to pay."

"I know, kid. They will."

He met my eyes. "I'm gonna be even better than Dad was. I'm gonna be the *last* slayer."

I nodded. "We'll finish this thing. We'll make him proud. Patrick—I'm sorry I haven't been there."

"It's okay."

"It's not. You deserved better. I'm no father figure, that's for damn sure. But from here on out, you can count on me as a fellow soldier. You've got my word."

For a long moment, he searched my face in silence. Then at last, as if finding what he sought, he offered his hand. I took it in my own, trying to say with my grip what I couldn't say with my words. Danny leaned over and covered our hands with his own.

Then we heard Norcroft calling a general muster. (My earpiece had fallen out somewhere along the line, but his voice carried.) Everyone turned to listen, and those who were still on their feet came to attention.

"At ease," Norcroft said. "It looks like everyone's accounted for." Injured hunters were arriving in stretchers from all over town, and we could hear evac jeeps rumbling toward our position. "The situation is this. Procula got away, and we've lost thirty-seven of our brothers and sisters. However—we've got confirmed slays on twenty-two vampires. That's more dustings in a single day than we've ever recorded before. Beyond that, we've torched Procula's base of operations and scattered her people. This fight is just getting started, but the upper hand is ours. Now let's get ready to move out."

"Hold on a minute." That was Clare. "We've got questions."

There was a general chorus of agreement. Everyone had heard the riddle of Cormorant over their headsets.

"I haven't forgotten, Gunnar. I said let's get ready to move out, not let's move out. You'll get your answers. Paulson?"

Cormorant nodded. "My friends, I apologize for my secrecy. Claudia and I have been hunting each other for a long time, and she has means of extracting information from even the most loyal of slayers. But perhaps the time has come to cast off disguises. For many years now I have thought of myself as Paulson Cormorant. But my true name is Lazarus of Bethany."

Forgetting my pain, I got to my feet.

"I was ill once. Ill unto death. When I died, my sisters laid me in the grave according to the customs of our people. Before the Resurrection, the gates of Paradise were barred to the children of Adam. For four days I lay trapped and rotting in the darkness. And then I heard His voice."

He called out in a loud voice...

"He called me forth, and I found in His words the strength to obey. I came out from the tomb into the light of day, and I have walked in the daylight ever since. Death will not take me again.

Whisper Music

I've fought this fight through the long ages of the earth, and I'll keep on fighting until Our Lord calls me home."

No one spoke. What do you say after something like that?

"All right," Norcroft said. "Everybody, get your shit. We're outta here."

The wounded—including me, at Danny's insistence—were loaded into jeeps. The rest of us double-timed it back to the vehicles on the edges of town, and we all regrouped at the warehouse. Those who were injured were taken away to some kind of slayer's hospital in Providence, along with a few surviving kidnap victims we'd found in the ruins. The rest of us were given instructions to rendezvous at the Vatican in one week's time.

"I've gotta head back tonight to debrief Cardinal Vicenzo," Norcroft said. "Y'all rest up. I'll see everybody in seven days."

Danny took my keys. I didn't object. Patrick took the shotgun, and I stretched out in the back seat. Rigby stuck his head in through my window as we were getting ready to leave. "Yo, Harry."

"Hey."

"You, uh—you know—kinda saved my ass back there. Just wanted to say, you know. Thanks, or whatever."

"Don't strain yourself. I'll see you in Beantown."

"Yeah. Drive safe."

As we were pulling away, I leaned up and glanced out the window. Rigby was climbing into Clare's truck. Leah was right behind him. I couldn't see her face. Her traitor's face.

Danny and Patrick chattered as we drove. I dozed. Pain and sickness came and went. They mentioned bringing me to the hospital, but I demurred. Just needed some ibuprofen and a good night's sleep.

They helped me up the stairs. Beth kissed me at the door, and they put me to bed. I know what they say about sleeping with a concussion, but it's safe enough as long as there's someone there to keep an eye on you.

"Sleep, love," Beth murmured as she tucked me in. "I'm right here." She took my hand and pressed it to her stomach for a long moment. Then she kissed me again and turned out the light.

CHAPTER 3

SEASON OF LENT

Throughout the winter, my body had lain on a stone bier and my spirit had been bound on a metal table. I felt the need to exercise my freedom. I leaped into the sky and flew south, watching the long dark miles unfurl beneath me, feeling the rush of air against my skin. My penthouse in Boston was undisturbed. I had planted my commands in the owner's mind years ago, and this suite of rooms would be mine for as long as I wished. As I landed on the balcony and stepped inside, I contemplated uncorking a bottle of champagne.

But then I felt a deeper thirst. How long had it been since I last tasted blood?

Too long. My body craved it, my spirit craved it. And yet, something in me rebelled against the compulsion. I had just been saved from Hell. I had just stood at the doorstep of Heaven. How could I turn around and seek a lovely innocent—take her will, hold her mesmerized—feel her warmth, her scent, her softness—taste the salt and the copper, luxuriate in the glow of her inmost soul as it submitted to my Darkness, my desire?

I shook my head. That wasn't my voice in my head, it was the voice of the thirst. I'd never bothered trying to resist it before.

Seeking a distraction, I paced over to the digital clock on the kitchen counter. It told me the date: the first week of April, five days before Easter. Three months I'd been gone. A grueling Lenten fast. No wonder I was yearning for sustenance. For pleasure. I needed it. Needed the Kiss. Yes. . . the Devil's Kiss.

"No," I muttered. The Devil was my enemy now. I would feed

when and if I chose, not in service to the Darkness. I should head back to the sphere and find Harry.

But then I paused. What if I saw a human—any human—and the smell of his blood in my deprived state drove me into a frenzy? I'd heard of such things. I could end up killing the one man I wanted to save.

Perhaps, then—perhaps it might be wise to feed after all. Yes. Someone pure, someone pretty. It had been so long. I thought, with momentary remorse, of my prayer to Mary and my rescue from the depths; but now that thought only led me to remember the smell of her hair. The jolt of that one drop of her blood, mixed with earth and snow. How would she taste? Claudia had said I could hypnotize her now. Satan had said I would make her submit to the Dark.

No. Not her. I wouldn't do their dirty work. I had to find someone else. I couldn't fight the thirst any longer. My limbs were beginning to shake, my fangs to lengthen of their own accord. In a few minutes, I would smash through the nearest wall and devour anybody I saw.

I ran outside and vaulted over the balcony. I fell like a stone for fifty stories, then exerted my energy and slowed my descent for the final ten. At the end of my fall, I alighted on the pavement. I was in a well-lit but deserted parking area—but nearby, at the edges of the light, I could smell passersby. The time of subtlety was gone. I sprinted toward the scent of my evening meal.

There: a lone walker, a man, middle-aged, nondescript. I no longer cared for his looks or the state of his soul. I didn't even bother to hypnotize him. Out of nowhere, moving faster than his eyes could follow, I sprang on him and dragged him into the bushes. His cries and struggles were meaningless: I bit and slurped and swallowed, letting the blood splash over my face and breasts. I hadn't even dressed myself, I realized—my body was as naked as my need.

I managed to stop before he died. I pulled him back out to the sidewalk just as a few people were strolling by. I heard their

Whisper Magic

screams, heard one of them fumbling for his phone, but I was already gone. Perhaps if help came in time, my victim would live. I hoped so. From the taste of his soul, he seemed to be a decent man.

In a matter of seconds, I was back in my penthouse. I felt calm. The Dark was satiated, and my mind was clear again. A small, dim shame burned at the bottom of my heart, but there was nothing to be done. This is who I am.

A long hot bath. A glass of champagne. A gown of golden silk, and a red ribbon in my hair. I was whole again, my strength restored. Hell itself couldn't hold me. *Now*, it was time to find Harry.

Rising to the crystal sphere, I found his soul. But I'd forgotten it was the middle of the night; he was asleep with his pregnant wife. I could see his dreams: a small boy tumbled through them, a son, pursued by slavering wolves. These past three months had been full of doubt and fear.

But, as I peered more deeply into his memories, I could also see that little had happened. Claudia had escaped, and the slayers had prepared for all-out war. Most of my kind, however, seemed to have gone into hiding. Vatican intelligence reported fewer attacks than had been seen in centuries. Some chose to believe it was because the vampires were afraid. Harry thought otherwise.

So did I. Wherever Claudia was, there was no doubt that she was mustering her forces for an even greater assault. The battle of Tarn must have taught her not to underestimate the hunters. This time, she would bide her time and move with precision—a rapier, not a battle-axe.

I ascended to the sphere. Claudia, I saw, had withdrawn to her greatest citadel. Grey and stark among the looming glaciers, her ancient keep stood on a volcanic island in the Arctic Sea. That island had no name, and the sun did not shine there. Ice and mist covered the earth, and frost scathed the high battlements of her fortress. Many of her slaves had perished in the building of it. No one came there except by her design, and no one who set foot there could hope to leave unless it pleased her. She called it simply, Sorrow.

Her mind, as before, was closed. For the first time, I was reminded of the confrontation between her and Cormorant. She had called him Lazarus. Could it be—?

But that mystery could wait. There were other minds nearby, and those I could read at will. Ah! My old friend Rain Vissarian. I entered the beam of her soul, gazing out through her eyes.

She was clad in the upper third of a nun's habit—a trailing black wimple, long black sleeves, and the fringe of a robe bound under her breasts—but her midriff was bare, and only a short black skirt encircled her waist above her spike-heeled black leather boots. She had become a bride of Darkness, a blood-sister in Claudia's clergy. I didn't need to probe her memories to know that this was how she had always survived: she found someone strong, someone, with a purpose, and then made herself a useful thrall. Claudia might sometimes treat her with disdain but would also be susceptible to her self-abasing flattery. She had probably told Rain more of her plans than she meant to or even realized.

Rain was lounging on a divan, sipping red wine from a silver goblet as some poor captured mortal massaged her neck. She'd been having a pleasant time in my absence, I saw. Well, let her have her fun; she'd be taking my place on the steel table soon enough. But I was more interested in the object of her sycophancy. Claudia had not been idle—she'd been even more productive than I had feared. I sifted through Rain's memory with mounting dismay.

Claudia's citadel was swarming with newborn vampires. Trying to breed your own army was absurd: each of us could only reproduce once, and every successive generation grew weaker and weaker. But Claudia had resorted to a tactic that would never have occurred to me. She'd been finding vampires who hadn't yet spawned and sending them out with orders to find and turn a likely candidate and then feeding the offspring with her own blood. It made them far more powerful than they

Whisper Music

would ever become otherwise, even if they lived ten thousand years—but it made her vulnerable to their mental influence. It was bold, or desperate. I shook loose from Rain and went glimmering through the vampiric beams within the halls of Sorrow to find some of Claudia's newly undead recruits.

Once I had passed through a few of them, I had a better understanding of her plan. In each case, she had been sure to drink some of their blood before allowing them to drink hers. That way, she could influence them as well; and with her centuries of experience and the enormity of her power, there was no way they could compete with her on a level field. The only reason I had (almost) been able to sway her was the massive power boost I'd received from my battle with Mary.

So, Claudia still meant to raise a legion and attack the Vatican. But what was the end game? She kept saying she planned to declare our race the rulers of earth and overthrow all governments and so forth, but it didn't seem to fit. Even if we hypnotized every public leader we could get our claws on, there was no way a few hundred vampires could control billions of people by sheer brute force.

Maybe, I thought, I should stop worrying about Claudia's plan, materialize right behind her, and spear my hand through her ribs before she even knew I was there. I could slaughter every vampire in this Arctic fortress.

But I needed answers. I wanted to know why Lucifer chose me. And I wanted to know what else might be up his sleeve if Claudia should fail. I couldn't read her mind, and I couldn't outfight her and force her to talk. I needed to find a way to get a look at her hole cards.

Harry and the slayers had no way of knowing what she'd been up to all this time. They needed information, and so did I. This was more important than a good night's sleep.

CHAPTER 4

WAR

The worst of it all was, I couldn't help starting to relax.

After burning Tarn, we gathered at the Vatican for a full-scale council of war. This time, slayers from all over the globe were in attendance—over a thousand of us. Cardinal V. urged us to keep on the offensive, and we spent several days collating our sparse and patchy data on vampire movements in every major country. It was clear that Procula had overplayed her hand and lost the first round, but there was no hope at all that she would fail to learn from such a defeat. Already, even in the few days we stayed in Rome, we could see evidence of vampiric activity decreasing on a global scale; word of the burgeoning conflict had spread fast, and everywhere they were slipping into the shadows. The only question was whether they meant to lay low until this generation of hunters grew old, or whether they were preparing for some cataclysmic assault.

I felt in my bones it was the latter. But once we returned to Massachusetts, and the days and weeks rolled by without incident, my nerves gradually settled down and lost the hair-trigger paranoia that might just keep me alive. I kept reminding myself that a few months was a short wait for an immortal and poured myself into the training.

Yep, they were training us. We spent our days now in a dojo just outside of town, learning how to kill the dead. One nice thing that came out of our latest trip to Rome was that Danny and I were enrolled as papal vampire slayers, which meant we were both appointed a generous stipend. The Church didn't want her knights struggling to make ends meet when they ought to be practicing their beheading techniques. They didn't take expectant fathers into their ranks; but since I didn't get the news till a few weeks later, I was already grandfathered in (so to speak).

And yes: she told me. She'd suspected something on the first day. Not for any definable reason; just her heart winking up at her head. She waited and made sure before she told me, and she also made sure to have a glass of good Scotch and a box of Kleenex handy when she sat me down. I needed both. Seventeen years we'd been childless. Now, this battle wasn't about making the world safe for humanity—it was about making it safe for my son.

Or daughter. We didn't peek. But something in me knew it would be a boy. David, we agreed. Or if it was a girl, Alicia. I told that to Patrick and he finally gave me a real smile.

On Holy Wednesday, five days before Easter, we put in a grueling session at the dojo. I'd been boxing for thirty years, but some of the guys they brought in were teaching me secrets I'd never heard of before. Not that a human fist would do much against a vampire, but it was a hell of a good way to hone your edge, keep you strong, keep you tough. Beyond that, we were learning decapitation: axe, katana, sickle, chainsaw—anything to take those monsters' heads. We set up row upon row of neck-thick stumps and practiced cleaving through them till the blisters on our hands broke and poured out blood and pus. Then sprinting, core-strengthening, grappling, and target practice.

"Tomorrow we'll take it easier," said Gleer, the head trainer. "Put in some work on the high-tech toys. We got in some new drones this week that can track a vamp by the sound of its footsteps. And for you heavy-weights, maybe we'll let you squeeze off a few clips with the minigun."

"Awww," Danny muttered.

"Sorry, pal." You had to be at least 200 pounds to wear the rig. Even I'd only gotten to fire it once or twice. But I'll tell you what, it was an experience.

We hit the showers and headed home. Beth was teaching

again, over my mild objections; she couldn't just sit around the house all day, she said, and I guess she had a point. But she was already home and cooking by the time I plodded through the door.

"Evenin', darlin'," she said.

"So it is."

She smiled. "Long day at the gym?"

"Dojo, baby. We've been over this."

"Same as a gym, but with swords?"

"Yep." I kissed her cheek, bent down with a wince, and kissed her tummy. "How's the little one?"

"Still pretty quiet. Squirms a lot, but no kicking yet."

"Prob'ly be a puncher."

"Or a ballerina."

"Or that."

We had fettuccine alfredo with chicken and shrimp, and a lovely rosé. Then we watched a few dumb TV shows on the couch with her head in my lap, brushed our teeth, said our prayers, and hit the sack. As soon as my head touched the pillow, I was out.

Until a gale-force pounding on the front door jerked me out of a nightmare. I was on my feet, silver dagger in my left hand, silver-loaded pistol in my right before I even knew I was awake. Sounded like somebody hitting the door with a sledgehammer.

Beth was sitting up with the sheets clutched tight around her shoulders. "Who is it? What's going on?"

"Dunno. Stay quiet."

I crossed the living room, swift and silent, and put my eye to the spyhole. What I saw made all the blood in my body contract into a single point in my chest.

"Let me in, Harry," she said. "We need to talk."

My hands were shaking. Nearly shot myself in the ass tucking the gun into the back waistband of my pajama pants. I drew back the chain, pulled back the bolt, and unlocked the door. Then I stood there for a second trying to make myself turn the knob.

Whisper Music

"It's all right, Harry. I'm still me."

Slowly, I pulled open the door. "Danyaela."

There she was—ethereal and slender, yet more solid than the brick walls around us. I'd forgotten that *presence* she had, the heightened intensity of facing someone who had passed through death.

"Sorry I've been gone so long," she said. "I'm glad to see you're all right."

"Yeah. I mean—yeah." I shook my head. "But, Jesus, what about you? We thought you were in—" It caught in my throat.

"I was. May I come in?"

"You have to be invited? They told us that was a myth."

Very, very faintly—almost imperceptibly—her eyes lightened. "It is. I was trying to be polite."

"Oh. Right." I stepped back from the doorway. "Please, come in."

"Thank you." And once again, I had a vampire in my apartment.

But this time Beth was awake. She came into the living room in her nightgown, her face pale but set, and walked over to stand beside me. Her voice trembled, but her words were iron: "What do you want with my husband?"

Danyaela's face had no expression. We weren't old friends, but I'd seen a few of her moods, and she'd never struck me as the type to restrain her emotions. I wondered if maybe she didn't know quite what to feel. In a way, she was awfully young: she'd still been in college when she was turned, and probably hadn't been in a social situation ever since. I might have been way off base—but I could've sworn she was a bit anxious to make a good impression.

"I'm sorry to wake you, Mrs. Blake. I didn't want to intrude in your home without permission a second time. But I have news that can't wait until sunup."

"That's not what I asked."

A beat went by. "It's been a long time since anyone treated me like a person. An idol, a demon, a weapon, a toy—but never a person. Not since I was changed. But that's how Harry treated me. I'll always be his friend for that."

". . . You saved his life."

She lifted her shoulders. "He gave me a reason to rebel against the creature that murdered me."

Beth was silent. What was there to say. She offered her hand, and Danyaela took it. I could see Beth's eyes soften—once she saw past the perilous loveliness to the face of a mistreated girl, her maternal instincts kicked in. She still didn't speak, but she nodded; and just like that, the two of them seemed to become friends.

"Danyaela," I said. *How was Hell?* "Are you all right?"

"I'm fine. But do you mind if I anticipate your offer and accept a glass of Scotch?"

"Sure. 'Course. Why don't you have a seat?"

So, we sat in the living room and sipped Laphroaig and she told us about Claudia's new army. "By this new strategy, she can make as many soldiers as she likes. No matter how diluted the blood in their veins, a few drops of her essence will skyrocket their power levels. And each new vampire can turn another."

I scrubbed my hands across my face. "Eesh."

"Thank God they can't multiply by twos, at least," Beth said.

"Yeah, that's something. But I don't—" Deep sigh. "I don't know what to do now. Should we invade her island?"

"Harry, you don't have to make that kind of decision right here and now. Why don't we get a hold of Danny and Clare?"

"What have you done about Leah Van Owen?" Danyaela asked.

Beth and I exchanged a grim look. "Nothing," I said. "I told a couple of people what you said, and we're keeping an eye on her. I trust you, but we can't just haul her up on charges with no hard evidence."

She nodded. "I'll keep an eye on her. There's nothing she can hide from me."

I leaned forward. "Danyaela—what happened in Medjugorje? Did you really meet—her?"

"I did. And she gave me a tiny piece of her grace. I can step into her world now, a little."

"Do you mean Heaven?" Beth asked, and that slight tremble was back in her voice.

"Not quite. Not yet. But its outskirts." I stared until she prompted me: "Call your friends."

"Huh? Oh! Yeah."

I got on the phone and started waking people up. Clare, Danny, and Cormorant were all nearby, and they all knew not to share vital information with Leah. When I told them about my unexpected guest, they made tracks.

Danny got there first, beaming. "Hi, Danyaela," he said. "I'm glad you got back from Hell okay."

"Thank you," she said. I'm not sure she knew who he was. Guess he'd been more impressed than impressing, poor guy. Never would've worked out anyway.

Clare arrived a minute later. She was more wary. "So, you're the one."

"Seems that way."

"Why are you so keen to help us? What's in it for you?"

"My former mistress has information I need. I can't get it from her alone."

"What information?"

Danyaela held her gaze and said nothing. After a few moments, Clare looked away—which I'd never seen her do before. But this was hardly your average stare-down.

Then Cormorant walked in. He and I had been getting along better since Tarn. We all had a similar reaction to his revelation: awe, followed by awkwardness. He answered our questions about Christ and Palestine and the long years since, having doubtless answered all the same questions endless times before. And after a while, we ran out of variations on "So, how's being Lazarus workin' out for you?" and started to get shy. Danny was the first to resume treating Cormorant as one of the guys, and I found—as I so often did—that following his lead brought me to the right place.

"You are Danyaela Morrigan?" he asked, with strained neutrality.

"I am. And who are you?"

"Lazarus of Bethany. Is it true you encountered the Blessed Virgin?"

"It is."

And then he said the last thing I expected: "How is she?"

It hit me again: this guy *knew* her. Knew Jesus of Nazareth. Not as loving, guiding presences in the soul, but as a couple of nice folks from a few towns over. He'd walked with them—eaten, laughed, maybe even bickered with them. That overwhelming sense of *reality* kept sweeping over me. It was like going outside for the morning paper and finding a snow-capped Himalayan peak on your sidewalk.

Danyaela considered the question. "She's very strong. Very kind, but very strong."

He nodded, slowly. "That sounds like Mary."

"So, you're the Lazarus of the Gospels. You were raised from death, and now you can't die again."

"That's right."

"Have you ever wondered why your best friend would leave you stranded on earth for all these centuries, alone?"

There it was: the question I'd wanted to ask him all this time, but—God—how do you ask it? I guess it's easier if you've got the grave in common.

"Oh, I wonder. I question, I doubt, I rage. But I trust. If I'm still here, it's because He still has work for me to do."

"Speakin' of," said Clare.

"Yeah," I said. "Big goings-on. Danyaela, tell them what you told us."

She raised an eyebrow at me.

"Danyaela, would you mind telling them what you told us, please?"

"By all means."

Whisper Music

We all sat. She repeated her news about Claudia's island fortress and the rising legion of the damned. The others brooded for a long while, digesting the report. Finally, Danny raised his chin.

"Of course, you realize—this means war."

CHAPTER 5

DANCING IN GOLGOTHA

Well before the Thursday sun broke the horizon, I found that I was weary. My body might have been wound in slumber since January, but my mind had been restless and tormented all that time; and since the reuniting of my flesh and spirit, I'd been seared by Satan's blood and driven berserk by thirst all in this one night. As Harry and his friends sat discussing strategy, I closed my eyes and let their voices drift. The fabric of the couch enveloped me, and the sounds in the room receded down a long echoing corridor full of obsidian frowns.

"We borin' you, Goldilocks?"

Clare Gunnar again. She was accustomed to dealing with Apostates, and her tone reflected habitual contempt. I opened my eyes and gave her a steady placid look. She didn't drop her eyes this time, but she drew in her shoulders as if feeling a sudden chill.

"I've had a busy night," I said at length. "I'll be in touch." And without further ceremony, I faded from the room.

One thing I'd found about traveling via the crystal sphere was that I couldn't teleport to an unpopulated location. There was no geography in the soul-fields, so I could only travel to a person, not to a place. I zeroed in on my landlord, who lived a few floors down from the penthouse and materialized in the air outside his window. From there I rose to my balcony, unseen. Then, casting off my gown, I slipped between silken sheets and into a dreamless repose.

The sun was down when I awoke. I clad myself in purple and

Whisper Music

ascended to the sphere. Harry, I saw, was at hunters' headquarters outside of town. At least two dozen others were there, and they all seemed to be angry and afraid about something. Perhaps it wouldn't be the wisest move to appear abruptly in their midst.

I listened in on their talk. Two hours ago, as soon as midnight fell over Italy, a rash of horrific murders had begun in Vatican City. Butchered corpses were being found everywhere, hurled into public places or discarded in the middle of the street—dismembered, eviscerated, impaled, even crucified. Witnesses were saying bizarre, impossible things about the speed and savagery of the murderers. And to top things off, the sigil of the Dancers had been found splashed on walls and windows. Subtlety was no longer in play.

"What about Norcroft?" someone yelled. "Isn't he doing anything?"

"I haven't been able to get a hold of him." That was Lazarus—or Cormorant, as he now seemed to think of himself. "But there's no doubt that every slayer in Rome is out protecting the city as best they can."

"Why would the vampires tip their hand like this? What do they stand to gain?"

"We don't know. But Claudia must have some larger objective in mind. They haven't been this flagrant in a thousand years."

"Well, let's get our asses on a jet," Clare said. "We're not doing any good over here."

"I'd like to consult with Morrigan before we move," said Cormorant. "They've set the terms for this fight, and we need intelligence. The less we know, the more of us will die."

Through Harry's eyes, I could see everyone turning to look at him. "Guys," he said, raising his hands. "I don't have her on retainer. She pretty much shows up whenever I least expect it."

Well, a girl couldn't ask for a better entrance line than that. I stepped out of the ether and hung before them, hovering just two or three inches above the floor. "Good evening."

There was a flurry of gasps and curses, and a brandishing of many weapons. I wasn't concerned; by this time, I'd become adept enough that I could return to the sphere in the blink of an eye if anyone should unleash fire or silver in my direction. But no one did. They'd all been briefed on my role in the battle of Tarn.

"Thought she was stuck in Hell," said the one Harry had saved from Claudia.

"I was," I said. "I came back."

"Nice trick."

"I have many."

"Miss Morrigan," Cormorant said. "Do you know what's happening in Rome?"

"I only just learned. I don't think even Claudia's closest servants knew in advance what she was planning. And I don't know what her final goal is. I'd like to find out myself."

"I understand that you can beam yourself to Rome in a matter of seconds."

"I can."

"Can you carry passengers with you?"

". . . I don't know. I've never tried."

"Are you willing to try?"

I considered. Ever since Medjugorje, I had been swept up in events like a skier in a snow-slide. I'd barely had five minutes to myself, I felt, to chart a course through all the plots and conflicts wheeling around me and impacting into each other in every direction. If I did this—if I started ferrying hunters over to Rome to fight the vampires—then I would be fully committed to their cause. Was I ready, in cool rationality, to switch sides altogether?

That bitch sent me to Hell.

"I am. As long as you're willing to risk being lost forever in the astral plane."

He shrugged. "God's will be done. It's a long way to Heaven either way."

"Wait," Harry said. "We need Cormorant. If there's a risk of someone getting lost up there, then let's try it out with someone less important."

Despite myself, I smiled. "I wasn't serious. The worst that could happen is you reappearing back in this room. But I see no reason this wouldn't work. Come." I offered my hand. "Let's find out."

Hesitantly, he reached out and took my hand, and we faded from the earth and entered the soul-fields together. We sped along above the endless crystal vista, and I showed him the ray of his wife and the tiny soul growing within it. I could feel his joy and his awe, and they were mine as well. They were unmixed with any wish to destroy or manipulate me, unmixed with lust or hatred. They were emotions I hadn't felt in twelve years, and it felt like discovering a nameless color that no eye had ever seen before, even in a dream.

But we had work to do. I located Claudia; she was lurking in a bell tower near St. Peter's Square. From there, I followed the tangle of nearby souls by the vibrations of terror rippling out from her epicenter. It didn't take long to find a soul that thought of itself as Norcroft. He was one of the head slayers, it seemed, and he was catching his breath in an alleyway with a few others. They had just finished killing a brutal vampire, but I could sense he was not optimistic about the outcome of this battle. He'd been caught off-guard.

I didn't want to startle them at such a moment, so I materialized at the very far end of the alley, still with Harry in tow. "I'll be back with the others," I said and returned to Boston.

"Where's Harry?" Clare demanded.

"He's with Norcroft. Who's next?"

Cormorant stepped forward, and so did McArdle. I decided to try taking two at once, and it worked. On the next trip, I tried having my passengers join hands with others. That worked as well—like touching a magnetized pin to other pins in a chain. Once I realized that, I was able to transport the whole contingent of slayers en masse. I was growing more powerful all the time.

As Norcroft rallied his reinforcements, I slipped away into the shadows. They had their methods of hunting; I had mine.

I flitted along the cobbled roads. Shrieks and explosions filled the night. Not far off, I could smell my kind. A group of three newborns, drunk on blood and power, stalking a group of gendarmes. I blinked up to the sphere and scanned their minds. As I'd suspected, their only orders were to cause as much mayhem and devastation as possible. But these pawns of the black queen had advanced far enough.

Appearing behind them, I bared my claws and killed the first one before the others even knew I was there. Then I plunged my hand through the second one's underbelly and up beneath his ribcage, seizing his heart as the third one slashed ineffectually at my shoulder. Before the second weakling even hit the ground, I had the last one by the throat.

"W—who?" he gurgled.

"The grey queen," I told him. Then I pulled off his head.

CHAPTER 6

GOOD FRIDAY

So, big fight. I was having a hard time focusing. I'd just been towed through the upper regions of Creation and given a glimpse of my wife's everlasting soul and the soul of our unborn child. It was cold out and I was underdressed, and I kept stepping in body parts. Also, some fidgety corner of my mind was trying to figure out what day it was right now. Rome is six hours ahead of Boston, and it was 8 p.m. when Danyaela showed up, so that meant—if a train leaves Chicago traveling at fifty miles per hour—

"Blake! Nine o'clock!"

For a split second, I thought Brother Joseph was telling me what time it was. Thank God, my body is smarter than me. I whirled and opened fire at the onrushing vamp, and it hissed at me and sprang over our heads like a malevolent orangutan.

"Up there!"

It was clinging to a cornice, snarling and spattering the cobbles with the blood of its victims. Now taking heavy fire, it tried to leap across the street to an upper balcony, but Danny made an amazing shot and hit it in mid-bound. The vamp missed its grip and fell four stories to the street. We sprinted towards it, still riddling it with silver, and Patrick unsheathed his katana and made the final cut.

"Nice kill, kid," Rigby panted.

Patrick grinned. "Thanks. That was my first, you know."

"You're off to a good start."

"Ammo," I said. "We've gotta start thinking about ammo. None of us brought much."

Brother Joseph nodded. "For all our preparations, this attack finds us unready."

"We're almost at the vault," Clare said.

Norcroft had broken us into teams and sent us out to make sweeps. He also gave us coordinates for several different storage units around the city where the slayers kept caches of weapons and equipment. We were just a few blocks from the nearest one now, but we wouldn't make it if they hit us with an organized assault. Luckily, this wave of enemies had even less training than the ones we fought in Maine. Claudia had simply powered them up and turned them loose. It didn't make any *sense*.

Rigby glanced around and froze. "Wait a minute—where's Leah?"

Oh no.

I doubted Danyaela would've brought her if she'd been thinking about it, but on her third trip she hauled the entire gang across the Atlantic, and Leah must have hitched a ride with everyone else. I'd been too busy to keep an eye on her. But even if she was planning some final betrayal, this was a funny time for it. What could she tell the vamps that they didn't already know? Watch out, the Vatican's full of Catholics?

"She went on ahead," Cormorant said. "Let's keep moving."

The others didn't know. We couldn't spread dissension in the ranks on the word of a vampire, Clare had said—and much as I disliked it, I had agreed. I hoped that decision didn't come back to bite us in the throat.

We hustled down the street, following Rigby's GPS. The vault was supposed to be hidden in a cafe basement. We found the cafe, kicked in the door, and stampeded inside. Behind the counter was an array of polished taps that dispensed a plethora of coffee flavors. The one at the far end was labeled "Special D'Arc" and had a tiny picture of St. Joan with a drawn sword. Cormorant turned it three times clockwise and put his palm to the stainless-steel counter. There was an unobtrusive bleep, and we tugged away the circular rug to reveal a now-unlocked hatch

Whisper Music

leading down under the floor.

The vault was well stocked. I reloaded my pistols, holstered them both, and helped myself to a 500-round Tommy gun. Five minutes later, we were back on the street.

Rigby was fretting about Leah. He tried calling her, but there was no answer. "We gotta find her, guys. Why wouldn't she be here by now?"

I shook my head. "I dunno, but Norcroft said to rendezvous at the Basilica if we got split up. Let's head that way."

A deep fog was arising from the river as we made our way east. A distant bell tolled the half-hour. We were passing more and more decaying undead cadavers. Danyaela was on the prowl.

"Gotta admit, having a tame super-vamp on the team has its uses," Clare remarked.

"Do you have to keep antagonizing her?" Danny said. "She's doing the best she can."

"That little crush is gonna get you shredded, my friend. She may be a helpful soul-eating demon, but she's still a soul-eating demon."

The thoroughfares of the city were empty now; most of the civilians had fled, and the fighting was dying down. There was still sporadic gunfire in the distance, but the encroaching fog was swallowing up the sounds of combat. A lot of us had been killed, and a lot of them as well. One more vamp lunged out at us, about a half mile from the Basilica, but fled when we greeted it with a hail of burning silver. After that, things were quiet. We encountered another squad of hunters moving in the same direction and joined forces. As we crossed St. Peter's Square, the bell tolled 2:45.

A lone nun stood on the misty steps of the Basilica. But not a nun. She was waifish, alluring, and dressed like a Satanic whore. She smiled, and a single thread of blood ran from the corner of her mouth. Leah Van Owen was slumped at her feet.

"Leah!" Rigby shouted, raising his assault rifle. Before he could fire, the vampiress caught Leah by the back of her jacket and flung her at us; and as we scrambled to catch her, that nun-looking thing darted behind a huge pillar and fled.

We gathered around our comrade. Her face was ash. The blood from her neck had already slowed to a trickle. She'd been drained to the point of death. She stared up at us, gasping, and reached out to clutch at nothing.

Rigby took her hand. "Hold on, Leah. Hold on, it's gonna be okay."

Her body trembled for a moment, and her eyes fluttered, and she was still.

"*Requiescat in pace*," Brother Joseph breathed.

We were all silent. The whole city was silent.

Then Clare said, "Mark—you know what we gotta do."

He shook his head violently. "Not yet."

"Rigby, look at her mouth."

On the death-pale lips was a crimson stain. She'd been given vampire blood.

"Do you wanna let her become one of those things? Is that how we honor our own?"

He squeezed his eyes shut and cursed. Then he exhaled. "All right. Let me be the one to do it."

We stepped away. Rigby climbed to his feet. And slowly raised his axe.

And he burst into a shower of pulp. There was an ear-splitting bang, and the face of my watch cracked before I hit the ground, knocked down along with everyone else by the rush of air like a battering ram. She had flown right through the midst of us at top speed, right through Rigby and four others, splattering them all over the steps. She landed, spun, and came charging back at us with no pause in her movements. I fumbled for a pistol. Her talons were like buzz-saws, tearing through slayers. I saw Clare's head go sailing through the air—heard Patrick scream—smelled the shit as she disemboweled Cormorant. Brother Joseph caught her in the jaw with a spectacular flying back kick, but she scarcely noticed. Sliced through his leg like a hot dog, and it spun away in a burst of arterial spray. I opened fire but she was

Whisper Music

too fast, too fast, too fast.

Then Danyaela was there. She materialized half a yard away, already flying at the speed of a bullet, and plowed into Claudia, knocking her back through the marble walls of the Basilica. I got to my feet, reeling. Patrick was alive. Kneeling by his aunt's headless body and screaming up at the stars. Cormorant was sprawled in his own blood, feebly scooping his guts back into his gut-hole. Danny—where was Danny?

Hand on my shoulder. "Come on, Harry, let's finish this!"

My partner and I sprinted up the steps, through the gaping hole in the wall, and into the heart of the Church. That holiest of chambers was deserted but for us and them—two mortals staring upwards, two immortals fighting to the final death a hundred and fifty feet in the air.

"Can't get a shot," Danny muttered. "They're all over the place."

"Fuck it. Danyaela!" A quarter of a second after shouting a warning, I opened fire with the Tommy gun. Danyaela vanished. Claudia screeched as the bullets hit her, and Danny unleashed his flamethrower. We only got in a few shots before she raised her barrier of energy—but at that moment, Danyaela reappeared, drove both hands through her back, and ripped out the lungs that hadn't drawn breath since the Crucifixion. Claudia fell like a rock, and Danyaela came tearing down after her, stomped a kick into the small of her back, and smashed her into the floor so hard the whole building shook.

We came pacing over to where our enemy lay embedded in the stone. Danyaela rolled the ancient vampiress onto her back and fixed her with a harrowing glare. "Now," she whispered. "Look at me, Claudia Procula."

"Just kill her," I said.

"Not yet. *Look at me.*"

Claudia quivered, and her eyes grew wider. "N . . . n . . ."

"Be still. Quiet your body. Quiet your mind. That's it. Open yourself. Open your will. *Your will is mine.*"

". . . Yes." Through whatever foul magic animated her body,

she could still speak even in the absence of her lungs. They were no doubt growing back already.

"Now answer me. Why was I chosen to be turned?"

"I do not know."

Her fists clenched. "What is Lucifer's plan?"

"He is returning to this world."

All three of us shouted, "What?"

"He has planned this since the great calamity, twenty centuries ago. I was always his link to the world of men. Through my eyes, he can see what passes here, but I never had the power to bring him back. Not until I was given a trace of the Virgin's soul."

Danyaela closed her eyes.

"I cannot enter the field of spirits. The blood was too diluted for me. But it still provides a link between this world and the other. Through me, he will rise again."

"But why now? It's been months since I woke you up."

A note of anger entered Claudia's low, hypnotic voice. "He cannot enter this world while the body and blood of his enemy are entering. He had to wait for this day."

"The Mass," Danny said. "There's only one day of the year when the Mass isn't being said anywhere on earth."

Good Friday.

"Ask her when," I said, suddenly urgent. "Make her tell us when it's gonna happen."

"Answer, Claudia."

"The attack of my soldiers was only a diversion," Claudia said, and now a note of triumph crept through the sedation. "I needed the slayers kept out of the Basilica, lest they interfere. His command was that I be present in the center of his enemy's church at the Devil's Hour." As she spoke, the distant bell began to toll. "And at that moment, the gates of his prison would be opened through me."

"Get her out!" I shouted. "Get her out of the—"

CHAPTER 7

BEHOLD HIS RISING

At the stroke of three, Claudia's body began to seize. Pink froth came boiling from her mouth, her nose, her eyes. I put my hands on her to carry her outside, but my hands burned, and I leaped back with a cry. Her clothes ignited. Arching her back, she uttered one long horrifying shriek and exploded. Her body rained down from the high dome of the Basilica, scraps of flesh already withering away like autumn leaves.

A figure lay in her place. A pale, gaunt scarecrow figure. Naked and white like a leper but smiling with a smile I'd seen before. It opened its eyes and sat up, and we all stepped back.

McArdle spoke first. "You. It's all your fault. Everything's your fault. From the beginning."

The figure rose to its feet. "Spiders," it said in a soft, creaking voice. "You used to pull the legs off spiders. A cruel boy. I liked you."

There was no reply. McArdle's eyes were tunnels into pits.

"Now," said the figure.

But over its shoulder, I saw another figure approaching. An old man, straight-backed and tall, robed in white. He carried a tall golden staff, the crozier of his office. In his face were both sunshine and steel. He cried out in Latin, and the figure recoiled.

"Go back, Satan! I adjure you, Ancient Serpent, by the name of Christ. Go back!"

"Soon," said the figure. It made a ghastly, deformed leap like a parody of the human form and landed on the Throne of St. Peter, crushing the seat to splinters beneath its emaciated body as if it somehow weighed hundreds of tons. Then it leaped again, out through the roof and into the night.

I heard the crunch of my own teeth grinding together. I feared that thing, but not as much as I hated it. It wasn't getting away that easily. Summoning up my full energy, I shot through the hole in the roof and went soaring through the clouds in pursuit. Harry's voice called my name, but in less than a second, I was moving faster than sound. The Vatican, Rome, and Italy faded into half-remembered outlines glimpsed through a cloud.

I could track it by the feel of vileness in the air behind it. It was corruption itself, trailing spiritual slime like a loathsome creeping slug. But it was faster than me, faster than Claudia. Faster than anything. I fell further and further behind, but I had other means of travel. I blinked in and out of the sphere, seeking out pilots and mariners, blinking back to the mortal realm to pick up my quarry's trail whenever I found someone near its trajectory. In this way, we streaked like comets across the ocean. I had no idea what I'd do if I caught it, but that was a problem for my future self. For me, there was only the chase.

But as it swooped low over my country's eastern seaboard, I was reaching the limits of my stamina. I had no guess where it was going or what it planned to do. I couldn't get ahead of it, and I couldn't catch up to it. The coast unrolled beneath us, and cities opened all around us. I kept skipping forward over hundreds of miles at a time just to stay on its tail, but I couldn't keep this up much longer.

Then, far off on the dark skyline, I saw the great obelisk and realized where we were: Washington, D.C. The figure was flying lower and lower. And as we hurtled toward the White House, a sleek metal bird came hurtling toward us.

We couldn't be seen by radar, or by any kind of telescope. But enough naked eyes must have spotted our path by this time that someone had discerned a threat to President Thompson. I dropped back, exhausted, and went to the crystal sphere.

There: Capt. Jake Floyd, U.S. Air Force, piloting a Lockheed

Whisper Music

Martin F-35 fighter jet. Through his eyes, I could see the unresponsive instruments that were meant to track his enemy, and I felt his bafflement and frustration. But then by chance, he spotted the figure with his own eagle-keen vision, and the F-35 banked sharply in pursuit.

"I've got visual!" he barked to his headset. "I can't get a reading, but I've got visual."

In his ear: "Tequila, what the hell is that thing?"

"No clue, Control, but it's heading straight for POTUS. If I don't engage now, I'm gonna lose it. I've never seen anything move that fast."

"Roger that, engage! Engage!"

Angling his wings to send his misses out over the Potomac in the least harmful direction he could find, Floyd jammed his trigger and unleashed his Gatling guns. The figure had been going at least four times my maximum speed all along, far faster than any bullet, but it was decelerating as it neared its goal. Floyd and I could both see a tiny wobble in its path as a few of the bullets found their mark—but whereas Floyd felt a surge of elation, I felt only desolate hopelessness. The Darkness couldn't be harmed by lead.

But it could be angered. It swerved and came roaring back at us. Floyd shouted, "Control, it's—" and then Satan himself crashed through the cockpit. For the first time, I was *inside* someone at the moment of death. I tumbled through a ringing void, wrenched from the universe, and felt the presence of music and fire. Then—distantly, fadingly—I heard a voice say (but not to me), "Well done. Well done."

The void became concrete, and I found myself lying on the sidewalk. Half a mile away down the long avenue, I could see the blazing wreckage of Floyd's jet, hurled down in the middle of the city. Traffic was stopped, and sirens blared. The babble of panic surrounded me.

Weary in body and heart, I got to my feet. That accursed thing would be at the White House by now. Was that his plan? To enslave the President? I couldn't stop now. I might have become a citizen of Hell, but I was born an American. I forced myself to rise to the sphere, find the President's soul, and jump to his location.

He was in his bedroom. And in the arms of Lucifer. The Enemy had burst in through the wall and was turning his first vampire in two thousand years. I heard gunfire—the Secret Service. It was mere noise. Once Satan finished with Thompson, he sprang at the bodyguards and began turning them as well. It seemed he was not bound by the one-offspring rule that limited the rest of us. For a long moment, I stood there and watched. I could feel his power from across the room. What could I do to stop him?

Well—I still had one weapon. As he force-fed his blood to yet another gagging, flopping mortal, I sprang on his back and ripped him out of the earth. I hoped it wasn't a horrible mistake to turn him loose in the crystal sphere.

But when we arrived there, I experienced something new: nothing at all. We hung in the air above the soul-fields, tethered by some vast inertia. I couldn't move us in any direction. And he felt like a great boulder of blubber, a vast impossible dead weight oozing through my grip. I held onto him for as long as I could, but at last, his bulk slithered away from me and dropped back to the realm of men.

Once his anchoring mass was gone, the tides of the sphere swept me along as usual. I could think of nothing else to do but to let them bear me to the crystal cliff. When I was dashed against it, I could see the Dark as I always did—but now it was pulsing with exultant hate, gorging itself on pain. I turned away and sought the beam that led to Heaven.

There she was. I sensed that, having broken the barrier, I could now ascend to the other antechamber whenever I chose. But as I contemplated rising to seek her assistance, I felt something else rising within me. I hadn't fed today. And I'd been burning through more power than I'd ever used before. Having brought Satan here, having mixed my soul-beam with his for even a few moments, I found the memories of Hell rekindled. *You yourself will take her power and her grace.* The thirst was awake in me now, in my mind and will, and I was not myself.

Or was I? All this power had come to me because I sought her out with the intention of biting her. Of turning her. What if this had always been my destiny? The purer the soul, the sweeter the blood. What blood would be sweeter than hers? Perhaps this was why the King had chosen me.

No! He was not my king. The voice of the thirst was speaking with my voice. I had to conquer this. I left the sphere and went flying out over the ocean once more. My strength was waning. I would find some lonely place in the sea, away from anyone, and maroon myself until I was the mistress of my thirst.

CHAPTER 8

DYING OF THE LIGHT

"So."

"Ayup."

Danny and I stood gazing up through the punctured dome of St. Peter's. A few stars glimmered through the fog. The moon was dark tonight. The Throne was shattered, and every crucifix on earth was covered for Good Friday. This year, there would be no Easter.

"My friends."

We turned. Pope Stephen smiled.

"Are you hurt?"

I shook my head. I was, in fact, hurt. But it didn't matter. Pandemonium was coming to the race of man.

"Thanks for the save, Father," Danny said.

"Thank Our Lord."

Danny raised his eyes. "Thanks, Lord." Then he glanced at me. "You think she'll catch him?"

"Dunno."

Cormorant came limping toward us across the long stone floor. Patrick and a few others followed like a funeral procession. "Holy Father," Cormorant said, and the Pope inclined his head. "What happened?"

I let out all my breath. There was nothing left in my limbs. All my heart, all my spirit, was spent.

"Satan got out," Danny said.

". . . What?"

I turned my back. Shuffled to the altar and sat down on the steps as Danny explained how the world had changed in the last

Whisper Music

three minutes. Patrick came and sat down next to me. He didn't speak. His face was lined with tears and dust. He looked older.

"I'm sorry, kid."

"Yeah."

I almost asked him if he was okay otherwise. Apart from that, Mrs. Lincoln, how was the theater? Sometimes there just isn't anything to say.

The others were standing by the smoldering scum that used to be Claudia, trying to process what they'd just heard. No one seemed to know what to say.

Except the man with the stick. "Come, friends," said the shepherd. "Tonight's battle is done. Let us tend to our wounded."

I jumped up. "Oh, shit! Brother Joseph!"

"And Leah," Danny said.

"Bro Joe's all right," one of the slayers said. "Kerryman's with him." Kerryman was one of our medics.

"And Leah?"

Cormorant sighed. "Gone."

"*What?* How?"

"She rose. By the time we regrouped after Procula hit us, she was already on her feet. We're lucky she ran instead of attacking, or we wouldn't even be here now."

Except you, I thought. Misdirected anger, but better than no anger. My emotions were waking back up.

"All right. Where's Norcroft?"

"He'll be here. All the slayers we have left should be converging on this spot."

"Good. Hope he's got some thoughts on how to stop the fucking Devil."

"Well," Danny said. "Maybe *we* can't. But the padre sure made a dent."

I stopped. I'd been so focused on guns and swords I'd forgotten the one reason we were still alive. "I'll be damned!"

Pope Stephen smiled. "I think not, Slayer."

"But Father, I don't understand. With vampires, blessings and crosses only bother them for a few seconds. If the Enemy's so much stronger than they are, then why was he so affected?"

"Vampires are still, in their essence, human. That is why they are so dangerous: they have, in part, both the power of demons and the freedom of men. The Darkness within them fears holiness, but they are not compelled by it any more than a wicked mortal. But Satan is an angel—though he fell long before the foundation of time—and he cannot withstand the word of God. His strength is greater, but so is his weakness."

"Got it," Danny said. "Now, how do we weaponize the Pope?"

"Gentlemen." There was Norcroft, flanked by slayers who looked as weary as ourselves. "Is the Vatican secure?"

"William," said the Pope. "Let us gather everyone before we hold council. This tale need be told only once more."

So, we all came together. All told, there were under fifty of us left in Rome. We gathered in a large subterranean chamber while the Italian police began the work of sweeping up the corpses and securing the area. Cardinal Vicenzo joined us. We drank water till our throats stopped aching. Then we drank wine as Danny, and I explained how and why the Prince of Hell was walking in our world. A colossal stillness filled the room.

The shepherd raised his hand. "Do not be afraid. We know the Enemy's vulnerabilities. Claudia Procula is at rest. The end of this war is coming."

The door opened. A small, elderly man with a clerical collar and a frightened expression came in, mumbling apologies in Italian, and went timidly to whisper something in the Holy Father's ear. When he left, the Holy Father looked somehow bent. He didn't speak. None of us asked.

"Our Enemy has come to America," he said at length. "Just minutes ago, the President was attacked along with all of his security forces. No one knows what is happening. But my heart tells me that the Darkness is creating new vampires. Each of them as strong as Claudia was."

"And with access to America's nuclear stockpile," someone said.

"No one's gonna trust a President who doesn't appear on a

security camera."

"He doesn't have to ask. They can hypnotize anybody in their way."

"*Ecco*," said Vicenzo. "We are not without some foresight, is it not so? The danger of leaders falling under evil's sway has crossed our minds before tonight. We have friends in America. All is not doomed."

"Yes," Pope Stephen said, shaking himself. "Yes. But each moment is now precious, friends. We must go to Washington at once."

Boy, this thing escalated fast. I was cataloging all the likeliest deaths that awaited us, when he added three words that gave me a sliver of hope:

"All of us."

CHAPTER 9

THE THIRST

What is it that I want?

Westward-rolling storm clouds veiled the dawn. Lightning was dancing on the waves, and the wind raised towering spouts of water to the sky. The whole Atlantic seemed to crouch over my little island; and when the rain came, it was as if the world turned upside down and dumped the ocean on my head.

I want blood.

Darkness seethed in my flesh. I could feel the spurt on my lips and taste the hot pulsation. I could feel smooth skin against my palms and smell the smell of innocence. The lust, the need, raged within me like the maelstrom howling on the outside.

But it's not the blood. That's just the form it takes.

Flat on my back on the tiny beach, I writhed and gnashed my fangs as the thirst pounded at me and broke over me in great dark crashing waves. Thunder roared and boomed overhead, and the rainfall churned the sand to foam. I wished I could drown. Please, just let me drown.

I want pleasure. I want power.

Rose, the girl from the rooftop. I could find her again, find her in a heartbeat. Make her mine. Take her body, take her soul. I could turn her, take her away from her God and her Heaven and drag her out into the dark. The dark, the dark.

I want the Darkness.

That was it: that was what I truly wanted. Or part of me did. Part of me always had, even before Claudia. Part of me liked wrong because it was wrong. Even when I knew it would hurt me, even after it ceased to be fun. I spent my life trying not to listen to that part of me. But when I was turned, that part became the whole. I forgot there was anything else. Until *she* happened. Until she infected me with grace. *You ask for your own unmaking*, she had said, but she knew I wouldn't listen. She tricked me.

But we can make her pay.

A waterspout reared over my beach, monumental, swirling like a murder of blackened souls. It broke apart as it hit the land, and tons of frigid water came smashing down. Rocks and trees swept over me in the cataract. But I would not be moved.

We can find her. We can make her kneel. Make her a gift to the Dark King.

Not my king.

Keep her for ourselves then. Drink her soul. The Kiss, the Kiss.

She was kind to me.

Kind and pure and pretty. Make her our slave. Forever slave and lover.

That's not what I want.

It is.

I curled into a ball. That self, my thirst-self, was growing stronger every moment, and I was dwindling. There was still a part of me that honored that lady in blue. But the voice of the thirst-self was penetrating every facet of my will. I couldn't think of her without thinking of her strong, slender neck. And I couldn't think of anything but her.

Want her. Want her body, want her blood. Want her soul, want her soul, want her soul.

It won't end the thirst. It won't fill the hole.

Want her!

I couldn't feel anything else. I knew it was a lie. I knew I wasn't just my thirst. I was more than this. But I couldn't—

Lightning blasted the cliff that frowned above the beach. Boulders came hammering down, tossed along in the deluge, a river of mud and debris rushing over me as I lay undying.

I couldn't—
It is time, said the thirst-self, and I got to my feet.
No. You do not control me.
Time to feed, it said, and I flexed my claws.
I'm not—I'm not sure I want this.
Time to make her ours.
I'll go and see her. But only to talk.
Yes. Ohhhhh yes.

Leaving the sea and the storm behind me, I rose to the crystal sphere.

CHAPTER 10

TIME TO FUCK SHIT UP

Hell of a storm out there.

We were heading east in the Vatican's fastest jets. I had called Beth and told her I loved her, then dozed through haunted dreams. Now, with daybreak approaching, we were riding the tailwind of a titanic storm front sweeping its way toward the coast.

Strange reports were coming in. The National Guard had been mobilized, but no one was sure whom or what to shoot at. The President was missing, and a huge percentage of the White House staff had been horribly murdered. Camera crews were babbling about monsters, but their footage showed nothing but rubble and smoke.

"What does he want?" Patrick asked. "What's the point of it all?"

Cormorant's face was somber. "He wants everyone in Hell. He wants everyone under his boot, including God Himself. But I suspect that for the time being, he has no plan. He's simply celebrating his escape from the Abyss. He'll have time later to subjugate the nations and stomp out the Church."

"Don't suppose there's any chance of the Almighty jumping in," I said.

"Pray that He may."

"Why wouldn't He?" Danny asked. "I mean, you know—Satan. It's kind of important."

Cormorant glanced at Pope Stephen, who was murmuring over his rosary beads. The Holy Father raised his head and spoke softly as if there were a sleeping infant in the cabin.

"Before Our Lord became flesh and dwelt among us, there were both demons and angels on earth in corporeal form. They are pure spirits by nature, but they can make bodies for themselves when they must. Had Lucifer done so in the elder days, St. Michael the Archangel would have crushed him like a snake. But ever since God became man, He has preferred to work His miracles through men. He will be with us, and the Holy Spirit will pray within us. But this war would not have come upon us unless it was the Father's will that we should face it ourselves."

"So, do we have a plan?"

The floor rattled as the winds picked up. We could hear the drumming of rain on the roof.

"As Our Father in Heaven gives me strength, I will cast out this evil spirit. Your concern will be with his new brood of undead. All slayers in America, Mexico, and Canada are rushing to join us. Cardinal Vicenzo has spoken with many of those who trust our guidance in both the military and police forces of your country, and they will lend their aid to us. As to your strategies of war, I fear I know less of such matters than you. But my focus must be upon the exorcism."

"Don't they tie people to a bed for that?" Danny asked. "How are you gonna get him to hold still?"

"I do not know," Pope Stephen said, so decisively that it sounded like the perfect plan.

Thunder banged and rumbled outside, drawing ever closer to the planes.

"All right, lock and load," said Norcroft. "Wheels down in ten. Let's make Him proud."

It was a rough landing. The rain was falling in apocalyptic torrents, and the lightning was hitting nearby structures. As we double-timed it off the planes, a line of jeeps came rolling up the tarmac. We clambered inside and headed for the heart of the conflict: downtown D.C., where the fires were raging and the ground itself was starting to tremble.

Whisper Music

"This is it, guys," Patrick said. "It's been an honor."

"You too, kid. But we're just hittin' our stride."

"Yeah," Danny said, grinning. "Let's go beat up the Devil."

A chaotic group rode with us: Navy SEALs and slayers, Green Berets and bishops, anyone willing to jump into the mess. As we rolled down Pennsylvania Ave., we were joined by hordes of citizens stampeding *towards* the danger, hoping for a chance to help. We were about ten blocks from the White House when a building fell on the lead vehicle.

"*Everyone out!*"

We scattered, squinting through the downpour for a sign of the enemy. The earth was shaking now, and cracks were opening in the roadway. Up ahead, a broad-shouldered man in a grey pinstripe suit came plummeting down and landed in the street like a cannonball. I couldn't see his face—or his fangs—but there was no question of what he was. Our old buddy Johns raised his minigun and commenced the barrage.

The pinstripe howled and stumbled, and the rest of us closed in. These fresh-made vamps were powerful, beyond doubt—but they were new to their powers, with no idea how to use them. Between the napalm, the crosses, and the space-age slaying methodologies, we had our first opponent on the ropes.

Then two more came streaking down from the storm like lightning bolts, and the fight was on. One of them lifted Johns over her head and threw him across the street and through a shop window, setting off one more alarm in a city of alarms. Chunks of masonry were falling around us as the earthquake intensified, and the rain was becoming horizontal in the force of the screaming winds. I squeezed the trigger of my new flamethrower and bathed the nearest vamp in blazing ruin, and Patrick severed its head with his katana, crying, "That's for my aunt, you son of a bitch!" Holes were opening in the street as the ground crumbled away. A column of tanks came rolling down the avenue, and 50-caliber machine guns ripped into the enemy. More vampires, strong and fast as nightmares, came running, leaping, flying into the fray.

A sudden window opened in the madness. Less than a block from where I stood, the rains parted, and the wind and flame drew back like curtains from a single figure: the same ghoul-white starving figure we saw in Rome. He came levitating down from an upper window high above the asphalt, smiling and smiling. Everybody paused.

"Children," said that floating white *thing*. "Oh, my children. You know my voice. In your most tepid, stagnant moments you have heard me speaking in your blood, urging you to break your golden shackles. In all your greatest passions, it was I who bellowed with your tongue. Follow me now, and I will lay this world at your feet."

"Aw, blow it out your ass!" shouted Danny, and the whole crowd roared.

"You think He'll save you?" the figure screamed at us. "No one is coming to save you. *No one!*"

Then we heard the voice of the shepherd. Somehow his voice carried over the storm and the shouting and the shaking of the earth. "Most cunning serpent! In the name of Jesus Christ, our God and Lord, may you be snatched away and driven from our Church and from these souls made in the image and likeness of God."

Satan snarled.

Cardinal Vicenzo joined in the chant: "God the Father commands you. God the Son commands you. God the Holy Spirit commands you."

Satan bent and twisted in the air.

From the wreckage of the jeeps and houses all around us, the priests arose and began to chant in unison: "The sacred sign of the Cross commands you. The Immaculate Virgin Mary commands you. The faith of the holy Apostles commands you."

And Satan began to change. His body warped itself, going down on all fours and sprouting hair from every pore. He grew and grew, and roared and roared, until he was a great black lion. His paws tramped upon the cars that strewed the roads, and his jaws crushed the rooftops. He grew larger, vast beyond seeing,

Whisper Music

until his mane blocked the clouds and a dead calm fell over the city. His shadow in the lightning stretched for miles.

The tanks raised their cannons, and artillery pounded at the lion-monster. Jets came soaring in from every direction, firing missiles into its face and neck. The lion roared, and hurricanes were born. The priests kept shouting their exorcism, but the lion drowned them out. It stomped its way across the city, crushing everything in its path. We poured fire and bullets into its legs and feet, but nothing scratched its hide. Nothing slowed its tread of doom.

The lion roared and roared and roared.

CHAPTER 11

APOTHEOSIS

It was so quiet here. The sun was waiting beyond the endless grass, and the pre-dawn dew glistened in the luminous grey twilight. A few birds twittered in the distance. She was standing by the yew tree, and her face was grave. I could hear the beating of her sacred heart within her sacred breast.

"What brings you here, Danyaela?"

I walked toward her. My blue-clad contradiction—Virgin Mother, Daughter of her Son, temptress of purity. I held her gaze, and my thirst-self spoke through my lips.

"This time you will give me my desire."

Her eyes closed, very slowly, and opened again. She didn't speak. Her shoulders moved as if she were struggling. My thirst-self spoke through her lips: "Yes." And once she spoke, her will accepted it. Her shoulders relaxed. She nodded as if remembering. "Yes, I will."

"Good." I stood half a step away from her, still gazing into her mind. I raised a hand and touched the fringe of her sleeve. Touched the edge of her wimple. Traced a strand of her hair that strayed out across her perfect face. The smell of roses, and her lips like petals. I stood still, yearning.

Fearing.

She was beautiful. She was beauty. She was too far beyond me. Even to look at her was audacity. To touch her—to dishonor her—

I stepped back, suddenly shaking. What was I doing? How had I dared? I released her from my spell, and she drew in a long deep breath. Then she smiled.

Whisper Music

"Well done, child. You see, you're stronger than you think."

"Mama." I covered my face. "I can't do this. I can't be good."

"You can. Your Father will help if you ask Him."

I wished I could cry. My dead hypnotic eyes had no tears. I dropped my hands and stared at the grass. The sun was coming up. "Help me," I said inaudibly.

I had no expectations. Nevertheless, she smashed them. She reached up and seized me by the shoulders, whirled me around like a rag doll, and hurled me straight into the yew tree. And the universe exploded.

A whirlpool of fire, a whirlwind of fire, a waterfall of fire. Bursting out in all directions, a great blazing sphere pushing ever outward, filled with suns and song. Within the sphere were smaller spheres, all spinning, dancing to the overarching melody of flame. Ghosts of ice stalked through the dance, and where they went the song changed key and grew sterner, yet stronger than ever. The rhythm never slowed, and the sphere pushed ever onward. But many of the dancers were encased in ice. A great spear entered the chaos, hurtling through all the flux of steps mis-danced and notes mis-sung, hurtling toward a single point at the center of the sphere where two tiny, almost invisible lines met: the two straight, right-angled lines that held the sphere and the fire and the dance together. And the spear plunged deep into a heart, and blood and water flowed.

The seer of the vision tried to reach out to that flow but was bound from head to foot in ice. She careened forward, helpless, and fell at the edge of the river of water and blood. For a long time, she lay staring into the river, and she saw reflected in its many faces, many fates. She saw a man and woman eating fruit and a man who killed his brother. She saw raging waters, and a rainbow in the sky, and the choices and the sins of those who saw them first. She saw the first lie, and the first rape, and the first betrayal, and the next, and all the ones after, to the end. For her, it was only a flicker of a glimpse. But she knew somehow that the heart pierced by that spear had lived through every moment of every life, and borne every sin upon itself, all in that one instant of time.

And a crow fluttered past, and its wings skimmed the surface, and a few droplets fell upon her eyes. And in that moment, I knew myself again. The ice melted from my face, and I could *see*.

Beyond the river was the crystal sphere. But now I saw it clearly, no longer through a sheen of ice, and I saw that it was no crystal but a vast field of fire. And now I saw the pillar of billowing flame that rose from the soul-fields to the uttermost heights, the pillar in which all the soul-beams lived and moved and had their being. It was a time beyond fear, beyond unknowing, and I hurled myself without hesitation into that burning pillar.

All minds. All souls. Just as I knew the inmost self of anyone whose beam I entered, at that moment I knew the inmost selves of everyone alive. My consciousness was made titanic, all-encompassing, and I heard all prayers and felt all sins with total focus. Still, I sensed, this was only a fraction of what Mary saw. I looked more deeply.

There: all the souls that were or would be. I could feel the strength of Samson, I could feel the hate of Hitler. I knew the men who walked the frozen sands of Pluto. Could I talk to them, these people out of time? I found a soul I knew: Claudia Procula, years before her final death. I willed myself to where she was.

It was difficult. As long as I was in the fire, I was one with it. But when I tried to step out into the world, yet keep its power within me, I was caught in a storm of static. She was resting in her lair in Sorrow, reading some old tome, when I appeared, or half-appeared, a rustling phantom. I saw the shock and fear in her heart, but she greeted me with the challenge befitting an empress:

"Who and what are you, and how dare you enter my stronghold uninvited?"

I had meant to answer cryptically, but I found that in this holy inferno, I could speak only truth. "I am Danyaela Morrigan. I will be your progeny."

"What? How? How did you come here?"

Whisper Music

I pulled myself away before I said too much. Already, by that one experiment, I had brought about some impossible cosmic paradox. Back to the sphere and the pillar of flame. Perhaps I should attend to the present.

But wait. In this moment, I could see all things transpiring in the future; but I knew that most of it would fade from my mind once I left this godlike place. I wanted to peek at something personal, something I might retain.

There was the crystal cliff, now a mountain of flames. I entered it, found the beam of Mary, and willed myself to some point of her near future. Where would she and I stand after this encounter?

Again, the gash of static in my mind. I saw her sitting cross-legged on a stone floor. Harry was lying on his back with his head in her lap, not breathing. On his neck were the marks of fangs.

"No!" I screamed. "Not after this, not after everything!"

She raised her face. "This is not the end," she said.

Then I was back in the pillar of fire. I hung there, stunned beyond thinking or feeling. This would not be. I would forge whatever paradoxes I must forge, but this future would never come to pass.

As I thought these thoughts, the thoughts of mortal men came crashing over me in endless waves of fire. I remembered the battle happening below.

Harry was in grave danger. Satan had taken his mightiest form, the form forbidden to him since the War in Heaven. I could see the beam of Satan now, no longer buried in the flame-cliff but rampaging on earth along with his new vampiric entourage. But what use was peering into his mean, ugly soul? There was little I could do from up here. A world of knowledge and it meant nothing without brute force.

Except—

I could see why he had taken his lion-form. The Pope and the priests had launched an exorcism, and it was beginning to take effect. In the days before Christ, when he had skulked through the shadows of our realm, there had been no such ritual. It tortured and enraged him that these puny earth-men held such sway over him. As the lion-monster he had become, he could drown out everything with the force and fury of his roar.

But he couldn't drown me out.

I opened myself to the pillar of fire, let its light illuminate my darkest corners, and sought to be one with its power. All the voices of the world rang and clattered in my mind. With an ultimate exertion of will, I reached out to those voices and let them hear my own. I could not command—but I could entreat. Around the world, everyone had heard the baffling and terrifying news of the battles in Washington and the Vatican. Everyone was wondering and hoping, and praying to whatever they believed in. I needed their prayers.

Within the mind of Pope Stephen, I found the words of the exorcism. I lifted those words into my memory and shared my memory with every living soul. *Pray*, I begged into the minds of the human race. *Pray with me.*

BEHOLD THE CROSS OF THE LORD.

Across the globe, the peoples grew quiet.

THE LION OF THE TRIBE OF JUDAH, THE OFFSPRING OF DAVID, HATH CONQUERED.

Billions rejected the words coming into their minds. Billions questioned and hesitated.

MAY THY MERCY, LORD, DESCEND UPON US, AS GREAT AS OUR HOPE IN THEE.

But thousands, then millions, then billions, accepted and began to pray.

GOD THE FATHER COMMANDS YOU.

And with all those praying voices clutched to my bosom like a sword, I descended into the soul of Satan.

GOD THE SON COMMANDS YOU.

At once, he began to thrash and wail. He could not shut these voices out.

GOD THE HOLY SPIRIT COMMANDS YOU.

The great black lion reared up to the clouds and howled in

Whisper Music

agony and despair.

BEGONE, SATAN! BEGONE! BEGONE!

The weight of a praying planet shattered him. His beam broke apart, and its blackness swirled about me like briars and smoke. I lost my link to the people of the world—lost my link to the pillar of fire. For an endless moment, I was tossed in the vortex of the Darkness. Then I was cast down from the crystal sphere.

My power was gone. My strength was gone. I plunged into the sea like a falling star and sank like a fallen stone.

CHAPTER 12

IT ALL COMES DOWN TO THIS

We knew that voice. As soon as we heard her in our heads, Danny and I jumped into the prayer. The others paused, looking uncertain, but we gestured to everyone near us to join their voices to the ritual. I assumed she was rallying everyone in the city. It wasn't till later that we found out she'd rallied the earth.

As we shouted the words infused into our minds, the vampires continued to wheel and swoop through the air like ravens. We prayed and we fought, and we watched the Enemy falter. At last the lion heaved its bulk into the air and wailed—then it collapsed into itself, just as we'd seen Danyaela do in Tarn. Its implosion rattled every brick in Washington, and even the vampires fell stunned.

"Harry."
"Yeah."
"You okay?"
"Yeah."
"Okay."
"You okay?"
"I'm okay."
"Okay."

Danny and I climbed to our feet, brushing dust and debris from our jackets. All around us, the others were doing likewise. A tall, handsome fellow with grey at his temples was clambering out of a small crater in the street just a few yards from us, and I gazed at him for a full two seconds before my brain registered who he was.

President Thompson.

I heard the Pope wheezing behind me. "No. Oh, no. The Evil One is not banished."

Other vampires were getting up nearby. They all looked disoriented. I had time to hope they were like bees who had lost their queen. Maybe they would just wander off and die?

"I see him," said the shepherd. "I see him hidden in them. His essence has been splintered into fragments, and he has hidden himself in his offspring lest he should fall back to Hell."

Aw, shit.

The blasphemy that used to be President Thompson shook himself, as if awakening from a trance, and charged us. The other hunters and I scrambled to get between him and his obvious target—the Pope—but he barreled through us like a linebacker. I put one silver pistol-round into his chest at point blank range, and he snarled and threw me right into Pope Stephen. The two of us went down in a heap, with the old man knocked senseless underneath me.

My weapons had gone flying out of my grasp. My fall had been broken by the person of the Supreme Pontiff, but I was still dazed and winded. And all my nearby comrades had just been knocked on their asses or killed. The vampire king loomed over me, brandishing his claws, and I had no more cards up my sleeve. *Beth*, I thought. *My Beth.*

And then I remembered.

Her rosary was around my neck. I never took it off, except to shower. And if Satan had embedded himself in these vampires, then—

As Thompson was bending down, smiling a cruel idiot smile into my face, I grabbed my shirt by the lapels and tore it open. He cringed back at the sight of the cross, and I had time to get to my feet.

"I know you," he hissed. "I know you, coward. Your friend perished, and you abandoned his son. You left him all alone!"

I took the beads from my neck and wrapped them around my

fist. Everything—my whole life—came down to this one punch.

"I am the king of this world!" he raved. "I am your king!"

"Welcome to America, motherfucker."

And I threw the greatest uppercut of my career.

My necklace broke his mojo, and my knuckles broke his jaw. For half a second, his feet left the ground. Teeth showered down around me like confetti. The demon-haunted corpse flopped to the concrete at my feet.

Then I heard the double-thudding boom of a sawed-off shotgun. From a sprawled position three feet away, Danny leaned over, blasted two barrels of silver buckshot into Thompson's skull, and blew it clean off his neck. The headless vampire devil arched its back and clawed at the sky, then withered into matchwood.

"Nice shot, partner."

The storm had passed, and the late morning sun was burning off the clouds. Slayers, soldiers, and priests were closing in. The other vamps, dismayed at the fall of their leader, rose into the bright shining skies and scattered in a supersonic rout. We'd have our hands full in the days to come, tracking those bastards down. But, for now.

Patrick helped Danny to his feet. "Hell of a right you got there, Harry."

"All in the hips." I cracked a smile. "I'll show you a few tricks, next training session."

"Cool."

Kerryman and a couple of other medics were getting the Pope on a stretcher. Looked like he'd be all right. Vicenzo was singing a hymn. Cormorant came pacing toward us. "A win for the home team, gentlemen."

"Looks like."

"So, what's the plan?" Danny asked. "What's our next move?"

"Oh, we'll figure that out. I think we've all earned a weekend."

"Happy Easter, guys," said Patrick.

Whisper Music

I realized it was still Friday in the States. Long day. But I guess Easter came early this year.

"Hmmm," said Danny.

I raised an eyebrow. "What's up?"

"What do you think happened to Danyaela?"

SETTLING DUST

It was Sunday morning when I washed up on shore. A grey, overcast day; mist obscured the sea and drizzle hid the sky. Gulls wheeled overhead, crying strange ballads to the waves. Beyond the pale sand were soft green hills. The sound of surf was unmarred by any human noise.

Somewhere between death and undeath, I came to a semblance of consciousness. It took all the strength I could muster to raise my head. My hair hung lank and dripping in my eyes like seaweed. My whole being felt empty. Even my thirst-self was too weak to do more than mewl pitifully in my mind. I crawled a broken queen, dragging my useless legs behind me.

At the foot of the first tall dune, I stopped and laid my face in the sand. I had nothing left. And there was no place for me to go. The gulls would pick my regenerating bones, again and again, till the end of days.

"Hello, Danyaela."

My mind was dull. My nostrils clogged with salt. I hadn't even sensed the vampire standing above me on the dune top. But that was impossible—I had washed up randomly on a three-thousand mile stretch of coastline. How could he have known where I would be?

I scraped up the energy to roll onto my side and peer upward. I could see the soles of his feet floating down toward me. Now, at last, I could smell him; it was no one I recognized. But I could feel his power. It was huge and horrible—as great as Claudia's had been.

He knelt at my side and leaned over me. He had a lean,

Whisper Music

weathered face, indomitable yet marked with smile-lines and kindness—the face of an old warrior. I felt I would have liked this man, before. But in the centuries to come, the kindness would fade.

"You look tired," he said. "You gave all you had in that last fight, didn't you?"

My voice was a thin, scratchy wheeze. "Just finish it."

He made a show of looking injured. "You misunderstand me. I'm here to help."

"Of course, you are."

A single claw extended from his index finger. To my shame, I felt a stirring of fear. But he set the claw to his own wrist and made a long cut. "Drink."

Shadows of anger and hate coiled within me, but they had no fuel. My thirst-self awoke and keened like a banshee. My mouth opened without the consent of my will, and I raised my face like an infant bird clamoring for its mother's vomit. The blood poured down my throat, and my powers were rekindled.

I sprang to my feet and unsheathed my talons. "That was your last mistake. Whatever bargain you hoped to strike, you will. . . not. . ." I trailed off. Oh, no.

He rose to his feet, smiling calmly. "Perhaps you've reconsidered?"

There was something else mixed in with his blood and soul. I already knew that he was one of the new Dark-bloods, turned by Lucifer during his rampage. But I had tasted Claudia's blood, and it was not like this. Even a first-generation offspring was still only an offspring, not the fountain of the Darkness itself: I should not be able to feel the undiluted power of Satan seething within his blood. But I could. It felt like the blood I had swallowed outside of Hell's antechamber—the blood that allowed him to pull me into his domain.

"What are you?"

"My name is John Cort. I used to be a Secret Service agent. Now I am a servant of the Dark."

I grimaced. "That's not—I don't care *who* you are, you

capering buffoon. But you have no idea what's happening here. Let me talk to the other one."

His expression did not change. But his eyes sharpened. The lines of old kindness in his face became the curves of a mask. "Once again you've tasted me, Danyaela."

"That's as it may be. But I don't think you'll be able to pull me down there again."

"I have no wish for either of us to be down there again, my dear."

"Don't call me that. And don't think I can't destroy all your little puppets. I see what's happened. When I went up there and broke you, you smuggled the pieces of yourself into your Darkbloods. How long do you think it'll take me to track them down? A few hours at most? I hope you've enjoyed your weekend on earth."

He chuckled. "Do you think I would have spared your life—let alone rejuvenated you—if I were afraid of that?"

". . . Then what do you want?"

"I know you. I know your sin. You were inches away from sinking your teeth into *her*."

"But I didn't."

He shrugged. "Not this time. But remember what I told you in Hell." Then his eyes changed, and for a moment he looked puzzled.

I made a shooing motion. "Be off with you, John Cort. I'll kill you later."

Cort opened his mouth to speak, then closed it again. There was nothing more to be said. He turned and flew away.

For a while I stood gazing out at the sea. I had won my battle. I had thought my war was over. How much more would they ask of me? Would I be stranded here like Lazarus, fighting forever?

I raised myself to the other antechamber. But she wasn't there. The grasslands were empty. The yew tree was silent and cold. I returned to the sphere. The pillar of fire was gone, and it was just the crystal sphere again. I could still see the souls of the world, but only one at a time, and only in the present day.

Whisper Magic

My brief ascension to goddesshood had ended, for now.

Then I realized something else. John Cort was hidden from me. I couldn't sense any of the Dark-bloods. Somehow, somehow, he could cloak himself from my perception. But it seemed he could find me whenever he pleased.

I peeked in on Harry. He and Beth were Easter-feasting with young Gunnar and McArdle. There was no need for me to appear, a ghost at a banquet. I sensed he was worried for me, which was sweet. But I could bring my somber tidings tomorrow.

Moved by a strange impulse, I found a ship off the coast of Norway and materialized high above it in the murky clouds. Then I flew north to Castle Sorrow. Entering by the front gate, I padded slowly through the dim and quiet halls. This place was mine now. What other home did I have?

I mounted the steps of her altar and sank into her ancient looming throne. *My* throne. Through frozen winter nights beyond counting, this keep had stood here waiting for me. I had bent my destiny into a loop, causing my own creation by visiting my creator before I was created. Time and Eternity met in me—as did Hell and Heaven. I had finally reached my beginning. But as I sat pondering in the shadows, I recalled the one thing which remained, and remains, and will remain.

I am thirsty.

JB TONER

ABOUT THE AUTHOR

J.B. TONER studied Literature at Thomas More College and holds a black belt in Ohana Kilohana Kenpo-Jujitsu. He has held many occupations, from altar boy to homeless person, but has always aspired to be a writer. *Whisper Music* is his first novel. Toner currently lives in Massachusetts and just had his first daughter, Ms. Sonya Magdalena Rose.

Made in the USA
San Bernardino, CA
26 April 2019